Anne Griffin

The Island of Longing

sceptre

First published in Great Britain in 2023 by Sceptre
An imprint of Hodder & Stoughton
An Hachette UK company

1

A CIP catalogue record for this title is available from the British Library

Hardback ISBN 978 1 529 37202 1
Trade Paperback ISBN 978 1 529 37203 8
eBook ISBN 978 1 529 37206 9

Typeset in Sabon MT by Manipal Technologies Limited

Printed and bound in Great Britain by Clays Ltd, Elcograf S.p.A.

Hodder & Stoughton policy is to use papers that are natural, renewable and recyclable products and made from wood grown in sustainable forests. The logging and manufacturing processes are expected to conform to the environmental regulations of the country of origin.

Hodder & Stoughton Ltd
Carmelite House
50 Victoria Embankment
London EC4Y 0DZ

www.sceptrebooks.co.uk

The Island of
Longing

Also by Anne Griffin

When All is Said
Listening Still

For Adam, may you never be lost to me.

PART I

She recognised the girl.
She definitely recognised her.

My father's back pocket is always full of rubber bands and safety pins. You never know when you might need them, he says, ignoring the listener's curious smile that sometimes borders on the brazen. A smile that Dad graciously forgives by looking off to the kitchen windowsill, finding something of great interest there – the teapot when not in use, or perhaps, if we're on the ferry, Cairn Rock, that he has seen a thousand times as we pass the north end of the island. It's a look that holds the weight of wisdom that is wholly and undeniably him: Danny Driscoll. Seventy-seven. Ferryman. Father of three. Grandfather to ten. Crooked of leg and bent of back.

My father has always known how to forgive a man's belief that he knows better than the next, possessing, as he does, an understanding that the need to survive in life often leads to the crossing of a line or two. And, well, what harm? he'd say. Have we not all tripped over our own cockiness at one stage or another? Once there is no theft or murder or cruelty, then what of it?

But this last year has changed him, and those enviable sentiments, exactly as it has changed me.

I have loved my father and his assured belief in the strength of his own flaws since I first set eyes on him, forty-nine years ago. Not that I remember my birth or the original moment of my seeing him. But it is as real to me as if I could. As certain as the fact that I had arrived in our small island home in West

Cork, with Patsy Regan by my mother's side telling her she had a daughter, just as she'd predicted, with ten marvellous fingers and toes, and a mop of black hair that refused to lie down, no matter how hard my mother and my two curious brothers tried in the coming days.

They christened me Rosie Driscoll. Twenty years later I would become the ferry skipper just like my father. Twenty-nine after that, I would return from Dublin to the island totally broken but willing to stand at the boat's helm once again. Still a wife – although my husband back in the city might have had his own opinion on that – and mother.

Mother.

The rounded wholesomeness of the word made me shiver on the occasion of my momentous return to this place, unconvinced as I was that I deserved that moniker. I have two children: Colmán, Cullie for short, twenty-three, still in Dublin, and Saoirse. Saoirse, the elder by two years, who would, when small and on our annual holidays back here on Roaring Bay, follow her grandfather around as if he had a rope attached to her, and who would trip in her wellies as she tried to climb the steps to the ferry's wheelhouse and would laugh joyfully when he sounded its departure.

Both mine, and both wholly bereft of me.

Eight months ago, I took refuge on this strip of land, two miles long and one mile wide, alongside all the other lost souls gathered into her arms. I suppose the island has always been that way – a haven for those blown off course, like the Siberian and American birds that take cover from the ravages of the Atlantic Ocean on our cliffs and in our scrub, needing to step out of the world for a while, to mend wounds that might never heal fully but somehow in this place are soothed. While I have loved the island my entire life, I had never before felt that I would simply crumble if I could not breathe the purity of its air or listen to the water nestling against its shore, but that has become the way of things.

Very little has changed here since I first left aged twenty-two. A community of natives and newcomers, our speech is still loaded with rich guttural sounds left over from our long-ago Irish-speaking days but that sometimes make visitors wonder if we are using English at all. We have a primary school, but older students have to travel to the mainland for secondary, a church and one and a half pubs – the one being Páidíns in the harbour, spelled incorrectly without its apostrophe, as my mother liked to point out every time we had passed its door, and the half being the Wagtail that theoretically opens in late spring, depending on whether the owner, my uncle Michael-Fran, is in the mood and not too distracted by the wellbeing of his animals, and closes at the start of autumn. We have two main beaches, one at the harbour creatively called An Trá, the Irish for 'beach', and the other south-east, Carhoona Beag. There are small strips of sand to be found at other points around the coast but none big enough for a body to lie on or on which a sandcastle might be built in any comfort. We have cliffs and birds and cows and sheep and goats and horses and a donkey. We have tractors and ride-on mowers, though drones were quickly banned – no one believing it fair that their washing be scrutinised by anyone other than themselves and their livestock. We are an island of fishermen and writers, farmers and potters, ferry folk and beekeepers. We are all hues and sizes. We are as grumpy as they come and as light and wistful as the soft breeze that skims the lands in June and reminds us that we are the luckiest people in Ireland.

It is a place of noise. Comforting sounds breaking through the steady silence: the bleat of one of Críostóir's goats, or the

sweet call of the skylark, or the chatter of those walking up
Hare Hill, so clear they could be standing beside you, each
voice rising above the constant hum of the ebbing and flowing
ocean that hugs every jutting rock, every slab of harbour wall,
leaving us gifts of sand and stone on which we walk to look
out at its splendour. And then there is the roar of a car engine
a mile away, a unique cacophonous delight bellowing in the
air, so that we know who is on their way without having to
wait to see them appear around the bend. We aren't ones for
fancy cars. And why would we be? We drive roads no wider
than a path – potholed, stony and bendy. You would be a fool
to drive your brand new Audi around here. We own cars that
have long since forgotten the suck of a Hoover, with indica-
tors that may or may not work given their humour, boots that
close with the help of a bit of rope, and engines in constant
need of assistance, crying out their pain that we ignore until
they stop in the middle of the road, refusing to turn on again
no matter how much we pray and implore. But by then that
car has done its duty, getting us from A to B more times than
any mainland mechanic may have thought possible. Those
sounds are my familiars now, my comfort, my safety.

The foot-ferry is our lifeline, carrying as it does the grocery
shopping from the mainland, the children home from secondary school on a Friday evening, and the visitors who come
every summer with their pockets full of money and a desire
to spend it. When they leave, they go with reluctance in their
hearts and a longing to return; their bags filled with our honey
and pottery, destined for the stomachs and shelves of relatives
and friends to whom they will rave about how on Roaring Bay
they forgot which day of the week it was and which disaster
was currently upsetting the world. And how they had gladly
left their phones in their Airbnb or yurt – oh, yes, we have

three of those – and sauntered down to the harbour to sit for hours on the low wall that runs in a curve from Diarmuid's shop-cum-café around to the top of the pier, watching their children play in the water below, perhaps popping back in for a second coffee or maybe to Páidíns for a welcome pint of cider if the hour of the day permitted.

Roaring Bay lies eight kilometres away from West Cork's mainland. Forty minutes' ferry ride. In recent years, the ferry, *Aoibhneas II* – *Aoibhneas I* survived until 1985 when her engine finally packed in – in all her navy and white brilliance has battled through more storms than ever before. Journeys when no one can leave the passenger cabin to stand outside, looking out onto the sea to spot a pod of dolphins or porpoises, or simply to chat and watch the mainland's approach. In the roughest tempests it is a journey with little or no talking, when the natives decide to lie across the benches and catch up on some sleep while others produce brave grins for their fellow travellers. For those less fortunate, it is a white-knuckled grip of the seats, their stomachs heaving as *Aoibhneas* dips and rises. And there are times when it is far too dangerous for the ferry to run at all. There have been more days like that in the past couple of years than at any other point in my father's memory, he says. The climate has changed. That is why you will find the cupboards and chest freezers of the islanders full of dried goods and meat, and a diesel generator in every second garden in case the electricity gives way.

But, above all else, the thing I love most about Roaring Bay is standing in the ferry's wheelhouse and looking out onto the vastness of the sea as I drive through the waves. I fit there as I did many years before, when I was a young woman just out of school: as if it has been measured and crafted specifically for me. I feel calm at that window behind those controls, knowing that is where I need to be, that there my harried heart and mind can rest. She has become so much of a necessity now it is hard to believe that once I had actually walked away from her, knowing I was destined for something more amazing. And I was right, of course, there should be no question about that. I left those shores for the greatest gift I was ever given. Love. And I never looked back, never ached so deeply for the boat that I counted down the days until I could steer her again. Until, that is, the ferociousness of Fate, and the love of three men, led me back to her.

When I first returned last May and wasn't at *Aoibhneas*'s helm I felt ill at ease. The solid island earth of road and hill and field all forced me to face the truth of who I was – the bereft mother of a missing child, Saoirse, my eldest, who had disappeared right outside our Dublin home eight years prior as if it had been predestined.

Yet at sea I did not feel her loss so crushingly. Instead she felt close. As though we were there together, racing the waves and dolphins. As though she were only a breath away in some portal, which if I could just unlock, I might reach my hand inside and pull her back into my world. I could sense her beside me at the helm. Sometimes still seventeen, sometimes younger, but always confident, black of hair and pale of skin, smiling, telling me that when she qualified from her degree in film production every one of her movies would be about the sea.

I had not expected it, to feel her so intensely there, or to feel that if I could not skipper again, that I would surely wither into a grave. No one had, not my father who had asked me to come back to Roaring Bay, not my son who had encouraged me, not my husband of twenty-six years who had all but insisted.

No one.

She had nearly fallen off the bike as the car had pulled up outside her house. She'd had to mount the pavement.

I hadn't wanted to go back to Roaring Bay at all, that's the ironic thing. Nothing had been further from my mind when the phone rang one morning in my Dublin home last April and I looked at the screen to see Dad's number. I'd barely said hello and he was off, in one long, panicked flurry in which I couldn't detect a breath being taken, telling me that he'd been finding it harder and harder on his own since Mammy had died the previous October, and now, with the pain in his back getting worse, he wasn't sure about skippering any more, and what would the island do if he had to give it up? What would *he* do? Give the boat to Michael-Fran, his brother, who might run it if he was in form that day but, if he had the desire, might sit instead with the cows in his lower field for an hour or two – then what would happen to the frozen fish waiting on the mainland, dripping all over Rossban pier? No, perhaps it was time to sell. There was a man up on White Island who was interested. Had been for years. Sure, he could lease it to him, if there was no other way. Because there wasn't, was there? he asked, finally stopping and allowing the significance of that question to be felt, waiting for my reaction.

Despite the darkness of my mood, I had made myself take the call, stepping out onto our back patio, trying to ignore the overgrown disaster that was our garden to watch instead the seagulls perched on the neighbours' rooftops, making their creaking-gate calls. I always did that, if the weather was dry, took my father's calls outdoors so I could hear the creatures of the Irish Sea that hemmed the coastline of Blackrock village not half a mile from my front door. It somehow made me feel closer to him.

'You mean Coady Maguire, Dad? I thought you said he was a shyster. That all he's interested in is profit and that he doesn't give two hoots about providing a safe and reliable service.'

'Well, who else is going to do it? You think I can ring up those brothers of yours in the States and ask them to take her? They've no more interest in her than I have in those skyscrapers they're building.' As soon as my brothers had been old enough they'd hopped on planes, one after the other, breaking my mother's heart to head west to LA to find careers on building sites, coming home rarely, except, of course, for Mammy's funeral. All far too late, she'd have said, if she'd been alive for the occasion. 'And no one round here has the wisdom to run it. They'd make a hames of it, as well you know.'

It wasn't like Dad, I thought, peering up at the blueness of that sharp April sky, to talk like that about people. He was normally more generous about them than the evidence warranted.

'What about Liam? Or have you forgotten about his want of the ferry?' Liam Ó Kiersey, my nemesis of old, had long since become the other skipper who worked the boat week-on-week-off with Dad.

'I'd have to leave the place,' Dad continued, 'I couldn't watch him constantly banging *Aoibhneas* off the harbour wall with not a care about it. We both know there's only one person other than me who treats that girl with the respect she deserves. You wouldn't crack an egg against the pier when you bring her in, you're that smooth.'

His compliment drew a reluctant smile from me. As it lingered, however, I considered how far my father's loneliness and aching back had brought him from his normal kindness about Liam and his ferrying abilities. Life's cruelties were stretching us both it seemed, making us tetchy, unkind perhaps, or was it more allowing us to tell it how it really was?

'Don't think Liam sees it the same way, Dad. Anyway, I don't have the time to be dropping everything to go to Roaring Bay if that's what you've been wriggling towards – getting me back down there. There's . . . well, there's a lot going on.'

But in truth, I couldn't list one thing that was so pressing right then. I had simply needed my father to stop talking.

'Well, now, I hadn't been thinking that at all,' he said, brazen as you like, as if butter wouldn't melt, 'but it's not a bad suggestion now that you say it. I mean, you're up to date on all your courses and your ticket's good for two more years.' A ticket was parlance for ferry licence. He was right. I'd kept it all going, doing the courses – sea survival, first aid, among others – at his encouragement never to let it slip, even though my heart had not been in it any more. You might be glad of it some day, he'd said, as if he was some kind of seer.

'What about the summer?' he continued. 'You could come just for that. You know, a couple of weeks. This old back of mine will surely mend with a few days off here and there. And, sure, it might do you good. Maybe it's exactly what you need – a distraction.'

'A *distraction*?'

'Now, love, I'm not trying to upset you or anything. It's . . . well, you know . . . I'm worried about you. It's been a tough auld time for you and Hugh, especially this past year.'

For a moment I couldn't reply – when people spoke the truth about our situation it often caught me off guard. Saoirse was gone eight years but that past year we, or I, had finally collapsed under the weight of her loss. I closed my eyes, letting my head drop and my tongue tip at a burgeoning ulcer on the inner left cheek of my mouth.

'And you do love the boat, Rosie. Ireland's only female skipper. God knows how much that made me smile the day you got your ticket. Would you not think about it? That's all I'm asking. I can hold out a month or two yet before I have to talk to Maguire. I never wanted it to come to this, but . . .'

'Ah, Dad.' I felt the exasperation as I returned to our patio doors, leaning against their cobwebbed hinges, unable to stand the thought of being at the centre of another loss. 'Isn't there another way?' My hand rubbed back and forth across my forehead, so fast that I could feel the heat rise in my fingertips. 'Look,' I said, with determination, finally drawing a line under this ridiculous quandary, 'I don't need this on my plate right now.'

I had expected him to let me off the hook. To say, Don't worry, love, I shouldn't have been bothering you with this. I'll figure out a way.

But he didn't.

'Rosie,' he said, cutting across my panic. 'Please. Just talk to Hugh.'

I had no intention of doing anything of the sort. As soon as the call ended, I went back inside and dropped the phone onto our L-shaped couch that looked out over the garden, vowing not to touch it for the rest of the day. There would be no more discussion of the island and going back there. Instead, I returned to watching out of windows, walking the rooms of the house and staring at the newspaper without reading a word.

No, Hugh would hear nothing of such things.

And yet he did.

'Any calls?' he'd asked, as we sat to eat that evening. This, too, was unusual, us sitting in that way.

I had assumed he'd meant calls about Saoirse, so I assured him all had been quiet, no update on the case had arrived, as was the norm.

'And no one else? Cullie or your father?'

It wasn't odd for my father to ring regularly, but it was Hugh's asking and my sitting there to hear him do so that was unusual. How naive of me to feel it like a kind of kismet, something in the universe divining that I should tell him all my father had asked, and not a considered plan to which I had not been party.

'He wants me to go down and help for the summer.'

'To skipper again,' he'd replied, a statement rather than a question. Even that nuance didn't strike me as odd, not then anyway. I'd simply watched Hugh wipe his mouth with a sheet of kitchen paper that I had left on the island counter. (Hugh had put in an island way back, long before they were *the* thing; the benefits of being married to an architect meant we were always way ahead of the curve.)

'It's his back, and, you know, Mammy.'

Hugh scrunched up the paper and laid it beside his plate at which he looked, fascinated, it seemed, by the remnants of red sauce pooling in the middle.

'I've said no, Hugh, it's OK. Don't be worrying.' I was so ashamed for even bringing it up that it forced me out of my chair. I was already clearing the condiments away to the press, tipping the last of the bolognese into a plastic container for its saving in the fridge, wiping out the dirtied pot with more kitchen roll and filling it with soapy hot water.

'Rosie, can you leave that for a minute?' His request was soft, yet determined, and when I turned, his open palm was indicating my stool. Unnerved, I shook out my hands and reached for the tea towel to dry them. As I did, I caught a glimpse of Hugh's electric piano through the open door into our garage conversion. I remembered the night he had brought it home two years before. I'd come out to the hall to find the long cardboard package with a picture of a young woman engrossed in playing a keyboard, leaning up against the banisters. I'd looked at it, then him as he came back in from the car with a folded-up stool that he laid beside the tallness of the other. I just need something, he'd said, putting his keys in the ceramic dish on our hall table. Nothing more, just that – I need something – looking at me as if I had been the one denying him all along whatever that something was. And then he'd manoeuvred the package through the kitchen door and out into the small room that had once been our garage but was now a gatherer of all things that didn't seem to fit in the rest of the house. A dumping ground of our odds and ends, including a desk with a computer that Cullie had sometimes used when he was studying but that was years ago by then. As I leaned against the door frame, I'd watched as Hugh carefully took out this supposed saviour and placed it on its stand. He'd stood back then to contemplate it before plugging it in, unfolding the stool and laying his hand for the first time on its keys. Every night that followed, straight after he had eaten and cleared up, that was where he had gone to.

I sat to the counter again, this time like a child, with my hands between my legs, watching him in worry. I could see it, the small white patch that appeared right in the centre of his forehead. When he was troubled it would come, an alabaster oasis surrounded by pink skin.

'I think you should go,' he said.

I laughed a little, sure that somewhere our wires had crossed and that he didn't quite understand what I had said. My hand had even steadied, my fingers circling on the marble surface as I formed the words to explain it again, but he got there before me.

'It's all too much.' It was almost a whisper but there had been enough breath in his words to reach me. Sitting poker straight now, his hands combed rapidly through the grey hair that had once been black. 'It's not in me, Rosie, it's just not in me.' He looked at our patio doors, beyond which lay the unloved garden, doused in spring sunshine. 'For years, it's felt like I've been trying to keep up with you.' His shaky voice appealed to the stone pathway that led to our shed, barely visible now for the weeds. 'Every waking minute has been about coming up with another possibility. Another angle. Another way to find Saoirse. You've been on the phone to Mick more than to me.'

Mick. Inspector Mick Malone who headed up Saoirse's case.

'But . . .' I said thrown by his reaction, as if he was a man not up to speed on this life we were being forced to live, an understudy coming in far too late on a script the rest of us knew off by heart '. . . I . . . I've had to keep pushing or they'd forget. You *know* this.' As soon as it was out of my mouth, I knew it wasn't totally true, at least not for that past year. But before that, it was undeniable that doing, searching, questioning, had been my life.

'I know, I know.' He closed his eyes and ran a hand down his face and neck almost to his clavicle. 'But it feels like I'm, no, *we*'re, not able any more, Rosie. We've . . . well, we've struggled, and we just aren't who we were, are we?'

Losing my mother on top of our daily burden, and the aftermath, *my* aftermath – we need to own our breakdowns in this life, don't we? It had been inevitable, I suppose, a thing that had changed us, had changed me. Once the warrior, I was a whisper of the woman I had been.

'No.' I agreed quietly.

'God, it doesn't stop, does it?' His weariness slipped across the counter, landing gently on my skin and soaking in. I felt as if I could sleep a thousand nights and still turn over for more. 'I just want . . . I want a break. I want to come home and feel silence for once.'

Silence? What was there left but silence? I thought. We didn't talk any more unless it was something practical about the case. A question from Mick, a decision we had to make. We spent our evenings apart, him at his piano, me in the sitting room, running away from each other to separate corners of the house, unable for the other's grief.

'I'm not giving up, you know.' His voice had found a momentary centre again, its assured strength that was so very him had returned. 'I know you think it.'

'No. I don't think that at all.' But he did not hear me, or perhaps chose not to.

'I've never once forgotten that she is out there somewhere without me, Rosie.' His finger stabbed towards the patio door, as if all along she'd been hiding there in the undergrowth. 'I will never stop looking for her. This isn't what this is. Do you understand? But I need something we have control over to change.'

Here we sat, two lost people unable to glue anything back together properly enough.

'We see it all so differently, don't we?' he continued. 'And it's so exhausting, you believing that she's—'

'Don't, Hugh,' I said, 'please. I can't do this again.'

I curled my head down, shoulders hunched, hands making fists against the softness of my belly, sinking away from this place we had always arrived back to: Hugh having long given up the belief that we would ever find Saoirse alive, and me knowing she was out there, waiting for her chance to return to us.

'I think that right now we need some time apart. Space, Rosie. We need space.'

It took me a moment to fully comprehend what he was saying. I looked up to see him rub his scalp again.

'So,' I began tentatively, 'you *want* me to go?'

'It might help both of us.' He must have realised how his words might be misconstrued, as he tried to qualify them. 'This isn't us breaking up. This is just a moment, a short space in time when we get to breathe again. I mean you said yourself it's only the summer.'

'But Cullie?' I retorted, unable to bear his honesty.

'Colmán is twenty-three and has a life. He doesn't actually live here anyway.'

'I know but he'll think I'm abandoning him . . . just like Saoirse.'

'Jesus, Rosie, how many times? None of this was your fault. *I* don't think it, *Colmán* doesn't think it. You're the only one who has ever believed that.'

I was unable to accept those words he had tried to console me with so many times before. Words that, no matter how much I wanted to hear them, I'd never let in, never fully believing in them.

'He'll understand. He's always understood.'

'He's like you. Saoirse is me and he is you.'

'I should go, then?' I suggested, after another moment's silence, in which every molecule, every speck of dusk, every cobweb hanging in the corners of those rooms waited for his response.

Hugh turned to observe the wildness through our patio doors once more. It was only then he nodded in affirmation.

As the passenger window had wound down, she could see it was the girl from that shop, Angelo's, with the clothes she liked so much.

And so, in early May, I reluctantly returned to a place I had at one point in my life never thought I would leave. On several occasions on that journey down the motorway, I thought of turning back. In Tipperary, my first stop, I stood watching the trucks and cars pull in and out of the busy service station as I leaned against my passenger door drinking water and eating a very greasy croissant that I gave up on, convinced that when I got back into my car I would take the Dublin road. But not ten minutes later, I stalled at the junction, the eager Prius behind me tooting in disgust at my hesitation. It wasn't right, I told myself, as I eyed that driver in my rear-view mirror. This leaving, this running away, was not right. And yet on I went.

At Innismahon, I stopped again, another service station, smaller this time, less busy. I got out to walk the forecourt three or four times, stopping every now and again to watch the road, raising my hand to guard my eyes against the glare of sunshine as I was drawn to the delighted shriek of a child further on up the street towards the churchyard. I was pretending interest, concentration, normality, like here I was, your everyday woman heading off shopping maybe, going on holiday even, when I was utterly and totally lost. I twisted, I turned, I bowed my head in disbelief at myself. 'This is just . . .' I said repeatedly, not even allowing myself the word that, above all, defined my actions: madness.

And yet on I went once more, driving through Boyerstown, Clonrath, Clonkill. I arrived in Rossban and sat with the car idling at the harbour car park waiting for someone to leave. If no one arrived, I told myself, it was a sign that I should turn back. But within two minutes, I was waving my thanks to a man who trotted by my window, indicating with his car key that he would be pulling out. I watched him take off his lifejacket and fling it onto his back seat, then take to the road as if he was late for his own wedding.

When I got out of the car, despite the sunshine and the relative warmth of the day, I zipped up my hoodie. It was 4.30 p.m. and soon *Aoibhneas*'s navy flank and white bridge would show herself from around No Man's Haven. I'd know then for sure. Once I saw her, I'd know if this was to be.

'Rosie? Well, my goodness, it *is* you,' Patsy Regan called from my right. 'I said to myself that looks awfully like Rosie Driscoll, but sure what would she be doing here this time of year? And then I took a step closer and there you were. Unmistakable. The picture of your mother.'

I was pulled from my concentration into the arms of the woman who, forty-nine years prior, had assisted in bringing me into this world. Patsy must have been in her eighties but still had an elegant prettiness to her. Was she even five foot tall? She had tiny everything: waist, wrists, fingers, nose. Everything she wore, which I always thought had to have been bought from the children's section of a department store until Rita, the island postwoman, put me right and told me it was all handmade by a woman in Galway, fitted her perfectly. She stood out from the raggle-taggle rest of us, like the first daffodil of spring in a winter-weary garden. Her golden-trimmed oval glasses curved up at the sides like a beautiful wave at its zenith.

'You're coming into us for a few days?'

'Well,' I shrugged as I let go of her, 'something like that.'

'Isn't that marvellous?' She clapped her hands in delight. 'You have the weather for it anyway. It's been glorious. Hugh not with you?'

'No, no. Not this time. He's working.'

'Sure of course he is. He'll be down later in the year, please God.' I liked that Patsy had offered up an answer, letting me off the very hook she'd hung me on. 'Is this you?' She pointed to my car.

'Oh, yeah.' I, too, pointed at my Golf, giving more confirmation than was necessary.

'The bus was following you out the way, and I was killed trying to figure out whose reg it was. I'm not as familiar with the Dublin ones. I'll know the next time now. I'll be able to wave you down on Clonkill Main Street and get a lift instead of taking the bus. Although I don't mind the bus, actually. It's good to catch up with Tim, the driver. Do you know Tim at all?'

I shook my head, although I'm not sure Patsy noticed or even took a breath.

'Lovely man. Liverpool. Ended up over here by sheer chance. Do you have much luggage, Rosie?'

'Oh, em, just the suitcase,' I said, thrown by her segue.

'Sure that's grand so. Would you be a pet and help me with my shopping? I left it over there at the bus stop when I saw you.'

'Of course.' I followed her to where six bags of Super-Valu shopping stood to attention.

'Tim was insisting on taking it down to the boat for me but his sciatica is playing up and I told him a white lie saying that that lovely woman over there by the wall had promised she would help me. I didn't even know it was you, would you believe that? It was meant to be, Rosie, it was meant to be. Now, that one has the eggs in it so be careful with it.'

'Why didn't you just ring an order in, Patsy, like the rest of the island?' I took two bags and Patsy had one and we checked the road before crossing it to the pier.

'I only went in for bread but I just can't resist all the treats they have. And sure, they are so helpful in that place that they gave me a young girl all to myself to do the shopping and carry the bags to the bus stop where she waited with me and loaded them on. But the way I look at it, Rosie,' she said, halting our trek to explain her theory, 'haven't we islanders been the loyalest of customers all our lives to them? Quid pro quo. Isn't that the phrase?'

We continued on to drop what we had and then returned for the rest. When we had delivered all of the bags, Patsy walked back to my car with me, chatting the entire time as I unloaded my case and a smaller bag that she insisted on taking, despite my protests. By the time we had finally stopped at the pier wall, every item now present and correct, *Aoibhneas* had arrived, offloaded her passengers and was ready for us. The low-lying water in the mainland and island harbours meant passengers always had to descend the pier steps to board. On our way down I cupped Patsy's right elbow as her left hand clasped the guardrail. It wasn't until I was seated in the cabin, Patsy updating me on how Rita's ankle was repairing itself from a fall at the community centre in February, and I heard *Aoibhneas*'s purr as she manoeuvred from the pier wall that I realised there was no turning back now.

It was Liam at the helm, but he hadn't noticed me yet. As Patsy began to chat with a young couple to our right whom I didn't recognise, I wondered had Dad mentioned to him that I was coming back for the summer to be his counterpart. I imagined his eyes lifting to Heaven at that. I pulled my legs in to allow a man of about my age, lanky and long, pass by. A man who'd winked at Patsy.

'Wait, Iggy,' Patsy called to him, excusing herself with a little pat to the arm of the young woman. 'This is Rosie. Danny's daughter. One of our own. And this is Iggy, Rosie. Our latest arrival. A man who can turn his hand to anything.'

Iggy smiled. 'I don't know what I'd do without this woman. She's got me so much work since I arrived. The government should hire her. Unemployment would be a thing of the past.'

His accent was northern, yet soft. Donegal, I thought.

'Rosie, I knew the minute I set eyes on him, he was one of the good ones. You know me, I can sense these things.' She wagged her finger in my direction for emphasis.

Apart from being able to deliver healthy babies, Patsy also possessed a sixth sense she had inherited from no one, at least none that any islander could figure, gathering up that talent all by herself, making it her own. We islanders eagerly grasped hold of that gift when we needed a web-thin thread of hope against some awful tragedy. Back early on, when Saoirse had first gone missing, Patsy had said, 'I can't see her yet, but I know she's there, and she's coming.' Her story had never changed. From when I rang her, four days after Saoirse disappeared, to sitting beside her on that ferry, her words had always stayed the same. And I knew she was right. No matter what the rest of the world thought, I knew some day I would have Saoirse back, alive, holding her in my arms again.

'How long have you been on Roaring Bay, Iggy?' I asked.

'Four, five months now.'

'He works for Diarmuid, and for Christa up in the B-and-B and—'

'Anyone else who'll have me.'

'And he's a powerful swimmer. Oh, my word, Rosie, there he is up at the crack of dawn, diving through those waves like he was born to it.'

'Ach now.' Iggy beamed at the compliment. 'Are you a swimmer yourself, Rosie?'

'Oh, I . . . well, I used to be. Not so much in the last while, though.' Truth was, I hadn't swum with abandon since Saoirse, but before then whenever we were on the island, it seemed we hardly ever left the sea.

'Really?' He sat down beside me. ''Cause you know, I've been amazed at how the islanders *don't* swim. I'm always on the lookout for someone to enjoy it with.'

'Well, I'm . . .' I was regretting the impression I'd given that I was the opposite of all those others who had disappointed him. I felt the sudden return of doubt about going to the island that Patsy, simply by being herself, had helped distract me from. I looked out through the cabin doors to see the mainland far in the distance, my chance of a quick exit now long disappeared.

'I've already started a petition, Rosie,' Patsy said, leaning into me, 'that we're not going to let this one go. I've told him I don't hold with people coming to live on the Bay, making me fall a little in love with them and then leaving. Liam and your father have been warned not to let him get on the boat if they see even a hint of a suitcase near him.'

'You're wasting your time there, Patsy. I travel light, they'd never know.'

'But you're not going anyway, Iggy. I know that, pet, I know it.' She gave a little chuckle before returning to her conversation with the girl to her right.

By the time the journey had ended, I'd talked with Críostóir, Phelan, Dad's crew hand, and Nancy his wife, and Sarah, the island's potter. No one produced those knowing glances as I'd thought they might, seeing deep within my soul and understanding that here stood a failed woman, come back to where she'd started because nothing could save her. At least, if they had thought it, they never let on, for which I was grateful. We talked of ordinary things: the goat farm with Críostóir, the price of petrol, fishing quotas, families, which children were in what years in school. They wanted to know about Cullie and Hugh and, one or two who were brave enough, Saoirse. 'No update, then?' they asked.

'No,' I replied, and there we left it, I as much as them moving us back to more palatable fare. No one seemed even to know that I was back to skipper the boat. Dad, it appeared, had not breathed a word.

On docking, I attempted to help Patsy but Iggy was there before me with all six bags divided equally in two hands. I gathered my own and got in line to climb the stone steps up onto the pier. As I neared the top, I looked up towards the wheelhouse where I saw Liam leaning over the guardrail, watching us all disembark. If he knew about my arrival, his sudden jolt upright made a good job of covering it up. We nodded in acknowledgement of each other before continuing with our business.

Dad was waiting for me. Hugged me so tightly that I dropped the suitcase he hadn't let me put down first.

'You're glad to see me so,' I said, smiling as he let me go and patted down my clothes, rumpled in the embrace.

'God, love, but I surely am.' He reddened, sniffled and rubbed at the weather-beaten creases of his chin. 'Let's get you up home,' he said, reaching for my bag.

'Your back, Dad.'

I batted away his hand and shooed him on, following his slower-than-expected limp up the pier. I waved goodbye to Patsy as she got into the island taxi that would take her and her shopping all five hundred metres to the top of the pier and the gates of her house.

'Call in for a tea, or something stronger.' She giggled.

Iggy passed me too, much quicker than my father and me. 'Seven a.m.,' he said, over his shoulder as he went. 'Over by Diarmuid's. Rain, hail or shine.'

I laughed, and it felt as if I was another person, an imposter, an actor stepping into my life and pretending all was perfectly fine. Those who passed me coming in the opposite direction, heading to pick up the shopping from the ferry, called out, 'It's yourself. Good to have you back.'

'Where have you got us parked, at all?' I asked Dad. 'Were you planning on us walking all the way?'

He pointed on up to the right to his Ford Cortina sitting patiently at the top of the pier. 'I can't be dealing with the reversing and sudden braking any more down there when eejits decide to pull out without looking.'

As I sat into the passenger seat, with no other ears now listening, I was, at last, able to bring up the obvious. 'No one seems to know that I'm back to work the ferry.'

'No, I thought I'd wait.'

'Wait to see if I made it, you mean? Wise man, I wasn't sure myself.'

'You're here now and that's all that matters. Now, like a good girl, have a look around there and tell me if there's anyone coming.' Wing mirrors were a luxury on the island.

'All clear.'

We passed Diarmuid's shop, which seemed, even for May, busy enough.

'So, how are we going to do this?' I asked. 'I just rock up on the boat and say, "Surprise"? Is that the plan?'

'Well, I could see if RTÉ's *Six One News* has a slot for us, but, yes, that's about the size of it.'

'So even Liam doesn't know?'

'It's none of his bloody business.'

The sharpness of his words made me turn to check that this was still the same man who for years wouldn't say a bad word against Liam, not even when as a boy in the playground at school, Liam had refused to let me play Ferry, a game he'd come up with, which involved stealing the skipping ropes so he could cast them up onto the sports equipment shed as if he was throwing the line onto the pier as *Aoibhneas* docked.

'You can't play,' he had levelled at me, the one and only time I had tried to take a turn.

'Well, I need to practise too. It's my dad's boat and he says I can work for him when I'm older.'

'I don't think so. Girls aren't allowed work on ferries – they're too weak. And anyway, when I'm bigger it'll be *my* ferry. Not yours. My uncle says so. And you won't be working for me.'

Liam had lived with his uncle Tommy, his father's brother, the other skipper on the boat back then. Liam's mother had died in childbirth and his father, an alcoholic, had gone the same way not long after when Liam was four. Tommy was softer than his brother but still had a hint of the Ó Kiersey edge. He fished and skippered and taught his nephew that life was about making sure you got what you could from the sea.

'No, it won't!' I'd cried in horror at Liam's suggestion that one day *Aoibhneas* would no longer be ours. After school I had run as fast as I could to the harbour to find my father.

'There now,' Dad had said, having heard me out. He pulled me into a hug, trying to help quell the tears. 'Look, you know Liam's daddy and mammy are gone and that's very sad for any child to take. And sometimes that hurt means that something might get said that can be cruel. It's not his fault.'

'But he said *Aoibhneas* would be his,' I managed, between sharp intakes of breath.

'She won't, little lady, I can assure you of that right now. That boat is ours and always will be. I promise you. OK?'

'OK,' I relented, mostly for my father's sake because I loved him so much and would never dream of doubting him.

Over the years that followed, I'd tried to be as kind as my father about Liam, but I had failed, battered as I consistently was by Liam's continued pronouncements that I would never be as good as him and that, one day, I'd see it for myself.

But now, back in the car on our way up home, Dad would not acknowledge my stare, not turning in my direction, his eyes on the road, not letting on for a second what had shifted in his attitude towards Liam.

'Right,' I said, not pushing it and looking left, taking in Michael-Fran's pub as we passed. 'Seems I've a lot to catch up on.'

Dad dropped down a gear, wincing as he did so, readying for the steep climb home up Mac's Hill.

Nothing had changed in the house since I'd last seen it seven months earlier at Mammy's funeral. Everything was as she had left it before she'd died. It seemed sadder, though, as if all of the colour had been watered down, a damp cloth laid flat on it for days so all that was left was the dullest suggestion of what it once had been. I sat to the sofa, my bags beside me, allowing my eyes to trail from the empty grate over to Dad's chair opposite, tucked in as always under the wooden stairs that lead to the two bedrooms above, the open steps of which give him a shelf for his cup of tea or pint of Guinness or glass of Baileys on Christmas mornings. Over the months that had bent him, he'd had to raise the seat height with cushions, making it easier to sit and stand. Donations from other islanders, I supposed, from thrones long since past their prime. I took a breath, sharp and unexpected as if my father had leaped from a darkened corner to frighten me, and felt it again, that loneliness, that desperation of the full circle my life had taken. Suddenly I could not comprehend how I would manage one night here, let alone a summer.

'I'm thinking you should start tomorrow.' Dad came into the room leaning on a stick I had not seen him use on the pier. It seemed the effort to collect me had caused more pain than I had realised.

'On the ferry, you mean?'

'No, Rosie, in the shop serving scones with Diarmuid,' he joked. 'Yes, the ferry.'

'Oh, right.'

'Liam's finished his week on so it's me tomorrow. I'll be with you by your side, you needn't worry.'

I watched this leaning man whose face flinched whenever he had to make the slightest movement, whose body seemed to have barely hung on until I'd finally made it to those shores and now simply, desperately, wanted to stop.

Behind him, a scratching had begun at the back door. Ergo, the dog, announcing his want of getting in.

Dad smiled. 'It's himself. The welcoming committee.' He began to turn but winced almost immediately. His free hand grabbed for the banister as I jumped up.

'Jesus, Dad. Sit, would you? Come on now.' I coaxed him to his chair, not wanting to lay a hand on him in case I made it worse. He moved gingerly to his hideaway refuge and let out a deep sigh.

'There now,' I hunkered beside him, rubbing his knee in comfort, in solidarity with his plight. 'And I'll be fine on my own tomorrow. I know *Aoibhneas* like the back of my hand, and you need to rest. Sure isn't that why you got me here in the first place? I'll let this man in and then I'll make us a cup of tea and we can all just breathe.'

He looked at me with such sadness that I imagined he could see them there, my mother and Saoirse. I felt the guilt of that, my physical features a constant reminder of all we had lost. He dipped his head eventually, closing those weary eyes of his, and nodded.

It was hard being back in that place without my mother. When I went to bed that night, I ran a finger over the spines of the books she had bought me when I was younger and that still sat in my old bedroom. She wasn't your ordinary run-of-the-mill Irish mammy, not in the housework and baking sense. No, when time allowed, she chose a book instead of a duster and would happily sit amid the chaos of a house with two boys and one girl and read whatever novel she had taken on loan from the library or bought in the charity shop in Clonkill. Purchases in the main bookshop were reserved for us children and only when she had saved up enough. Once a year, or twice if times were good, we'd make the trip to the town. She'd push open the shop door telling us there was no budget on books and we could choose what we liked, only they had to have some words in them, not just pictures of diggers and trucks – that, she directed at Nathan, the brother next to me in age who had not taken after my mother in her love of the written word and was to become the head of one of California's biggest construction firms. I loved the worlds she had opened up for me in those novels, allowing me to retreat there whenever I desired.

I bent to pet Ergo's black and white patched mane as he lay on the rug by my bed, ready for his night's sleep.

'We miss her, don't we, Erg?'

He raised his head showing me his blue eyes, those black lids drooping a little in sorrow, I was sure, and gave a whine.

Ergo's full name is Ergonomics. As the story goes, the day Uncle Michael-Fran brought him all cuddled up in his jacket to our front door, ten or so years ago, Dad had the business section of the *Irish Times* in his hand, reading about the importance of work-area design for staff and wondering if adjustments to the wheelhouse were required.

'Mighty had her pups,' Michael-Fran declared, handing over the son of Mighty, his own dog at the time. 'I promised you one of the litter. D'you remember? He's a beauty, what? Pedigree he is.'

'Pedigree? And where is it, Michael-Fran, you reckon the pedigree is from?'

'They told me in the pound she was pedigree. And that the father was too. Can you imagine someone abandoning a pregnant dog? I mean that's just not right, is it?' Michael-Fran's one addiction is animals, particularly waifs and strays. He has to work hard to stop himself going to the dog shelter every time he's on the mainland as he'd simply want them all. He nearly cried when they opened a donkey refuge, not just because of the poor neglected clients but mainly for every time he'd have to pass its gate and not go in. He did, of course, in the end. And brought home Tallulah to live among his cows and sheep, where she likes to stick her head over the hedgerow to show her full set of stained teeth when anyone passes. Michael-Fran says she's smiling, her way of asking that you give her a clump of the long green grass growing on the other side of the road.

'We have a dog,' Dad announced to Mammy, when he'd come in from the porch from which Michael-Fran had near run for fear that his sister-in-law might refuse to take the wee thing at all.

'Right,' Mammy had said, not even lifting her head from her book. 'Did you not bother telling him I'd said no?'

'There was no point, my flower, as you well know. Michael-Fran thinks people don't know that they want an animal until they have one. He feels it's his duty to human-kind, especially you mainlanders, to teach them that.'

Dad had liked to call Mammy a mainlander, like it was a flaw she had to bear.

Mammy looked up from her book but didn't shift her pose, clearly indicating that she would be returning to her reading presently. 'What are you going to call him, then?'

'Haven't a clue.'

Dad sat again. The paper now returned to his lap, he watched the pup try find a comfortable perch on top. 'Ergonomics,' he said, sighing sadly at the article he would not now be able to finish.

'Funny name for a dog,' Mammy replied, her attention now fully back in her book.

Dad had laughed and looked from pooch to wife, before admitting he supposed it was.

The girl was beckoning her.
Quickly, she'd encouraged. Quickly.

The morning following my return, at breakfast, Dad circled the kitchen table, his stick tapping its way around me, Ergo eagerly following it, as he gave instruction after instruction on how to manage the journey. I'd done more stirring of my porridge than eating, my appetite waning as the directives grew, leaving a nice big gloop in Ergo's bowl for him to eat later after his day's hunting of the island rabbits – although, it wasn't really a bowl but a margarine tub, one of those big plastic ones, catering size, now a sickly yellow from nearly ten years' use.

'Dad, honestly, I *know* what to do.' My patience finally giving in after he had followed me to the bathroom to continue his onslaught while I dropped toothpaste on my hoodie. Ferrying was a dirty business, one at which it was rare to keep clean, but couldn't I have managed it that morning of my first day back? I lamented, rubbing at the white stain. In truth, I was trying to control my own worries. Dad was right to be concerned: it had been a while since I had skippered *Aoibhneas* on my own. Back before Saoirse's departure, I had often covered a couple of days here and there when we were down on our holidays in the summer when the children were little, but this was different. Everything was different.

Despite my reassurances, Dad pursued me to my jeep, which I'd bought years ago to have on the island when we'd visit. Even its bellicose cough into life hadn't halted him.

'Could you leave it now, Dad?' I asked, as politely as my strung-out nerves would allow, with him standing in the opening of my driver's door. 'Might you not go back in to rest?'

'Maybe I should come along, just for the first outing.'

'Dad, we've been over this. Your back isn't up to it. And, besides, you said yourself I'm the best skipper *Aoibhneas* has ever had.'

'Of course you are. But in this game you can never be too cautious. I'll not apologise for that.'

'Listen, old man, you know I love you but if you don't take your hand off my door, I'll drive that boat right over to Rossban and head back to Dublin.'

He let go of the frame, stepping back slightly. I hadn't meant it to sound so harsh, my desire had been levity, my nervousness, however, had settled on miffed. I steadied quickly and smiled.

'Honestly, Dad, I've forgotten nothing. I promise you. And, look, if there's any sign of a wobble I'll be on that phone to you before I even attempt to pull her away from the harbour wall, OK? And, besides, Phelan will be there, right? Haven't you always said he's the best crewman anyone could ever have? He'll see me right, Dad, you know he will.'

The air stilled, laden with all that had led us to this exact point, both of us worn out far more quickly than either had ever wanted.

'He knows, by the way,' Dad admitted. 'The only one I told that you were coming back.'

'He never mentioned it yesterday when I met him coming in.'

'You could trust that man with your life.'

'See, we'll be OK, so. Me and Phelan will mind her.'

'It's not only her I'm thinking of.' He gave me a quick, knowing glance. 'Go on so,' he said, pushing the door closed and raising a hand in goodbye.

Phelan was already waiting for me by the time I got to *Aoibhneas*.

'Skipper,' he called, saluting me as I alighted from my jeep and walked towards him. 'Good to have you back.'

'Thank you, Phelan.' I gave a bow. 'My father told me he'd let you in on his secret, but you know this isn't a permanent arrangement. I'm only here for the summer.'

We were already on our way down the pier steps, pulling across the bolt of the ferry gate, closing it again and making our way up to the wheelhouse.

'A day, a summer, a lifetime, it matters nothing to me. I'm just happy to see you.'

I opened the wheelhouse door and stood looking at the control panel for a moment before slumping to the stool.

'To tell you the truth, Phelan, I never thought I'd be back here. This isn't how my life was supposed to turn out.'

'I know it's hard, girl, I know. But, Rosie, life has funny ways of sending you places you never intended to go. I mean, whoever thought I'd be heading off on a cruise of the fjords in Norway, but I'm booked in for September once I retire. Nancy's idea, I might add.'

He sighed in contemplation of said trip, good or bad, I couldn't decipher, his hands buried deep in his pockets giving the coins there a good jangle.

'Skip, you'll be fine,' he continued, coming back to me. 'This will all be fine. I promised the captain I'd keep an eye on you this summer, told him I wouldn't retire until his back was mended and you were heading home.' *Captain* was how the crew referred to Dad, a mark of respect for so many years of service to this island. Except, of course, for Liam. For the man my father had spent most of his life defending, never once had that word left his lips. 'So, do you know what we're going to do now? We're going to check the oil, the water and the belts, and when that's done we're going to sound the hooter and let the world know we're ready.' He nudged me in the ribs. 'How does that sound?'

'OK,' I said, allowing a reluctant smile.

'Grand so. Let's get started, no point in waiting for the bould Fergal. He likes to cut it fine.' Fergal was a cousin of Phelan's a third of his age, barely twenty-five, and with half his work ethic, at least when it came to the boat. He saved all of that for his Friesian cattle — or freezing cattle, as Cullie, aged five, had pronounced them the day we'd passed some of my uncle's and had asked why Michael-Fran didn't just give them coats — which he farmed on his week off. That was his life, plain and simple. He only worked the ferry for the money to finance it.

Within a half-hour, when all the checks were done, all of the crew in place and all of the passengers aboard, it was time finally to do what I had come for. I breathed in, turned the key and she was there again, the familiar purr, her deep sonorous voice welcoming me back. I laughed. I'd forgotten how much I had loved to be there in the heart of her, feeling her life and power calling out to the world. The stuff of past lives, never expected to be lived again.

'Isn't she a beauty?' Phelan confirmed, patting my shoulder. 'If you're OK now, Rosie, I'll leave you both to it. Those ropes won't untie themselves.'

'Of course,' I replied enthusiastically, a far cry from the woman who had entered that cabin earlier. I was sure if

I'd turned to see Phelan's face as he left, I'd have seen a smile there, perhaps even a hand reaching for his phone to text my father that all was going well. That moment was truly the closest thing I'd felt to happiness for eight years. I tapped my water and temperature gauges, my eye swinging right to the plotter, then left to the radar, all familiar to the eye and touch as I ensured we were ready. Then I smiled a small, involuntary smile as I steered us out of the harbour, throttling forward as we met the open sea. Fergal arrived with the passenger numbers, and soon I was calling them into Mercier Station – they welcomed me back, word of my return having reached them already. The logs filled, I listened out for weather forecasts on the VHF, checking the GPS. I had forgotten nothing. I guided *Aoibhneas* through deep waters and let her carry us over the waves. I was twenty again, as light as a rogue hair skipping on a breeze.

And as I counted down the nautical miles to Rossban, she was there with me – Saoirse, alive in my imagination, six years old, amazed and delighted, watching me drive *Aoibhneas* when I covered for Dad on our summer holidays that year.

'Mummy,' she'd announced, after we had left the harbour, Hugh holding her in his arms in the wheelhouse, 'Sophie's mummy can only drive a car. But you can drive a *boat.*' Her voice was high in wonder, her two hands splayed out, palms up as if fully comprehending only then how unusual that really was. She'd leaned over to wrap her arms around my neck so suddenly that Hugh had nearly dropped her. I delighted in the attention for as long as I could while trying to keep an eye on our progress, eventually having to unleash myself in order to ensure our safety.

I answered her questions all over again as if it were the first time of her asking.

'What's that for?' Her finger had pointed at the Automatic Identification System.

'It tells other ships that we're here so we don't crash into each other.'

'Can I press this?'

'No! Leave that now, we need the GPS to work properly so we know where we're going.'

'What happens if we hit a dolphin?'

'We won't. They're too clever for that to happen.'

'What's a "haven"?' she had asked, as we rounded No Man's Haven.

'It means somewhere safe. It's called No Man's Haven because if you were to fall into the sea you could climb up on it but it's a bit spiky and your bum might be very sore by the time *Aoibhneas* came along to rescue you.'

I imagined I could still touch the curve of her cheek and the cut of her hair that hugged her chubby face.

'Now watch this,' I told her, as I finally steered *Aoibhneas* into Rossban harbour, feeling for the first time in eight years the excitement of pulling her in so gently that no passenger would feel a bump. I tipped the rudder, the gear low, the throttle silenced, inching forwards until I felt *Aoibhneas* rest against the rubber tyre Fergal had thrown over the side.

'*Yay!*' Saoirse had called, at my prowess. I replayed the moment of my taking her from Hugh's arms to let her hug me, to smell her hair. I laughed, so loudly that I had to put my hand to my mouth in embarrassment, checking the door in case Phelan came running.

By the time I leaned over the rail outside the wheelhouse, I was almost euphoric, waving to those who disembarked, those I had hidden from at the start of the journey behind the closed wheelhouse door.

'Great to have you back, Skip.'

'You're looking mighty up there.'

'The pirate queen, what.'

All shouted up to me.

The journey back to Roaring Bay brought much of the same. When we pulled in, I would gladly have turned around and driven her straight back over. I could see myself going back and forth, never letting up, letting go, happy to avoid my life on land and stay right there at the helm with my imaginings for the rest of my days. But there was an hour's break before the next sailing. Instead of following Phelan and locking *Aoibhneas* up, I set about cleaning the control panel and sweeping out the wheelhouse, so afraid was I to leave that place, to lose all that I had regained, of Saoirse, but also of me, that sense of self, that happiness in my skin at *Aoibhneas*'s helm but that out there, on land, I was so sure, would fall away.

Phelan watched me Windolene the glass of the cabin door. 'Well, that's a first.'

'What? It's all grubby. You need good vision in the wheel-house.'

'Break time,' he stated, turning so he was side-on in the doorway, his right hand showing me the way out.

'I'm grand. You go on.'

'I told the captain—'

'This place needs a good cleaning.'

'He's waiting.'

'Who's waiting?'

'Your father. Over at Diarmuid's.'

I looked out of the main window and sure enough, over beyond at one of the benches, I could see the white hair of my father, who was turned in our direction. He checked his watch, then looked again to *Aoibhneas*.

Phelan took the cloth and spray from my hand and laid it down on the stool.

'Come on,' he coaxed. 'It's OK now. You'll be OK.'

'I thought we might need a small non-alcoholic toast, to mark the day,' Dad called to us, as we approached him and the three filled mugs, two teas and a hot chocolate, alongside the mountain of ham and tomato sandwiches, enough to feed the crew of the navy's LÉ *Eithne*.

'Like old times, Captain,' Phelan said, as we sat, harking back to when I was sixteen, working crew with those two men, having our breaks looking out over the harbour. Granted, back then we'd have been on the wall, further up towards *Aoibhneas*, but age had brought us there, closer to the throng outside Diarmuid's and the relative comfort of a wooden bench, not to mention the toilets.

'Why aren't you at home resting?' I asked.

My father chose to ignore my question. 'Well. Was it like you were never away?'

'Something like that,' I replied, with a shy smile.

'There's no one like her, Danny. We always said she was the best.'

Phelan and Dad raised their mugs in salute to me. I added mine shyly.

'The best? Is that so?' a familiar voice asked from over my shoulder, disturbing our toast. Liam. As if he had been hiding under one of the tables or lurking inside Diarmuid's shop or crouching the other side of the wall on the beach, keeping watch on my progress that morning. 'Rosie,' he said, 'good to have you back.'

I looked up to check that face, but there was no sarcastic grin, no scowl.

'Are you well, Liam?' I shook his hand and smiled, wanting to show that I came in peace, not to continue our rivalry of old.

'Couldn't be better now. You're back, I see.'

'I am.'

'And skippering the ferry too. Danny never mentioned that at all.'

My father looked away to concentrate on the water to his right, ignoring Liam's stare.

'How's Teresa and the boys?' I asked, moving us away from that topic of conversation.

Liam's wife Teresa was the principal in the primary school, although I always felt this was a loss to the business world. In college in Limerick, she had run a clever little enterprise delivering sandwiches from the local Spar to the stressed-out students in the library at exam time. From Tipperary originally, she had fallen for Liam back around the same time as Hugh and I were dating. Lar and Paul were his sons, teenagers, still in school.

'All grand now, not a bother.'

'The lads still wanting to be ferrymen?' Perhaps it was nerves, but I was on a roll, it seemed, engaging with Liam like I had never done before. I could get good at this, I realised, if I really wanted to.

'Would you stop? Once school's over they're down with me on the boat. Every minute of every day if I let them.'

'Put you in mind of anyone? We were the exact same, you with Tommy and me with Dad.' I was making such an effort.

Tommy had long since given up skippering the boat once his nephew, aged twenty-one, had qualified.

'Course it does.'

But he said no more, shutting me down, too soon I felt. Had he chosen to join me in reminiscences of our shared growing up and want of the same thing, we could have painted our past relationship to be brighter and happier than the rancorous rivalry it had always been. Instead, he looked over at *Aoibhneas*, the serious stare I had expected earlier finally arriving to cool the little warmth the May day had thus far managed.

'So tell me, is this going to be a permanent arrangement, then, or were you just feeling nostalgic this morning and decided to take herself out?'

I opened my mouth to reassure him that I would not be staying long, but was interrupted.

'Rosie is here under my request, Liam,' Dad answered firmly. 'It's the back, you see. I need to rest it. It's been a tough year, so Rosie agreed to come to my aid. She'll be staying for as long as I need her.'

As long as he needed me? I didn't think that was the arrangement I'd made, but I knew better than to argue that in front of Liam, who nodded, taking in the ground, disturbing the earth with the sole of his shoe. 'I see,' was all he said.

Dad was watching him intently, as if trying to read any twitch. Liam dutifully pulled at his ear, and with his head still bent gave a small smile that I don't think was meant for us.

'Whatever you say, Danny,' he eventually offered, meeting Dad's eye. 'A tough year. It's surely been that.'

Phelan coughed and ran a hand over his mouth.

To all intents and purposes, they were both referring to my mother's death, but Liam's tone insinuated something else, something I couldn't quite put my finger on. In the end, he let it drop, addressing me instead.

'I'll let Teresa know you were asking for her, Rosie.'

'Yes, great.'

He left then, his head bent in concentration as he paced up the hill, not once looking back.

I turned to the two men, Phelan, now digging into a sandwich and diligently avoiding me. And Dad, Dad whose eyes were locked on *Aoibhneas*.

'That went well,' I said sarcastically.

'Ah, you know Liam,' Dad replied. 'He thinks he's king of the castle, even though he's not. Doesn't like his fiefdom to be challenged.'

Perhaps I should have dug a little more, caught the moment and drilled down, but I didn't. Would it have made a difference anyway? It felt more pressing to clarify what Dad had said about my length of stay.

'You do know, Dad, that I'm only here till the end of August, beginning of September at the latest, and then I'm gone. Even if your back is still not a hundred per cent. Hugh and I agreed that this was only for the summer.'

'I know. Haven't I already said that?'

'Yes, but you just told Liam that I was staying until you no longer—'

'Don't you know not to be minding what I said to Liam? Sometimes you need to say certain things in a certain way to assert a bit of authority.'

I watched for a flicker in his eye, but it held steady. 'Right so,' I relented. 'Just so we're clear.'

'Right,' he concluded. 'Now drink your drink. We all know how much you hate a cold hot chocolate.'

'Sandwich, anyone?' Phelan held up the food mountain between us.

I took one and put it on my plate, then had my first sip of my, by then, warmish hot chocolate. I gulped it quickly to feel the remnants of its silky heat. As I did so, I couldn't help but feel that Dad hadn't wholly been truthful, and that when August came, I might have a fight on my hands.

The urgency meant that she had to leave her bike abandoned on its side to run over to the car to find out what was wrong.

For the rest of May, outside my time on *Aoibhneas*, I was on edge, unsure of myself. Generally, I stayed away from people. Dad could not even persuade me on those days when his back wasn't so bad to join him for a scone in Diarmuid's. I had no energy for conversations. I avoided Páidíns where most congregated at night. My father and uncle, when he dropped by, were the sum total of any serious interactions. Not even Patsy had heard my knock on her door since I'd arrived. When I met people on the road, I'd stop to chat and was happy to do so when it was talk of the ferry and how it was to be at her helm again, but thereafter my will evaporated, like a dried-out water-butt in a summer garden with no final drip to offer. I'd hurry on with a smile and a wave and a supposed urgent need to get Dad's dinner on. That was a laugh. My dinners for Dad were dull and often last-minute – some frozen fish and a tin of beans from Diarmuid's shop.

'A feast,' my father would say, nevertheless, rubbing his belly.

'Sure,' I'd scoff, looking out of the kitchen window at the long summer evening casting its colour on the mainland, wondering about Hugh and Cullie.

When I wasn't working or fighting through a restless sleep, I'd walk the island roads. Early mornings, late nights, in the belly of the lazy summer afternoons, setting myself the task of visiting every corner, every cliff edge I'd never peered over, every sloping bank I'd never sidestepped my way down until a sheer drop stopped me. I could not sit still. I hopped over gates that bore the sign 'Bull in Field' knowing very well there was only one bull on the island and he was half a mile away on Críostóir's land.

I was outrunning my mind, trying not to let it think too much, which inevitably it did. I'd turn to my phone then. Thinking of Hugh, and how I imagined – no, wished – a conversation might go if I were brave enough to ring him. The man I wanted to hear was the one I had fallen in love with, right here on Roaring Bay. The one who had whisked me away to another world. The man who loved me and I him so deeply I thought nothing could ever change that. But the person who answered, when I took the chance, was always the one who had told me to go. The one who sounded exhausted and broken. And yet we tried to stretch out those calls, as if our hanging on and the ticking of a clock might bring us back to where we once had been. I'd wanted to tell him about imagining Saoirse beside me on the boat, but I worried he wouldn't get it and I couldn't bear another argument. We were masters of the awkward pauses. Silences broken with an abundance of 'sos' and 'wells'. I'd ask about the weather, and if he'd heard from Cullie, despite my perhaps having talked to him already that day, how work was, had they put in any more cycling paths on his route? We talked of more important things too, like the case – any advances? Any news from Mick? Those small things and big things filled our gaps and allowed us to tick the box that we two, husband and wife, were still communicating. When I hung up, I swore I would not do it any more, put us through that strain. But another day would dawn, another moment of feeling lost on a cliff edge and craving the comfort of the solid ground we'd once had, and I would ring again.

I rang Cullie more often. Cullie who lived with Nina, his one true love, whom he adored so ecstatically that it made me wince in pain to think that he might have to deal with it ending some day. It was Saoirse, Cullie always said, who had brought the pair together. They had known each other in school, mates of sorts. But the day his sister had gone missing, Nina had searched him out and taken his hand and hadn't let it go since. They lived in Dublin city centre in a one-bedroomed townhouse the size of a dog kennel. I'd dropped off leaflets and posters there so many times. 'HAVE YOU SEEN THIS GIRL?' flyers that for a while we taped to every lamppost and tacked on every noticeboard and handed out to wary passers-by on crowded streets, long after many might have thought it worth the while. Nina is very like Cullie, thoughtful and full of the type of kindness that makes me worry that they don't mind themselves enough. They volunteer with the Simon Community on Friday nights, delivering food to the homeless of Dublin. She works for an eco-charity and he as a youth worker in the inner city. They are happy. They want no children. They just want themselves.

I would listen eagerly, holding the phone close as Cullie filled me in about the youngsters he worked with, the ones he worried about, the ones he felt might fall off the radar, the ones whose doors he called at, to try to coax them back to the youth club, the ones who told him to fuck off but might then turn up two weeks later. They were the ones he loved the most. He felt guilty about that, not loving the others who turned up week in and week out as much, but he couldn't help it: *they* were why he did the job. Then he'd hand the phone to Nina, who would tell me how the environment was a mess and really was I sure an island was the place to be living given the rising sea levels? You live on one too, I'd laugh, to which she'd say I was right and, really, we were simply doomed. But how was I, anyway?

And when all of that was done, I'd ring Maggie.

Maggie Buggie, mother of Claire, same age as Saoirse, who went missing in 2000 from their holiday home in Killarney. In other lives, I believe Maggie and I would have been friends, too, had we not met because of our children. She held no fear, Maggie. A Dubliner who took no prisoners. We talked about our daughters, not only comparing our cases, but more who they were, what they thought, how they had amazed us and also driven us mad.

'No, but honestly, Rosie, you should have seen her. She walked out of the house in her pyjamas, bold as you like, and told the bin man to "put the fucking bin down". I mean I nearly lost my life. I was morto. But that was her, no flipping fear. I don't know where I got her from.'

'Oh, Maggie,' I'd say, wiping away a laughter tear. 'This one time,' I told her, 'Saoirse was doing a play in the Arts Centre. And she was furious because she'd told the director she didn't want an acting part, she wanted to do the scenery. And he was like: "To understand how a play works you have to be in it, live it, act it, tell the audience." So she comes home that night raging. Bangs her bedroom door and stays there and I'm like, great, what do I do now? So I go up and I tap on the door and I, ever so gently, ask if she's OK, and if there's anything I can do. And she snaps at me: "No. I'm fine. I'm learning my lines." And I think, Well, OK, maybe she's decided she'll just do this part and, you know, all will be well. So she does the same thing three nights in a row, makes a sandwich as soon as she's in from school and goes to her bedroom. And I watch the kitchen ceiling as she paces back and forth upstairs, worrying, as you do, wondering has she enough to eat, is she ever going to go to sleep, should I leave a glass of water outside her door. Anyhow, fourth day is Friday, drama day in the Arts Centre, which she goes to straight from school. She comes home later than normal and I'm all worried thinking, Oh, God, it's gone terribly. Anyhow, in she comes eventually and I say, as nonchalant as I can, "So, all OK with the part?" And she says: "Yeah, I'm not doing it." And I say, "But all that work you put in." And she says: "This is how it went. I learned the lines, and I went down there and I acted the whole thing out in front of the director. I mean no one, no one else, has their lines off by heart at this stage, but I do it all, bore the pants off the lot of them, and the director sits there with his mouth open in the front row and listens to me, I mean really listens, and when I'm finished he gets up and claps and turns to the others and says, "See, *that* is acting." And then I say, "Great, now that I know what it is to be an actor can you give me the set job?" And when he stopped laughing, he came to shake my hand and said OK. So, now I have the set job. What's for dinner? I'm starving." And then it was my turn with my mouth open, but somehow, I managed to say: lasagne. But all the time I'm thinking, Who the hell are you and how did you get that bloody smart?'

I could have spent an hour talking with Maggie about those things and never tired of hearing the same stories repeated.

One evening in early June, on one of my late-night rampages, I happened into Michael-Fran's bar. I'd survived a whole month by then, alive at sea, lost on land. It must have been close to eleven as I'd passed the Wagtail and, amused at it being open, decided to pop in to have a chat with him. Only there he wasn't. Instead, Iggy, the sea-swimmer whose invitation, needless to say, I hadn't taken up, was serving. I hesitated, about to head on, but he was already coming towards me so I couldn't back out. I was a reluctant returned islander but not rude. So instead I sat to the stool closest to the door.

'Rosie, here you are at last,' he said, as if he had been waiting for me days and weeks.

We hadn't actually talked to each other since that first encounter on the ferry. I'd seen him around the place, swimming his lengths in the early morning in the harbour as I scurried by, but I'd never stopped to talk with him.

'What can I get you?' His eager-to-serve fingers drummed lightly on the counter.

'I'm not sure. Coffee maybe?' I didn't drink coffee, but somehow I thought it a better choice than my usual hot chocolate. For some reason what this man thought of me seemed to matter, and I suspected he was more of a coffee guy.

'Ah. Well, now, all we have, to my great shame, is this.'

He reached under the counter to produce a jar of instant coffee.

'Decaf, by any chance?' At that late stage of the night, I'd realised my choice of beverage was perhaps not the best. My sleeplessness needed no assistance: it was masterful enough on its own.

He looked at me and then the jar. 'I find it sad that people opt for decaf. I mean, not to be judgemental or anything, but you know, if you're going to drink the stuff you need to dive straight in, take the full hit. Although, in fairness, this might be equivalent to a decaf.' He looked at the jar with such disappointment that it made me smile. 'Sorry,' he said, coming to his barman senses. 'Not my decision.'

Amused, I decided not to refuse. 'I'll take one anyway.'

For the rest of the time, not that it was very long, nothing much passed between us. I surprised myself by not drinking it quickly and leaving to carry on back up Mac's Hill to home. Instead, I found myself nursing a beverage that was as hideous as Iggy had implied, lulled by his swift yet elegant movement up and down the bar as he dealt with the other punters, all now on the wane as the end of the night drew in. He wore his skinny body with ease. The back pocket of his khaki shorts, which I presumed stayed up by somehow hooking onto his sharp-edged hip bones, held a book, upside down, so I couldn't read what it was.

Every now and again, he'd come back to my end of the bar and simply point to my cup. Mostly I declined, but I acquiesced once, and he boiled the kettle again.

As the last of the customers left and he began to clean down, unbothered that I showed no signs of moving, I pointed to his rear and asked: 'Who are you reading?'

As if it was a surprise to him that a book was in his pocket at all, he pulled it out and laid it on the counter.

'That,' he said, gently running a fingertip along the Sellotaped spine of *Tess of the d'Urbervilles*, 'was going to be my quiet read for the evening. But you all kept coming in and ordering things like instant coffee.'

I smiled.

'Are you a reader?' he asked.

'Not as much as I used to be. You are, though.' I pointed in Thomas Hardy's direction.

'Aye. I write a bit too.'

One of the things I grew to like about Iggy was that he didn't care that people might mock him for such pronouncements.

'Nothing brilliant, mind, but enough to get my head straight. Gives me time to breathe.'

'Isn't there enough good air round here to let you do that all day every day?'

'Not like that, though. Not where your mind is so pre-occupied in a kind of unforced trance of words that your breath is effortless, unhindered. And when I read, I'm constantly learning how to write better. I get so lost in how the author structures a sentence, or how they throw in something plucked from the everyday that I've never noticed before as if I'm seeing things crystal clear again. I walk the roads with renewed interest in the gravel, the weeds, the discarded Coke bottle. It's my meditation, I suppose.'

'God, my mother would have loved you.' I had to look down at my two cups, so strong was my urge to hug this stranger, with his silver-ringed hands and his tanned skin that I'd say had never seen a lick of sun cream in its life, for bringing her back to me so clearly for that one moment.

'Ah the famous Evie. I believe I arrived two months too late to meet her. I like the plaque they've put up for her at the library, though.'

My mother was the librarian on the island. I must have been about five when she first came to rule over the late returns with the enthusiasm of a newly qualified police recruit that never left her in her thirty years of service. She had retired eleven years before her death but that had never stopped her volunteering nearly every day thereafter. Darcy, her replacement, wasn't quite up to my mother's standard of addiction when it came to literature, but still, Mammy had admitted on many an occasion, she *was* eager. Eager maybe not to have the old librarian hanging around while she learned the ropes, I'd often thought but never said. But it was the immensely patient Darcy, who a week before this had organised a little ceremony to mark the reorganisation and renovation of the library, which was a simple Portakabin in the harbour, carried out over the winter months – new roof, no more waterlogging, new shelving and soft furnishing, the orange flat beanbags of my youth finally gone. Dad had been asked to cut the ribbon on the plaque erected that read:

> *To our beloved Evie who is missed and*
> *who'd still like to remind you to return your books.*

There had been speeches too. I had distracted myself from listening, fearing I would cry, by watching the drip from the *new* guttering fall right into a strategically placed potted geranium at the corner of the Portakabin. We'd stood on the small semicircle of grass that never managed to thrive because of the visiting feet and listened as Dad tried to speak but failed. It was Michael-Fran who had stepped in to save him, telling them all that there had never been a mainlander like her and that the island, thanks to her, had become a people with bigger hearts and bigger brains, with the best reading appetites around, and that he personally, a man who had hated reading in school, couldn't wait until the new Anne Tyler was out. At which there had arisen a cheer, clapping and whooping.

'I'm a big Anne Tyler fan myself,' Iggy continued, as he put *Tess* back into his pocket and completed his wiping down of the counter. 'She captures ordinary, everyday life with such humour that it makes me laugh. Not like a quiet inner chuckle, I'm talking an out-loud guffaw.'

He actually said 'guffaw'. I doubted that word had ever been uttered by anyone on the island before. It made me smile again and wish that Mammy had been sitting beside me to hear it.

'I didn't see you at the opening,' I said. 'Mind you, I didn't really notice who was there. I was a bit distracted.'

'Anything to do with books, you know. I was at the back.'

'So, you're from Donegal, I'm guessing?'

'Aye, and you're down from Dublin to help Danny with the boat.' He glanced over at me for a second.

'The boat, yeah. I'm here to help with the boat.'

There was sarcasm to my voice, which took me by surprise. A momentary recognition that what I was here to do was really somehow to right this life, this marriage, this battered heart of mine. It was quickly followed by a sting to my eyes. I grunted away the tears that threatened, coughed, then gave a tight-lipped smile that begged he'd ask nothing further.

With my permission, he took my cups and loaded the dishwasher's final tray for the evening. I watched him turn off the cash register and the lights that illuminated the bottles lining the shelves behind the bar. He rounded the counter then to sit on the stool to my left.

'I don't know about you, Rosie, but I'm here in this place to learn how to breathe calmly again, that's all. Nothing mysterious about it. We all have our baggage, don't we? I know mine weighs a ton.'

Wave after wave of dishwasher water filled the void he had left, so poignantly. I tried to ignore the feeling that this man had reached inside me, had a good look around and knew who it was he had found there. Exactly in the way Hugh used to, way back when we'd first met, and during the years and years thereafter when we'd shared a life we both loved. I felt it so clearly, that empathy, that kind understanding and gentle togetherness. I blinked away the memory, embarrassed by equating this man to someone I loved in that way. After a moment he rose and took the keys from his pocket. As he moved past me, he placed his hand on my shoulder and left it there.

'Come on,' he said, 'we'd better lock her up before your uncle thinks I'm serving after hours.'

I left my stool to follow him.

'I still go, you know,' he added, as we hit the night-time chill and he turned the key in the door.

'Go?' I shivered, the remnants of the Wagtail's heat falling from me.

'Swimming. Same time, same place every morning. Still looking for a swimming partner too.'

I smiled but remained noncommittal.

'It helps.'

'I gave it up a long time ago.'

'Didn't we all? Weren't we born swimmers in the womb and then we get out here and we seem to forget?'

'I didn't mean that way.'

'You're an early bird. I've seen you walking the roads and the fields at ungodly hours. Why not come and swim with me? Or you're welcome to simply sit on a rock and get a load of my butterfly stroke. I normally do that one for Patsy – she says it's her favourite event in the Olympics. Not that I recommend it on a Monday morning in the freezing ocean when you've worked the night shift in Páidíns.'

I laughed a little.

'What do you reckon? I'm always there, you know, if you're in need of being around another soul without having to say a word.'

'I dunno. Maybe.'

'I'm good with a maybe. And if you do come, I'll take you for a coffee, a real one. None of that muck you were drinking tonight.'

'Around here, at seven in the morning? Where do you plan on buying that?'

'Ah,' he said, tapping at his nose, 'that, Skipper, is a mystery you'll just have to solve.'

He left me with a wave. I watched him for a second or two before taking the road around to Mac's Hill where I started up the incline, up on my toes so as not to feel it in my calf muscles, moving sprightly, grinning as I went.

What is it? she'd asked, bending to the passenger window to see the girl more clearly and the man in the driver's seat.

Curious to know this man a little further, I joined Iggy three days later, pulling up my jeep to find him already powering away across the harbour. He must have been early that morning because my phone told me it was exactly 7 a.m. I sat on the flat-bedded rock at the back of Diarmuid's shop beside the small slipway, where Iggy had left his towel and clothes and where we, as a young family, had also left our things on our summer holiday dips. He was right, he was a strong swimmer, cutting through the water as if it took nothing from him. His stroke smooth, no jerk, no wasted motion. To watch him was hypnotic and I was glad that he had the width of the harbour to go on his return so I could remain entranced at his progress.

He didn't see me on getting out, or at least, he didn't make a big deal of it. He turned back towards the water as if saying his goodbyes, sweeping his hands through his hair. On finally beginning to make his way up, he called for me to throw him his towel, as if he had expected my presence all along.

'Well,' he said on sitting, 'I think Patsy will have been pleased with that.'

We turned to look over at her house to catch a glimpse of Patsy with her binoculars at her upstairs window. We waved, and she did too.

'Is it cold?'

'Definitely warmer than May.'

'So Baltic, then.'

'Aye. But glorious.'

His head disappeared under the towel for a second, as he rubbed at it vigorously.

'You know,' he said, on reappearing, 'the offer of coffee is usually dependent on the other person swimming, but I'll make an exception for you. The others don't get away with that.'

'The others?' I looked around in search of those hordes of missing swimmers and smiled.

'You've caught me on a good day, that's all I'm saying.' And then he hopped up and wrapped the towel around his middle. 'Shall we?' he asked, already heading for my jeep.

Within minutes we were sitting on the flat roof of his one-bedroomed house rental, our feet dangling over the edge, watching nothing but water, no mainland, only the vast expanse of for ever.

What I didn't know then, but came to, was that the money Iggy earned in the summer at his various jobs needed not just to last him all through winter – he refused to collect the dole, said he wanted to take nothing from anyone that he hadn't earned honestly himself – but also to pay for his one addiction: coffee, which he would grind with utter love and pour with concentration and devotion into his floral china espresso cups that had survived from his life pre-Roaring Bay. He said he would rather eat porridge all day than go without his organic fair-trade beans.

Iggy carried those delicate cups on a square wooden tray, gingerly climbing the ladder – one of Michael-Fran's, apparently, borrowed on the long-term permanent arrangement that was characteristic of the island, which meant that if ever you wanted something back you had to go looking for it, unless the borrower was German, or sometimes English, in which case the item was promptly returned to the owner, who would be lost for words at such efficiency and consideration.

'Wow,' I said, that first morning, on tasting the rich bitterness of his coffee, coughing a little.

'It's great, right?'

'Yeah, it's certainly . . . strong.'

'It is, surely.'

'You know, I should tell you, I don't actually drink coffee. The other night in the Wagtail, I don't know why I asked for one at all.'

'I like that.' He smiled broadly. 'Asking for something out of the norm, it shows spirit.'

'Yeah, I'm not sure it was really that.'

'Look, coffee like this is an acquired taste. All you need to do is give it time. Savour each mouthful, let it rest on your tongue for a moment.' He nodded encouragingly.

'Oh right, sorry, you want me to do that now.'

I let the liquid sit in my mouth as instructed. Its sharpness was so acute that I thought I might sneeze. When his hand gave a graceful wave, my cue to swallow, I did so in relief. He looked at me expectantly.

'Hmm, yummy,' I said.

'I'm not feeling the commitment, Rosie. But I won't give up on you. It's like sea swimming, it takes application.' He took a sip from his own cup, his eyes closing.

'I really only like tea and hot chocolate,' I admitted shyly, totally embarrassed yet feeling the need to be honest.

A little drop of coffee escaped his lips on hearing my admission. He swallowed, then wiped at his mouth.

'What are you – ten? No, I can't be having that. You're mine now, my very own lost cause. I'll save you from yourself, Rosie, I promise. Wave bye-bye to those hot chocolates. They are a thing of the past.'

It made me happy to hear that this man was taking me under his wing to try to mend me. 'OK, then,' I complied, swinging my feet in delight, as if I was indeed ten years old.

It became a regular thing then, most mornings during the summer in fact, that I would find myself there with Iggy, whose story I never pushed for. Not that I hadn't gleaned things. From the little I had gathered, while I was a parent with a missing child, Iggy was a missing parent, at which I could also have qualified. Iggy had three grown-up children, with one, his youngest at twenty, still living with his estranged partner, Hannah, back in Donegal. The other two were away, in Perth and Amsterdam. He was granddad to a granddaughter, who, he told me, he would never meet. He didn't explain why and I did not ask. But whenever we edged close to it, he looked away as if unable to bear it. No one on the island knew a thing about what had happened. Oh, there were theories, an affair, on his side, on the wife's side, on both, alcohol, drugs – you name it, it had been considered. But I didn't entertain them and simply stepped away from those conversations when I happened upon them in the pub, which I began to venture to after a time with Dad for the odd pint of an evening as the summer drew on, or outside the shop in one of the huddles that sometimes formed and that I no longer ran from.

He never asked me directly about Saoirse. Instead I would talk about her when I needed to and he would listen and laugh when they were funny stories and hug me when they were sad. But I didn't always want to talk about her. I liked that I felt young with him and had regained something long lost, which once I had had with Hugh, when life hadn't had the time to hurt me yet. Iggy and I began simply to exist around each other as though we had no history, laughing as if neither of us had lost a thing, especially when we sat on his rooftop when the rain was off elsewhere, drinking his beloved coffee and watching the sea. Sometimes, if we were in a giddy humour, we might transfer to the other side of the house where we had a perfect view of the glen road and we could see cars approach each other blindly around the bend and we bet on who would have to reverse first. The loser had to make the next coffee, for which I was beginning to develop a liking.

By July our routine was this: most mornings I would pick him up at 6.55 a.m., Iggy not owning a car, and I'd bring him to the harbour. I didn't swim with him. Not at first. No matter how much he encouraged me. I shook my head time after time and sat instead by the rock, watching him swim across the harbour to the pier and back again.

'You don't know what you're missing,' he'd call on getting out.

Normally I simply threw him the towel as he gingerly walked up the slipway.

But this one time, I answered him. It was 16 July, Saoirse's eighth anniversary.

'I do,' I said. 'I know exactly what I'm missing, and I don't care.'

He was baffled, but nevertheless sat beside me to dry his feet and put on his sandals. But he didn't ask anything further. He knew I'd continue if I wanted to, which, that day, I did.

'I used to swim here every day when we came on holidays with the kids. Every year, for a month or so, we'd be right here. And every morning the first thing out of their mouths was "What time can we go to the harbour?" You know, the year she left, unlike every other seventeen-year-old around, it seemed, she still wanted to go on holidays with us. She'd just finished the Leaving Cert exams and was wrecked. All she could talk about was lying on her back in that water, with the sun beaming down, and closing her eyes on everything. She was already packing. We weren't even going for another two weeks but she had her case open on her bedroom floor. Her togs, *three* pairs, already in there. God, the amount of times I tripped over that thing going in and out of her room. I was all, can you not just shove it in against the wall instead of leaving it out in the middle of the floor for someone to break their neck? But I might as well have saved my breath.' I smiled at the memory. 'You know, she'd swim up home at Seapoint and the Forty Foot but she always said there was something different about it down here. Something special.'

Beyond us the mouth of the harbour gave way to an expanse of deep hued waters, powerful and inviting, where once me, Cullie and Saoirse had often canoed.

'I'm a strong swimmer, you know. Dad started to teach me when I was three. He told me he'd make me the best swimmer in West Cork. And if I do say so myself, I believe I am. I taught them how to swim, Cullie and Saoirse. It was our thing. We three kind of bonded over that. And we all genuinely loved it. Hugh wasn't one for the water. He got into it, in a way, paddling along with us. He was our great supporter, making the sandwiches if we decided to go over to Carhoona Beag, or if we were here he'd get the food in Diarmuid's. He loved that he had three water babies even if he wasn't a natural himself.'

The water lapped at the base of the rock, like it might be trying to encourage me in.

'I haven't swum since. Well, not like that, not for enjoyment anyway. I've had to do safety stuff for the ferry. I just can't bring myself to do it otherwise. Halfway across I know I'll just let go, I know it. I'll let the water take me. Let the weight of my heart sink me. And I can't do that. Not yet. Not until I know where she is. So, you see, that's why I don't swim.'

I waited for his reply, concentrating on my hands as they twisted in my grief and embarrassment.

'OK,' he said finally. 'I get it. Not another stupid word will leave my lips.' It was so very him, no questioning, no cajoling, no digging just simple acceptance.

'No, honestly, I don't mind.' I searched for a tissue in my pocket. 'I . . . well, I wanted you to know, that's all. Not to stop you asking. I like that you swim, and that you nag me about it. It makes me happy. I do like being here in the peace, with something to fill all the bloody voids. God, listen to me. It must be way past time for coffee,' I said, getting up to walk back towards my jeep. Not waiting for him but knowing he wouldn't be far behind.

That night, it being her anniversary, Hugh left a message on my phone. I'd seen it ring, read his name on the screen. But I couldn't do it, try to speak, to fill the empty spaces on that day of all days.

'Rosie,' he said quietly, when I had eventually worked up the courage to play his voicemail. 'I . . .' and then there was a long pause and I thought he had hung up and I nearly did so myself but he spoke just in time. 'I wanted to hear your voice today.' He gave a sad, gentle laugh, 'And I have,' he continued. 'Hearing you telling me to leave a message is enough. Is that stupid? No need to ring back. That's all. Take care.'

I never did call him back. He was right, it was enough.

Dad's back was mending. Not having to skipper the boat was working as he had promised me it would. The island nurse, Steve, Diarmuid's partner of five years, had also given him a few gentle yoga stretches that, when time allowed, he would do with him for fifteen minutes in the morning. There they'd stand in the sitting room, with me at breakfast in the kitchen pretending I wasn't there, while Ergo cocked his head at the opened door, his ears alert every time Dad attempted an arch towards the window. Within a couple of weeks, he had progressed to a yoga mat I'd ordered online, by which time he was all about the 'seated child's pose' and 'half butterfly'. He liked to tell me about minding my core, as though he had discovered the thing himself. But it was good to see him interested in something other than his wayward daughter.

By late July, we were taking regular morning walks on the pier, which, more often than not, Dad was managing without his stick, the reward of breakfast in Diarmuid's after was always a helpful encouragement. When the weather would not allow the exercise element, Dad was still keen on keeping up the other half of the programme. One such thunderous morning found us heading for said place to find Patsy and Michael-Fran already there, both independently deciding a coffee and scone might be a good idea while the tourists were still tucked up in their beds waiting for the rain to pass. They were sitting at their own tables, but nevertheless engaged in a good chat. I liked that about us islanders: when the place wasn't packed, we all insisted on our own tables but would converse happily across them.

'Beautiful day,' Michael-Fran called in salute, raising his cup in our direction as we came in.

Iggy was behind the counter brandishing a potato peeler, which he tipped towards his head on seeing us. The counter was a large semicircle, big enough to allow space for the two or three staff members who would work the register and coffee machine at full tilt at the height of the summer rush.

'So tell me, Patsy,' Iggy continued the conversation our entrance had momentarily interrupted, 'if I were, for example, to invest my vast fortune in this here enterprise of Diarmuid's, would I be set to make a mint?'

Diarmuid stood beside him, looking up at the ceiling, enduring the thunderous downpour in worry. 'I'm telling you, the place is going to cave in.'

'Two of the usual there, Diarmuid, and a couple of scones,' Dad said, ignoring the proprietor's concerns.

'Well, now, Iggy dear,' Patsy replied, 'I don't exactly keep up with the stock markets so I'm not sure what to tell you about that kind of thing. Danny'd be the man to ask about that.'

'I would?' My father asked, amused, as he took his seat at the table to Patsy's left and I brought over the scones Diarmuid had produced, turning his attention then to my hot chocolate and Dad's tea.

'I'm more in tune with whether you'd be having a boy or a girl if you were in the pregnancy way or whether there's someone . . .' Patsy hesitated then, trying to find the right word that would make sense without actually defining what she often told me was totally indefinable '. . . *around* you, in the spiritual way, if you understand me.'

'And to be clear there, Iggy,' Diarmuid interjected, rounding the counter to bring us our two steaming white mugs, addressing his kitchen porter who was paying him no heed, 'I'm not actually looking for any investors right now. This place is doing perfectly fine with me all by my lonesome. I'm more interested in those spuds being peeled by eleven a.m., if that's all right with you.' He gestured towards the kitchen door to the rear of the building, which Iggy also ignored.

'Ach, you see me, Patsy, my child-rearing days are over.' Iggy shook his head in mock disappointment. 'I mean, I know I look like the picture of youth but I'm actually fifty-three.' He invited our appreciation of his Adonis-like physique with a sweep of his hands down his torso. 'I know, right, would you believe it? It's the swimming.'

'We'll be swimming in here in a minute if that rain doesn't give it a fecking break.'

Diarmuid's attention once again diverted upwards, a deep crevice burrowing between his brows.

'If you don't mind me saying so, Diarmuid, you've the cut of a fairly tense man today,' said Michael-Fran.

'And why wouldn't I be, with the mother of all downpours threatening my premises and keeping the punters away?' Diarmuid leaned defeatedly on the customer side of the counter, looking out of his shop-door window, the pathway to which promised no new arrivals.

'We're here,' I piped up brightly, quite proud that I was indeed there among these wonderful souls.

'I mean those who spend the big bucks, you know, the steak-and-bottle-of-wine crew, not just a couple of teas and scones.' Diarmuid's hand waved in our direction. 'No offence, Danny.'

'None taken.'

'Eh, yeah, none taken by me either, Diarmuid, thanks,' I added, pretending at disgust.

Patsy got up then and, to his surprise, took Diarmuid's hands in hers, as if they were about to engage in a dance. Diarmuid looked as nervous as Cullie had once been when I'd caught him, aged four, with a KitKat stolen from that very shop. Patsy looked him right in his eye.

'Is it Stella, Diarmuid, is that it?'

'Stella?'

'Yes, you know I feel it. Feel like there is something not quite right. Is she sick?' How often I had seen Patsy do this, announce something that took the listener by surprise?

'Well, actually,' Diarmuid admitted, 'she's been off her feed. She didn't take it this morning and only had half her dinner last night.'

Stella was Diarmuid and Steve's Scottish Highland terrier.

'I knew it!' said Michael-Fran. 'I thought she didn't look so well yesterday when I was passing. She's usually out that gate looking for the treat I always have in my pocket, but yesterday she turned her head away like she'd never set eyes on me before.'

'Perhaps a trip to Ted Boyd might be in order,' Patsy suggested, giving Diarmuid's hands an extra squeeze, 'simply to check her out, you know. To be on the safe side. I think that way everyone will be reassured that it's not anything serious, don't you?'

'But I haven't the staff to cover today. It's only me and Iggy. And Steve's on call.'

'I'll take her,' Michael-Fran offered eagerly, not passing up an opportunity to visit the vet in Clonkill, which whenever he was on the mainland he called into anyway for the chat and the nosy around to see who was in – not the people you understand, the animals.

There was a moment of tense silence as we waited for Diarmuid's reply, which came reluctantly.

'Well . . . I suppose you could take her.'

'There you go now, Diarmuid love,' Patsy said. 'You pop off and get her and her bits and bobs while there's no one around and we'll make sure everything is fine here.'

'OK,' he replied, like the worrying soul he was, taking off his apron and passing it over to Iggy who gave an encouraging smile.

'Spuds,' Diarmuid stated, resurrecting a small amount of authority.

'No worries, boss.'

Before he left, Patsy hugged him and told him she knew everything was going to be perfectly fine. Which it was, because, as I well knew, Patsy was never wrong.

It was at that moment I realised that this returned life, these people were growing on me. Where once I had attempted to hide from them, to lock myself away in my childhood bedroom, or to walk the outer edges of their lands so they had little chance to waylay me, I had begun to seek them out for moments such as this.

As I smiled to myself, my eyes wandered left out of the small window overlooking the bay, which had the deepest of windowsills holding the artwork and pottery of local artisans on sale, and there I saw Liam steer *Aoibhneas* into dock. Not ten minutes later, in which time Iggy, Michael-Fran and Patsy had become engaged in a conversation I wasn't taking note of, my father shouting over his opinions every now and again while also managing to finish his entire cream-and-jam-laden scone when I hadn't even started on mine, in he walked.

'Tea there, Iggy,' Liam called, nodding his greeting to all.

'With just a drop of milk,' Iggy confirmed, already with the teabag in a mug and the water steaming its way in.

'The very thing.' Liam turned to face us, his back to the counter, his elbows up on it supporting him. 'Rough day out there.'

'Aye,' Dad affirmed. 'Was it bad coming in?'

'You know yourself. Nothing I couldn't handle.'

As Liam looked around to gather up the appreciation of his mastery from all present, my father quickly glanced my way with a tiny smirk. Liam never gave up an opportunity to tell the world what a great skipper he was – open the door for him and he'd be sure to walk through it.

'Numbers are down, Danny.' Liam strode his length over towards us, after Iggy had handed him his mug of tea, to stand beside our table.

'I suppose the clue is in the rain, Liam. I wouldn't be expecting the numbers today. They'll pick up, like they always do.'

'If you say so, Danny.'

Liam took a good healthy gulp of his tea, with no worries that it would scald the mouth off him. He then sighed and looked at the liquid, like it was his first pint of the day, and said: 'I needed that.'

'Actually, Liam,' my father said, not letting his dismissal of him go just yet, 'd'ya know Rosie here has some great ideas about increasing the ferry's footfall, haven't you, love?'

This I had not expected. I looked at my father, wondering why I was being made the sacrificial lamb.

'Well, I mean it's nothing major or anything,' I said, trying to play down my many suggestions to Dad over the last couple of months.

'Now, now, Rosie, don't be putting yourself down there, tell Liam about the commentary yokey you were on about.'

Liam turned his full attention to me – if he'd been a car he'd have had his headlights on.

'Well . . . I was suggesting that maybe it'd be nice for the tourists in the summer to have a commentary of the landmarks on their journey over to the island. Cairn Rock, Shelley Island, Farnroe Lighthouse. It might, you know, be interesting for them – an added bonus for the price of a ticket.'

'A *commentary*? Are you really serious, Danny? I don't think that's going to bring in the big bucks.'

Dad did not rise to it, merely took another mouthful of his tea.

'Anyway,' Liam continued, ignoring my father's ignoring of him, 'I thought our job was to safely transport passengers, not to entertain them. This lot round here would get sick of it in no time. Don't they know exactly where they're going and what every bloody bit of rock sticking up out of the sea is?'

'I wouldn't,' Iggy called from the counter, where he was now peeling spuds. He had somehow, without my realising it, gone out to the kitchen and brought back a huge pot of spuds.

If I'd been beside him, I might have kissed him.

'See?' I was delighted. 'I'm sure they wouldn't mind it for the couple of months. It might up those numbers you seem so concerned about. More tourists mean more money. No one round here is going to complain about that. I'm sure Teresa would be glad of an extra few people buying her cards.' The entrepreneurial spirit she'd displayed back in college had never left her: as well as being school principal, Teresa also made greetings cards with the native flowers of the island that she would dry over the winter months. Come the summer, she'd sell them in this very shop. They were beautiful. I'd bought several in the previous month, sending them to Cullie and Nina and Maggie and even Hugh. Not that I was inclined to share that with Liam.

'Sure the summer is nearly out, why go to the bother now?'

'Well, maybe for next year. I mean, I could record it before I go and then you'd have it ready and all you'd have to do is press a button.'

'Oh, wouldn't it be wonderful,' Patsy interjected from the counter, 'having you with us all the time like that? It'd be like as if you weren't gone at all.'

Liam had turned briefly at her comment but soon came back to me. 'So you *are* definitely going home then, Rosie? Not staying around?'

I looked at Dad, who, not a few times in that last week, had suggested, as I had feared he might, that I could extend my stay, a week or two even, or perhaps more, if I was interested. On the first occasion, I'd said no. The next time I'd said: 'Dad, we've discussed this.' The last, I'd simply pretended he hadn't said anything at all. As time had worn on over the summer, my father had at least,

I was glad to note, stopped looking at me out of the corner of his eye, all concerned about how I was coping. Even I could see that I was doing well, thanks to *Aoibhneas* and my friendship with Iggy. My days were less erratic, there was less pacing, less sighing, less rubbing of my forehead. I had welded back into the shape of this place, seeping into its grooves, quicker than perhaps we had all expected. But I still reminded him whenever I got the chance that at the end of August I would be returning to Dublin, to Hugh. That somehow, despite the difficulties that lay between us, with both of us having hopefully rested, we would manage to forge a new path ahead, in which I could restart my search for Saoirse without it damaging him and us as it had been. Surely somehow, I thought naively on my good days, all of it was so very doable. We owed ourselves the will to try.

No, I would most definitely be going back.

Except I could see my father's sadness every time I mentioned my return, despite him trying to hide it by reading the headlines of the *Southern Sound* newspaper for a second time or checking if Ergo's bowl needed refilling. I knew his disappointment had the potential to weaken my position if I allowed it, so I too would find something that needed my urgent attention.

'That wasn't her only great idea actually, Liam,' Dad segued, before I could answer. 'She suggested we invest in another boat to run tours in the evening out to Farnroe Lighthouse.'

That was indeed another of mine. But I was surprised to hear Dad talk about it with such enthusiasm because the night I'd brought it up, on one of his bad-back days earlier in the summer, you'd swear I'd told him I'd swapped

Aoibhneas for a fishing trawler by the way he had raged at me, saying he'd enough to be worrying about with one boat rather than lumbering himself with another.

'Tours! That's a good one, that is.' Liam's grin bore an edge of distaste. 'You're a real expert at this, aren't you, Rosie, coming down here telling us how to do things, right? Did you learn all that from them up above in Dublin?'

'Liam,' I said wearily, 'I'm only trying to help.'

'Oh, really, Rosie? Is that what you were at when you were down checking the ferry before my shift even began? Do you not think I can do my job?'

Dad had warned me, told me not to do it. But in those early weeks of me being back when I was trying to outrun my mind, after another sleepless night I'd be up at five trying to occupy myself, filling those empty spaces of my life with something, anything, like checking the oil and water in the ferry when it wasn't even my shift, washing out the toilets, brushing out the passenger cabin. But in recent weeks I'd stopped, miraculously sleeping through whole nights on end.

'It's not what you think, Liam—'

'So it's not you doing what you've always done, having to be the first at everything and rubbing it in my face?'

'God, Liam, not this again. It was thirty bloody years ago. It wasn't my bloody fault I got my ticket first.'

'Really? Funny how the timing worked so perfectly, though, isn't it?'

Aged seventeen, while Liam had gone off to crew on the big ferries in Scotland for two years after the Leaving Cert, I had stayed around. But Dad had suggested that if skippering was the life I really wanted, it was worth my while trying other ferries as well. So for two years on and off, I found employment on the Galway island routes to the amusement of my new male colleagues who, like Liam, had never thought a woman would be interested in the work or have the brawn and wisdom to do it. Apparently, the ownership of a penis was essential in these matters. But despite them all, I not only hauled and manoeuvred as well as any man, I also studied at night, getting one exam after another to make up my licence. I had just turned twenty when I came home to ferry *Aoibhneas* with the surveyor by my side and to get my final pass. Uncle Michael-Fran opened the Wagtail in celebration. Unintentionally, it also turned out to be one of Liam's rare visits home from the ships. But I never saw a ghost of him for the whole time he was there. He never arrived to avail himself of the free drink that night, that's for sure. I was told his uncle Tommy had brought him back out to the mainland on his fishing boat when his holiday was up instead of having to ride the ferry with me as skipper.

'Do you know what, Rosie?' Liam continued, when I failed to rise to his taunt. 'You'd think you'd have more to occupy yourself with up in Dublin rather than poking your nose into things that don't concern you down here.'

Patsy gasped, a hand to her chest. Iggy rounded the counter, the peeler still in his hand, only to be halted by Michael-Fran who had grabbed his arm. While Iggy's disgust had quelled slightly under my uncle's command, both men took a step forward, standing guard.

'Liam, for God's sake, get a grip.' That was Dad.

My limit had been reached. I shot up out of my chair, the force of the movement knocking it over, and took the two steps I needed to stare into that man's eyes.

'Don't you *dare* talk about my life, Liam, here or up there. You have no right to pass any kind of judgement. Do you hear me?'

When word of Saoirse's disappearance had first filtered through to the island eight years before, Liam had actually texted me, his first time ever. Said he was sorry and that he and Teresa were praying for her safe return. I had replied, a simple but heartfelt, *Thank you.* I had thought things had shifted that day. But no: standing there, I realised my coming back had been so bad that he would use anything, even Saoirse, to hurt me.

He offered no reply but placed his mug on a nearby table as if I'd never said a word, as if I didn't exist at all. 'Danny,' he said, 'You need to remember, I'm employed to skipper that vessel and that is what I'll do, like I always have. But I'll not start turning cartwheels for you or for anyone else.'

He left then, striding back out of the door.

Everyone's attention returned to me. Trying to slow the quickened beat of my heart and steady my shaking hands, I busied myself righting my chair. But when the door opened again, I bolted upright, bracing myself for round two.

'Right,' Diarmuid announced, on walking in, a sad, bewildered Stella in his arms, 'this lady's ready to go. If you're quick, Michael-Fran, you'll catch Liam on the next sailing.'

It's Aimee, the girl said.
Aimee, my friend? she'd replied,
confused.

From those ragged beginnings in early May, by late August I had settled in that house, happy to be in my father's quiet presence of an evening.

'There's not a thing on the box tonight,' he might often have said. 'I don't know why I pay the licence fee. Will we break out the cards? Forty-five, what do you say?'

'If you're willing to take your chances despite the thrashing I gave you last night,' I sometimes teased, allowing the hot water to fill the sink for the washing-up.

'I'm biding my time, luring you in. I'm holding out for the paper money. That's when you'll know all about it, my girl.'

We played with ten- and twenty-cent pieces, throwing in a fifty cent if we were feeling daring. We had yet to move to notes, but Dad kept speaking of it as if, when it finally did happen, it would go down in the annals of Roaring Bay.

'You fool, old man, you fool.' I'd chuckle, swishing my hand through the hot water, making it as sudsy as possible.

Michael-Fran might call to join us, or even better, both he and Phelan, and then all three, as if they had planned it just for me, would talk about the sea and all the ferrying stories told so many times before over the slowest games of Forty-five perhaps ever played. And I'd sit back and sometimes close my eyes to listen to the murmur of them, the sudden leap when one contradicted the other, the slow rise as the dramatic end approached, the feathery, disbelieving laughs of them when something wonderful was remembered, an extra nugget pulled from the depths of the long-forgotten.

'You're making it up now, boy?' Phelan might say.

'I am in my eye.' Michael-Fran, on when he had, allegedly, brought a horse from the mainland on a fishing trawler and stood beside her the whole way, singing the national anthem quietly, as if it was a love song and not a call to war.

'You should have seen the weather. Dear God in Heaven, someone had committed some kind of mortal sin that night because I tell you now, boy, she was raging, and there I was, the throat drying up on me but I kept it going. Kept lulling that girl until, thank Christ, we hit the mouth of the harbour.'

Another round of tea. Another hand of cards.

'Do you remember when *Aoibhneas* broke down on us?' Dad, referring to *Aoibhneas I* in '74. 'Stopped mid-sea and wouldn't turn for love or money and her only new. Towed into Rossban, we were. And I sat with her that night, missed the dinner your mother had cooked. Do you remember she sent Danny junior over with it in your little trawler, Phelan, him carrying it all the way, one plate over the other and a tea towel wrapped around it? I was that upset and worried about her, like she was some pet lamb. I'd checked the lot of her but couldn't figure what was wrong. And then just before you were turning back for home and about to leave me there for the night, I decided to try her again, and up she purred, like as if not a thing had been up with her at all. She made a liar of me that night and several times again. But I didn't mind. I never did. Isn't that what it's all about, the rough with the smooth? When the smooth is good, nothing nor no one comes near it.'

A week before I left for Dublin, I swam with Iggy for the first time. It was not planned. He'd been halfway across the bay, his back to me, when something told me to do it, to kick off my sandals and get in. And I did. Fully clothed, I sank beneath the water with my eyes closed and stayed there for as long as my breath allowed, letting it surround every bit of me. And when it felt right, I emerged gently, seeing Iggy reaching the other side, turning to wave to where I should normally have been. I submerged again before he had time to locate me. Under water, I stretched out my arms and let my feet propel me forward and I swam, my heart refusing to let me sink as I had once feared. I glided over the rocks and skimmed above the sway of seaweed, totally unburdened.

Iggy, as was his wont, didn't make a big deal of it when he got back to find me soaked and wrapped in his towel.

'You've got a bit of water there,' he said, pointing to my chin at which he smiled, as did I, and then we laughed, the warmest of laughs.

Later, when we shared our last coffee together, watching the vast horizon from his rooftop, me having borrowed some dry clothes, he bumped me softly with his shoulder and asked: 'Who am I going to swim with now?'

To which I could offer no answer.

That night my father asked if I was sure about going home.

'Aren't you doing well here? At the start I know it was hard but look at you now. I haven't seen you so well in a very long time, love. Hugh wouldn't mind. I could talk to him.'

'It's all arranged now, Dad. I've already been on to Hugh.'

That afternoon after the swim with Iggy, so buoyed was I by that achievement, so sure it was a sign that things would be OK, I had called Hugh to let him know I intended to return to Dublin the following Saturday.

'Dad's back is good now and, you know . . . I feel better,' I'd said, as if that explained it all.

'Right,' he'd replied, then cleared his throat. 'So, what time will you arrive? Should I order a takeaway for you or . . . I'm not sure when I'll be home, you see. There's a backlog of work right now and I was going to work through the weekend—'

'No, no, don't worry,' I said, slightly deflated but wanting not to let it show. 'I don't know what time I'll get there anyway. No, I'll eat on the way.'

There would be no fanfares on my return, that was clear. But still, I reasoned, I had to try for us, for Saoirse.

I smiled at my father that evening, hoping he wouldn't press me further. He crossed the kitchen floor to kiss the top of my head. 'OK,' he whispered. 'OK.'

There's been an accident. Just up the road. And I saw you on the bike and I told Dad to follow you. We can bring you to her, the girl said.

On my arrival back in Dublin the following weekend, I had moved around that house like I was a guest who had got there too early. I ended up sitting on the couch until Hugh came home to give me permission to feel at ease.

That didn't work.

'Here you are,' he said, as I came to meet him in the hallway.

'Here I am.'

We kissed each other on the cheek nervously.

'So how was the journey?' He circumvented me, taking off his cycling helmet. I followed as he headed for the utility room. Hanging back in the kitchen as I listed off the usual: how long it had taken me, the traffic at the Jack Lynch tunnel, the dreaded ring road where I had stopped for a break. I said it all to the half-shut utility-room door where he took off his cycling gear.

'Great,' he said, on coming back out, putting his hands in his pockets and standing there, tipping back and forth, heel to toe, every second or so.

'How was your day?' I asked.

'All fine.'

'Good.'

There was nothing more to say, it seemed, so I decided on a yawn. I admit it was not genuine.

'Yes, yes of course,' he said. 'You must be tired.'

'The journey takes it out of you.'

'I didn't . . . um, I didn't make up a bed. I didn't know what you might want to do.'

'I think Cullie's room for now, don't you?' For the four months I'd been away Hugh still hadn't moved from the spare room, it seemed, where he'd been sleeping for the previous year. Our room lay empty of us, a relic of our past togetherness.

'Sure, whatever you think.'

I headed for the airing cupboard to find the sheets with which I would dress the bed. I cried silently as I pulled and pushed, finally tugging them free from their snug home, not wanting this now despite all I'd hoped for back on Roaring Bay, not wanting to be with my husband, who seemed unsettled by my presence in a house that no longer fitted us.

'Time,' I told myself, as I tucked a sheet into the corner of Cullie's single bed, 'it just needs time. You have to get through this, you have to, if for no one else but Saoirse.'

And, my goodness, how we tried to put it right, how we tried to stitch and mend us back together in that coming week.

The following day, Sunday, Hugh insisted on bringing me food shopping, as if I was some alien he was having to cater for, showing me things and suggesting food I'd never eaten with tightly wound hope. We walked up and down those aisles, filling the trolley with items neither of us wanted, proving to ourselves that we could do this, be together again by virtue of a packet of twelve-month cured Serrano. After, he brought me to what had once been my favourite restaurant in the village, Leaf. We ate sea bass and drank white wine as if he'd never asked me to leave. We smiled at each other when the conversation dried up and he filled it with the complexity of designing a building in the city centre on an overpopulated, under-serviced street close to the canal. He asked me about what it was like being a skipper again.

'Fine,' I'd replied. Fine, nothing more. I resisted the urge to elaborate, to tell him how it really felt for fear he would ask why I'd come home at all.

I did not tell him that my sleeplessness had returned, and that the previous night I had sat on Cullie's bed thinking about all that I had lost in leaving the island, leaving that ferry: the closeness to Saoirse, the calmness of my breathing, the level purr of my heart.

'You look well, Rosie.'

His words caught me by surprise. I had not expected them. But his shy smile told me he had meant them.

'And you do too,' I replied, encouraged by his compliment in this perfect little moment of maybe – maybe this, despite our awkward start, could still be OK. I had meant it. He genuinely looked at ease for the first time since I'd come home. 'How is the piano playing?' I asked.

'Well, I'm happy to report that I can nearly play pretty much all of *Blue Lights on the Runway*, the album not just the song.'

'Wow, I am impressed.'

'Yeah, you know, it's been good.'

And there we lost hold of it. That brief moment of relaxation between us had slipped through our hands as he seemed to realise how bad it might have sounded that he'd enjoyed my being away. He began to eat with great intent and speed.

I moved us on quickly, filling up the void, still trying to rescue us. I, too, after all, had found happiness in his absence.

'So I was thinking of going back down to Dún Laoghaire to see if my job is still open in the harbour.' The ferry ticket office in Dún Laoghaire harbour, the first and only job I'd ever held in Dublin. I'd finally handed in my notice a year ago, after years of leave-taking on and off after Saoirse went missing. The idea had come to me instantaneously. It hadn't crossed my mind before to do so, but I thought he might approve.

He nodded briskly, indicating his support as he chewed a too-large mouthful of sea bass and baby Italian potatoes.

'I thought I should at least try,' I continued, buoyed by his positive response. 'I think I might be able for it again.' But then I took a step too far. 'And Mick, I should ring him and see what needs to be done.'

How badly I had judged what we were able for. It was as if a charm fell off our chain of hope, clanging itself noisily to the floor.

Hugh finally managed to swallow, while he held his knife and fork mid-air for a second before replacing them carefully, silently, back on his plate.

'But it can't be like before, Rosie, you know that. It can't be you running in a hundred directions. I couldn't cope with that, not again.'

I felt an unbidden fury rise. How quickly the magic had been erased. Suddenly, all I could see was him sitting at our kitchen counter back in April asking me to leave.

'I can't be here and do nothing, Hugh. You can't ask me to go back to staring at the walls of that house like last year.' My armpits sweated and my stomach burned.

'You had a breakdown, Rosie. Cut yourself some slack. You needed to rest.'

'I know I had a bloody breakdown, Hugh, thank you very much.'

'OK,' he said slowly. 'Please just take a breath. You've come so far. I can see how well you've done. Don't ruin it now.'

'Oh, really, you can see that? You can tell all about what it was like down there for me by just looking at my face? You've no idea how hard it was being sent away by you. Knowing you wanted me gone. You couldn't even talk to me on the phone, for Christ's sake.'

I stood up, my napkin falling to the floor.

'Rosie, please, just sit.'

I wanted to go. I wanted to storm away as I had done once before at the beginning of said breakdown, but the memory of that time weakened me so much I was forced to sit again, forlornly. His hand reached across the table, asking for mine, but I didn't oblige and left it there until he took it back to drink his last sip of wine.

'I don't know how we got here, Rosie,' he said, before placing the glass back on the table and staring at it.

'No,' I agreed sadly. Our romantic evening had come to an end and neither of us had the will to rescue it. 'Neither do I.'

A moment lapsed and lolled as we considered what now, until eventually Hugh caught the attention of a waiter and asked for the bill. Instead of walking the mile home after, as we had always done before – linking arms, laughing a little drunkenly about the odds and ends of life – I hailed a taxi, in which we sat in silence and watched, out of opposite windows, a world we could no longer understand speed past.

The following day, and the day after that, the strain continued, the reach to comfort never ever achieving its goal. By Tuesday, I was exhausted. By Wednesday, after sleeping most of the morning and into the afternoon as a result of another night's tossing and turning, I got up to walk the coast line, climbing over walls and fences, giving up when they were too high and taking to the suburban pathways, but never veering far from the sea line, watching those huge tankers out there on the horizon, walking through the hours, returning only when I thought Hugh might be home and playing his piano or perhaps, if I was lucky enough, already gone to bed. But, no, when I got back, I found no lights on in the house. Ten o'clock and Hugh still wasn't home.

Cullie called in on the Friday. Despite my delight at seeing him and fussing over him and asking him a myriad questions, he cut through the jovial with the precision of a sharpened razor blade. 'You don't seem happy, Mum.'

'What do you mean?' I gave one of those false laughs. I didn't like being that way with Cullie. He was unworthy of such stupidity.

'Well, correct me if I'm wrong but I thought the island was doing you good.'

'Yes, it did, and here I am now rested and ready to go,' I lied.

'Ready to go? Ready to go at what?'

'Well . . . getting back to normal.'

'And that is?' We were standing in the sitting room, or rather I was, it seemed, shifting around it, plumping up cushions, wiping at couch arms, while he watched from the doorway.

'I was surprised you came back, actually. I honestly thought you'd stay.'

I stopped what I was doing to look at him questioningly.

'Mum, you have to do whatever it is you need to get through, even if that means not living here.'

To get through to where? I wanted to ask him, he who, despite all he'd had to endure from the age of fifteen, had managed to remain this uniquely kind soul. But he had broken through my flimsy defences.

'You're right. I don't know what I'm doing, Cullie, not any more. Not about here, anyway, this family, your dad, you . . .' How weak my voice sounded, as if I had been talking all day, and the saliva, the breath, the will was finally wasted.

'Mum, listen to me. I don't need you to do anything for me. I'm fine. Me and Nina are doing great.'

'But your sister? I'm letting her down.' I felt so ashamed to think back on how long it had been since I'd made one phone call on her behalf.

'How exactly?'

'I need to be here.' I swung around, indicating the sitting room as if he had no clue what 'here' I was referring to. 'Pushing for more. Getting the guards to listen again. Getting back on the TV and radio, like I used to. Reminding people that she's out there and still needs their help.'

Even as I was saying those words, I knew the truth was that if Cullie had told me to go on air immediately, I'd have panicked. Despite my protestations to Hugh the previous Sunday night at dinner, that woman who for eight years had waged war on a world that had robbed her of her child seemed a million miles from the person I was now, so lost and ill at ease.

'Mum—'

'No, listen. There was a time when my every waking moment was about my list of things we needed to do.

People we needed to call: TDs, chief inspectors, help lines. I had radio and TV interviews dripping off me. Now? Well, look at me, do I seem like a woman who could go on *Prime Time*? If I manage to brush my hair in the mornings it's a miracle.'

'Mum, it's—'

'And being back here reminds me that I'm failing her. I was hiding away down there on that bloody island, that's what I was doing. Ignoring that I have a missing daughter to find.'

'MUM. LISTEN.'

I stopped, shocked by Cullie's raised voice, a thing that was not naturally him.

'I've already lost a sister. I don't want to lose a mother too.'

My poor boy had no clue that he had lost me already. I realised that even in those moments when I was physically present I still wasn't really there at all, not in my mind. I was standing beside Saoirse at a window in some apartment looking out on a foreign cityscape, one of the many lives I had imagined for her. I wasn't with *him*, not like I should have been.

'What I mean, Mum, is if you'd continued as you were, we'd have lost you. And we nearly bloody did. And none of us wanted that, not Dad, not Granddad and not me.'

I didn't want to think about that, my breakdown, my time in hospital after Mammy's funeral. I concentrated on the carpet, wishing him away from the subject.

'Bottom line, Mum? Our lives changed from being in any way normal a long time ago. Stop putting that pressure on yourself, and us. Go back to Roaring Bay. You don't need to sleep in the same bed as Dad, or live in the same house, or the same city, or the same strip of land. We're not some happy suburban family. We need to stop trying to fit into that. We were handed a whole different script when Saoirse disappeared.'

How was he so wise? I wondered. I placed a hand on his cheek, then kissed his other. And then my arms surrounded him as my mind drifted to an office six kilometres away, to Hugh, who I imagined sitting at his desk, ignoring his computer, instead staring out of the window that overlooked the sea, his elbow on the chair's arm, fingers tapping at his lips, wondering how long he could stretch out his evening's work to avoid the journey home.

When he eventually returned that night, I met him in the hallway. Hugged him before he'd even had a chance to take off his cycle helmet. And there I whispered in his ear that I was leaving once more. He didn't protest, but took my hand, knitting his fingers through mine before eventually letting me go. I climbed the stairs to fill my case, and waited on the spare bed till the morning gave me light enough to pack the car and turn her south-west, once more heading away from him, the man I had once thought I could not take a step or breath without.

PART 2

Maybe I should just . . . she looked back to the house, wondering if she had time to explain to her mother.

I was sixteen when I met Hugh in 1984. He was seventeen and had come to work in the shop. The thing I'd noticed about Diarmuid's summer staff back then was that none of them could make a hot chocolate quite like the owner. I'd already had this out with Diarmuid well before Hugh had arrived, when I was still working the weekend ferry crew before school finished when I would work *Aoibhneas* full time for three long months. Every Saturday that May, I'd insisted Diarmuid make my hot chocolate himself. Out he'd come from the kitchen saying: 'Do you not think I have other things to be doing than making sure your hot chocolate is perfect, Rosie?'

'Not my fault if you can't train your staff properly, Diarmuid.'

Diarmuid was in his late twenties at the time and had come home from Cork City to take over the shop and restaurant from his mother.

'They aren't that bad.'

'Oh yes they are. That woman from Rathkilly is hopeless. It was more a freezing chocolate the last time. Where is she anyway? Haven't seen her around lately.'

I followed close behind as he wiped his hands on the tea towel that hung from the apron strings tied tightly beneath his belly, and made his way to the front of the shop. It being early in the season, he'd only filled one or two of his potential vacancies by then.

'Gone. Some family emergency. Her summer of writing by the sea evaporated before it had even begun – she got a phone call and started crying right over there by the Knorr stock cubes.'

'Best all round, I think.'

I knew Diarmuid was lost to me, wondering how he would fill her spot as he took the milk from the fridge and filled a mug before putting it into the microwave. He was used to it, though, things not working out, people thinking they could hack the long hours and pace of the work, then finding that, no, they most certainly could not, not even if the job came with room and board. Their images of long walks and creative flow were soon replaced by the reality of exhaustion and too many late nights spent in Páidíns bar. And not everyone wanted to go work on an island anyway. Diarmuid would always have to throw the net wide to find his staff, ringing aunties on the mainland wondering if any of their grandchildren might need the few bob, or friends he once knew when he'd worked his food truck on Cork City docks. Someone who could, like Diarmuid, be both shopkeeper and host, smiling as they served the tourists homemade scones, nipping back in to serve the eager children a tub of Críostóir's goat-milk ice cream, switching seamlessly to serving the midday menu of open crabmeat sandwiches and seafood chowder with a glass of wine, while at the same time making sure Patsy got her *Irish Times* and half-dozen eggs, rounding off that frantic day with the evening sittings of Diarmuid's salmon *en croûte* and steak or pizza, and finally, when the last customer had wandered home, mopping the kitchen and shop floors without flooding the place, to then, at long last, collapse in a heap on a single bed in whichever establishment Diarmuid had managed to rent them for the summer. No, Diarmuid knew, they weren't always easy to find.

'Maybe you could teach me how to work your magic and I'll make my own,' I suggested. 'That way I won't be bothering you all summer when it gets really busy.'

'Oh yeah, right.'

'Think of it as one less picky islander to worry about.'

Between milk, microwave, cream and the dinkiest little power whisk I'd ever seen, I watched Diarmuid create his legendary piping-hot, silky hot chocolate.

'I can't just be letting anyone in here, Rosie. I could be done for it.'

'By who? The guards? I don't think they're going to make a special trip out to arrest you for that.'

'There is such a thing as health and safety standards. And, anyway, it was more the whole island I was thinking of. They'll all be wanting to come in here and make their own, won't they?' He reached under the counter for his tin of marshmallows, taking off the lid and tilting it in my direction. 'Two or three?'

'Four. Employ me, then. I could be your orders person for the crew. Imagine no more *us* hanging around your counter making the place look messy. Meanwhile, I'll slip in here and Bob's your uncle. Dad and Phelan only want tea, and Phelan's is black at that. If I can handle making this, I'll surely be able to dunk a couple of teabags. And, besides, us crew can't be waiting in queues, can we, when we have the whole island dependent on our efficiency of service? I'll be in and out and no one will ever know.'

'I don't give discounts, Rosie, even if it is a do-it-yourself.'

'I know.' I was a little indignant that he would think I'd even ask that, before relenting. 'But maybe one free hot chocolate a month wouldn't be out of the question, you know, so you can prove to any health inspector that may come knocking that I am kind of staff.'

I grinned, then took the first sip from the mug he'd handed me. I could see he was coming round or, at the very least, amused. He leaned against the counter as I sighed in happiness at the creamy hot smoothness of my drink.

'And what about the week you're off and Tommy and his gang are on?' That would have been the other crew, or the 'shit crew', as I liked to call them, much to Dad's exasperation, made up of Tommy Ó Kiersey, Éamon and Séamus Ó Kiersey, Liam's older cousins, and Liam himself, working the weekend shift like me. 'I'm not having Éamon coming in here with those rotten hands of his. God knows where they've been – in his ear most of the time, as far as I can tell. I keep telling him to see Dr McArthur if it's that bloody itchy.'

'That lot like queuing.' I smiled, both of us knowing I had just put a huge dent in my argument of the ferry's need for speed and its crew not getting in the way of Diarmuid's other customers. 'And, besides, if they start to complain, I'll deal with them.'

'And this is all going to be worth it because you don't like your hot chocolate a little on the cool side?'

'Definitely.'

By the time Hugh Dunne, the son of a friend of a second cousin of Diarmuid's, had arrived at the end of June, I was working full time as ferry crew and was well into the swing of my hot chocolate-making: straight off the ferry once the passengers had disembarked at eleven, a quick sprint around into the shop's loos, two good hand scrubs and then a nip behind the counter, bobbing in and out of the way of the workers. I'd prepay at the beginning of the week, ensuring no more time than necessary was wasted.

'Rosie,' Diarmuid said, on Hugh's first day, 'meet Hugh. Hugh, Rosie. Hugh's down from Dublin to help me out till August.'

We nodded at each other, nothing special passing between us, like when Dad met Mam over the counter of O'Sullivan's supermarket in Clonkill where she was working, and the next day presented her with a bunch of sopping wet daffodils he had plucked from the local park. No, our beginning could most definitely have been described as sedate.

'Now, Hugh, you're not to be minding this one here. Rosie likes to make her own hot chocolate.' He raised his eyebrows. 'Leave her at it but make sure you get the money.'

'Oh, right,' Hugh said, noting it in the little book he carried around with him in which, I was to learn later, he wrote down details like how much the bottles of wine were, which for some reason bore no price, the code to the store room and where to locate the gravy granules – he'd been asked already that morning and couldn't find them.

He looked up: 'How much are they?'

'How much are what?'

'Hot chocolates.'

'Oh, a pound.'

Hugh wrote it down.

Diarmuid gave me a wink. I couldn't decide if he meant to impart that he had found an excellent employee who'd be keeping an eye on me, or if he was saying, Look who I found for you: a good-looking, black-haired, blue-eyed beauty. Either way I gave a sarcastic smile and continued with making my hot chocolate, unsure that this serious, diligent boy would have what it took to succeed there. But I needn't have doubted.

At my morning break I'd go in to do my thing while Hugh worked the counter.

'Rosie,' he'd state.

'Hugh,' I'd reply.

'How is the seafarer today?'

'Oh, fine.'

'Well, excellent.'

And that would pretty much be it. Except for when I was leaving, pushing open the shop door with my back, my hands clasping the triangle of three mugs, I'd watch him take out that notebook and mark down, I suspected, my one hot chocolate and two teas, the perfect little employee. By the time I got to Dad and Phelan, I'd be seething at such close tabs being kept on me by someone not a wet week in the place. As if I was the suspicious one. I mean, who the hell was he? A Dubliner, here, in the arse-end of nowhere – if that wasn't suspicious then I didn't know what was.

Dad and Phelan always sat on the low wall right at the top of the pier. They liked it there as it had a good view of *Aoibhneas* in case we were needed urgently. Behind us, by the road that ran straight from the pier right into the heart of the island, was Patsy's house and on the other side of the crossing was Páidíns bar, as yet unopened at that time of morning. Conversation was mostly limited to observations on the day or the calibre of passengers we were carrying.

It was while we were in that very spot, about a month after Hugh had arrived, sipping our drinks, that I became aware of a figure in close proximity. I hadn't looked up. The harbour was the most crowded place on the island on hot summer days, and even though we sat at the end of the throng, there would always be someone about, looking out at the harbour like us, or waiting for a child to catch up or even someone apologising for interrupting our break but asking when was the next sailing.

'Erm, Rosie?' I raised my hand to shade my eyes from the dazzle of the sun as I looked up, barely able to make out that it was Hugh before me. 'Sorry to interrupt,' he said, an air of worry about him, 'but I've been keeping a tally of your hot chocolates and teas over the last while . . .'

'Yes,' I said, 'I've noticed.'

Beside me, I could almost feel the sharp nudge to the ribs my father had given Phelan, delighting no doubt at the bravery of this boy and the tongue-whipping he was about to receive in return. Phelan gave a cough as he uncrossed his legs, then re-crossed them the other way, looking to the left-hand side of the harbour so I couldn't see the grin I knew was there. As I turned back towards Hugh, I noticed Dad taking far too long a gulp from his mug, trying to hide his smirk.

'And?' I asked finally, not looking up at him this time as I could no longer take the glare of the sun, instead focusing on the empty space to my right on the low wall. He took it as an invitation, and after he had seated himself, produced his notebook where he had written out each date I had been in and how many drinks I had taken. It was all there: 25 June, 1 hot choc 2 tea, 26 June, et cetera. He was diligent, I had to give him that – diligent and fearless, misguided though it was.

'So, as you can see, I've tallied up everything here.' He held out the book, as if he was a town crier about to 'hear ye' to the world. 'And there seems to be a discrepancy.'

'A discrepancy?' I put down my cup in the small space he had wisely left between us and folded my arms, at which both my father and Phelan shifted again. 'In what way?' I had my ace up my sleeve, ready to hurl at him as I began to blister at this boy's audacity, that I too was an employee of sorts, a fact that Diarmuid had obviously failed to mention, forgetting my one free hot chocolate that we had clearly agreed on every month that would need to be considered in this Dubliner's profit-and-loss statement.

'Well, I'm a little embarrassed to say but—'

'No, don't be,' I interrupted, 'I mean, I hadn't realised we'd come to this on the island. I know Dublin is a whole different kettle of fish, what with your penny-pinching, but round here we usually aren't that concerned with such pettiness. But if that's the way it is, that's no problem.' Indignantly, I pulled a fiver from my pocket, along with an unrequired stick of lip balm, a tissue and a couple of pound coins. One bobbed along the edge of the wall, in danger of falling right down onto the sandy beach until Mr Auditor saved it by slapping the palm of his hand over it. 'How much?' I demanded. I had already decided I would never go behind that counter again, and I'd make a flask of hot chocolate to bring with me every morning instead, saddened that a fork or my mother's large sauce whisk wouldn't be able to cut it like Diarmuid's dinky dynamo and that I would be having lukewarm milky chocolate for the rest of my summer.

It was then that he smiled broadly. 'No, it's we who owe you. The discrepancy is in fact an overpayment in your favour. And what I was really wondering was, do you wish it to continue this way as a rolling surplus, so to speak, or shall I refund you now?'

At this point, my father spluttered with laughter, and had he been able to reach him, I'm sure he'd have added a good hard slap to Hugh's shoulder. Instead, he leaned forward, and raised his cup in cheers to his courage.

'Well, my God, boy, I thought you were a goner there. But, no, you've risen yourself up to be a true hero.' He laughed again, then shook his head in awe. 'A discrepancy, that's a good one.'

I looked beyond Hugh, towards the shop door where Diarmuid, too, was standing laughing. This boy had known exactly what he was doing, walking over to me with my father right beside me, with that serious head on him and his list. I had been had.

'I'm going to kill that man,' I said, stuffing my belongings back into my pockets, before relenting with a smile. 'Tell him I'll be having two free hot chocolates this month for that.'

'I will,' Hugh replied, getting up and walking back to the shop, high-fiving Diarmuid on his return.

One had to admire Hugh's pluckiness. Seventeen years of age, without an idea of how the island worked, and there he was, taking his life into his own hands and doing Diarmuid's bidding. But as I was to find out later, it had all been Hugh's idea. He reckoned I'd be up for a laugh. For weeks he'd watched me slipping in and out of the place and exchanging a joke or a slagging with whoever was about. And, anyway, he said, he was a little bored.

'Bored?' I enquired, the Thursday of the following week when, at ten o'clock at night, we were sitting once again on the harbour wall, but this time with pints in our hands from Páidíns. 'You can't be bored in Diarmuid's, not in the summer. Sure you don't have time to breathe.'

I'd seen Hugh there on his own, watching the darkened water on a rare night off as I passed on my way to meet my brother Nathan and his mates in the pub on one of his last weeks on the island before he set off to follow Daniel to the US as soon as his stint in construction college was over. I'd stopped and chatted with Hugh for a minute before offering to buy him a pint. Although Nathan had had to buy it, given I was still under age.

'Yeah, no, I don't mean *that* way bored. I mean more in the head, needing to-do-something-else bored. There's only so long you can sell sliced pans and packet soups without feeling like you're dying a little bit inside.'

'So, you thought you'd have a laugh at my expense.'

'Well, it was more trying to break the ice, to get to know you a bit better. You're in and out so quickly that I reckoned I needed something big to get you to stop and notice me.'

'Oh,' I said, registering there was indeed more to this than boredom.

We sipped from our drinks while we adjusted to this admission.

'But what I *really* don't get,' he said, veering us away from the embarrassment of two teenagers realising they had crossed into new territory, 'is how you drink that stuff every day in this heat. I mean it's like drinking mulled wine in summer.'

'Well, I've never actually had mulled wine so I wouldn't know. But I don't see why a particular drink must be reserved for a particular season. Why deny yourself what you like because tradition demands it?'

He had turned to look at me, impressed, it seemed, by my non-conformance. 'Hmm. I like that.'

My stomach thrilled at how he lifted his chin as he considered me. I had the urge to reach out and touch the concavity of that slight dimple there. I shifted, embarrassed, curling my fingers against my glass in case they decided to go rogue.

'So, Rosie, what are you planning on doing with your life?'

'Skippering the ferry.' I gestured in *Aoibhneas*'s direction.

'Really? Isn't the ferry just a summer job?'

'It is right now, but it won't be once I've gotten my licence. Why? What's so surprising about that?'

'Well, yeah, I mean . . . I suppose I'm not usually around people who want to do stuff like that. It's great, though. Is it only *this* ferry or do you plan on doing bigger ones elsewhere?'

'Oh, no, here. She's all I want.'

'So, you're not tempted to travel the world? Which, in your intended line of business, let's face it, would be fairly easy.'

I had thought about it, plenty of times, how if I wanted to, I could skipper bigger ferries in the most exotic of places. But each time I imagined myself at the helm of a tanker on the Suez Canal, or even simply crossing the Irish Sea, it didn't feel right.

'No, she's enough for me.'

'It must get really quiet in the winter, though. Not sure I could live here all year round.'

'Other places aren't all they're cracked up to be.'

''Cause you've been to so many.'

'No, smartarse. It's because I think when you know you're happy you know, right. And why change that?'

'Well, OK.' But he didn't seem so sure.

'Oh, come on. So, what, Dublin's not good enough for you?'

'Yeah, I guess you're right, I do love it. You don't know what you're missing not living in a city. I mean, everything is, like, there. The cinema, the nightclubs—'

'We have night life!' I gestured to Páidíns.

'Yeah, quality.' He laughed.

'So why are you here, then, and not there trying to fool some other unsuspecting stranger?'

'Yeah, you see, they aren't that gullible in Dublin, so I have to do that stuff down here.'

'A man with a talent for compliments.'

He laughed again, then took a sip from his pint. 'In fairness, what I want to do with my life isn't half as interesting as you. I want to be an architect, work for one of the big companies in Dublin or maybe branch out on my own, we'll see. I'm hoping to get architecture in UCD. I'm here because I need the money for that.'

'Architecture in UCD? Aiming high.'

'We'll see. It's handy, you know. I live in Blackrock and my dad works as a security guard in the college so there's this reduced-fee thing.'

'Blackrock? Very posh.'

'Ah, yeah, there you go, falling for the belief that every-one who lives there is loaded. *We* aren't. We live on a council estate.'

'Didn't think they had them in that part of the world.'

'There are a few. But they hide them behind the private estates with the really big houses so no one can see them. We're only allowed out at night when it's dark. Actually, I had to get a special visa to come here.'

'Well, we can't just let any riff-raff in.'

'I know. I mean, I can see why. The cars alone say you're a refined people.'

He turned to put his hand on the bonnet of Phelan's Nissan that was parked right up against the wall. It was green, only the bonnet was black, and the driver's door red, with the window permanently down. He would need to fix it by winter, but right now the empty space held a sheet of clear plastic Sellotaped on to keep out the summer rain.

'No, I still don't get it. You decide to leave your beloved Dublin and all your mates to head here for the summer. There has to be more to it than money?'

'Really, does there? The opportunity was handed to me. Do you know how hard it is to get jobs in Dublin these days? Besides, my mates, such as they are, will still be there when I get back. I'm not missing that much.'

'Wow, popular too, I'm guessing.'

He placed his now empty pint glass between his thighs, his hands circling the top, and he watched his thumbs tip at the rim. 'Actually, I don't have a whole heap of people I hang out with.' He looked out towards the sea, illuminated as it was now in the oncoming darkness by the light of Páidíns bar from behind us on the left and Diarmuid's, still busy with night-time diners, from the right. 'One or two. But they're like me. We hang out when we want to, but we give each other space as well. I guess there are times when we all need a break, you know. I'm an introvert really.'

'Yeah, right. Don't think introverts play pranks on complete strangers.'

'You'd be surprised. We're an odd breed. Introverts do like people, and, yes, sometimes we also enjoy a bit of fun with other human beings. But then there are times that we need to get away, see other things, be on our own, have a bit of alone time. It's not weird, it's just me.'

This honesty, this understanding of who he was and what made him tick even at seventeen, coupled with his ability to tell me straight out without a hint of embarrassment, that right there was Hugh in a nutshell. Presenting himself to me as if on a menu, with all the ingredients and allergens out in the open, allowing me to choose whether I really wanted him or not.

'Another one?' he asked, holding up his empty. Our eyes held the other's for a simple, comfortable moment before we smiled, knowing where it was we were going, the future we were assembling.

'Sure,' I answered, handing over my glass as he swung his legs back over the low wall, heading for the bar.

I sat with him for the rest of the night and every night he had off thereafter that summer.

We have to go now, the girl said, watching her. Get in, get in.

Whenever Michael-Fran took the fancy and was spotted opening his pub, news would spread quickly across the island, like a good southerly gale. Soon people would be sitting on the bar stools in front of his counter, sometimes just having a mug of tea with the Cadbury's purple snacks Michael-Fran had behind the bar, enjoying the novelty of having another venue in which to enjoy a Saturday afternoon.

The Wagtail, at the base of Hare Hill, looked out over the glen where down below sat the school, the church and a round of houses, and where very little happened other than the arrival of native and exotic birds finding safety in this silent cocoon tucked out of the Atlantic's way. Michael-Fran lit the fire even in the summer, it being his firm belief that no one should be indoors when the sun shone (or in the chill of early spring, for that matter, but it was hard to win the crowd over on that one). Not wishing to sit in the sweltering heat, no matter how cold the beer, the customers would soon, much to Michael-Fran's delight, fill the wall over the road by the glen's edge that he had built himself to watch the birds flit in and out.

'And what inspired you this time?' That was Phelan wondering why it was that Michael-Fran had chosen that day, 14 April 1990, six years after Hugh and I first met, of all the days to open.

'Do you know, I haven't a clue. I got up this morning and had my usual egg from Fidelma and it came to me: open her up. There's something good going to come out of today if you do. And here I am now. Waiting.'

'Might it be the Lotto?' Phelan enquired. 'Perhaps you should nip around to Diarmuid's and buy a ticket.'

'Ah, no. I'd be thinking it might be something a bit more special than that. More on the lines of a sighting of that Eurasian Hoopoe that's been spotted around. Patsy said it was in her garden yesterday. That would make my day now,' he said wistfully.

But it was neither windfall nor bird. It was my engagement.

I had never dreamed it possible that I could fall in love with anyone who had the power to take me away from *Aoibhneas* and Roaring Bay. But I had.

For a man who thought he would do only one summer on the island, Hugh came back that first Christmas of our meeting to stay in my brothers', by then empty, bedroom. The following summer, when I had finally finished school and was working the boats in Galway he headed west to my grotty house share. Thereafter, once I had qualified, he returned to the island for his weekends off while he was finishing up his master's and working internships in Dublin firms. I'd go to Dublin too, to sleep in his bedroom, although without him in it. Even though his parents were from the city, a much more liberal place than Roaring Bay, as Hugh was killed telling me, Robert and Ursula weren't so free-thinking as to go for the whole sharing a bedroom, so Ursula would make up the couch for him when I was there, not trusting him to do it as neatly as she could.

He delighted in showing me the city, the bars, the night clubs and the cinemas. I'd get him to bring me to a bookshop or two, so I could go home to Mam and rave about how big they were. We'd walk down to Seapoint in Monkstown to sit on a rock moulded by the sea, and there the two of us would quietly talk about nothing and everything, falling deeper and deeper into the other's world, so that by the time my few days were up it would feel as if we were leaving each other for ever.

'Isn't it magnificent?' he'd say, looking out at Howth across the bay, and I'd smile, knowing exactly what he was at, trying to convince me I could most definitely fall in love with Dublin as much as with him.

I'd smile and nod, but not as convincingly as he had hoped, because he would sigh as if to say, honestly, you haven't a clue.

We were six years at this traipsing across the country to see the other. Those constant goodbyes were exhausting, not to mention upsetting. He asked me on more than one occasion to move to Dublin.

'But why me?' I'd reply. 'Why can't you move down?'

This one time we were on the couch in their sitting room, watching *Inspector Morse* while trying to decide whether to go to Morton's in Donnybrook where some of his workmates were meeting for pints or whether to go to a late-night movie in Stillorgan, when the topic had come up again.

'OK, so remind me,' he said, 'how many architecture firms there are in Clonkill?'

'But you've always said you'd like to have your own business, so why not do it down there?'

'Yes, but I have to prove myself first, don't I, to me most of all? It's important that I'm working for Kirwan's – they're one of the big guys. If I can last the pace with them then I know I can do it on my own. I don't want to settle for

"Donal Ó Shaughnessy" who has to do a bit of part-time farming on the side to make ends meet. Anyway, who the hell has the money down there these days to pay an architect to design their house? And before you say it, I have no more interest in designing the kind of bungalows rural Ireland seems intent on. Besides, nobody needs an architect for them – any builder could do them in his sleep.'

I didn't bother answering but looked back at *Inspector Morse*, having completely lost where I was in the thing.

'But do you know what we have in abundance up in this part of the world?' he asked, giving me a little nudge.

'Not this again.'

'Sea. Loads of the thing. And we have ferries. Huge big ones.'

'Not interested.'

'Well, what do you propose we do then?'

'Can we please leave it?' I laid my head back on the couch, resting it wearily there.

'OK, but you know I'm right. Up here we both get to do what we want. Down there, I'd have to become a fisherman, and these were meant to create, not kill.' He waggled his fingers at me.

These conversations could have gone on for ever if Hugh had not put a halt to it when his granny died. Granny Pat had passed the previous February, and in the coming months when her three sons worked through her estate they found, to everyone's amazement, that she'd had a nest egg that was less an egg and more a boulder of £150,000 that none of them could figure out the source of. She left thirty thousand to each of her three sons and twenty thousand apiece for her three grandchildren. It was this that allowed Hugh to begin his life, as he put it.

And so on 14 April 1990, when I was twenty-two, he turned to me as we sat in Michael-Fran's bar and said: 'Marry me.'

'What?' My abrupt response, a little louder than I had planned, caused the whole pub to fall silent. I wiped at the small amount of beer that had slipped down my chin when I'd halted my drinking mid-swig as I waited for his reply.

'I'm asking you to marry me. I want you to take a chance on us, on Dublin. I know it's not your ideal plan but what else can we do? Give me five years. If I haven't convinced you that this is the right choice by then I swear we'll move down here, and I'll become a farmer if I have to. But please marry me. Please put me out of my misery of being without you. I want you by my side every minute of the day, Rosie Driscoll. That's all there is to it.'

I squinted at him, still distrustful that this was really happening.

'I'm serious, Rosie.'

And so we were finally at that place where a decision had to be made. Once again, I felt the panic of giving up the island life I loved and had worked so hard for. Despite knowing it was too late, I began to run through the options again, a life lived half in Dublin half here at breakneck speed. But as much as I had wished for them, there were no viable alternatives. It was Dublin or losing the man who made me happier than I had ever felt and that was something I could not let happen. I had no choice. I loved him. From the top of my black-haired head to the tip of the big toes on my insanely small feet, he had me. I would do anything for him, follow him anywhere, just as long as we were together.

'Yes,' I said, with a shy smile, and the whole pub breathed out. A roar went up and he laughed and I laughed, as he took my face in his hands and drew me in for a kiss.

My uncle rang what felt like the entire island and they all came to celebrate. There were rounds being bought for us by complete strangers, birdwatchers who couldn't help but be caught up in that joyful occasion, which, when I think of it, might have been more their luck at finally seeing the Wagtail open, having returned year after year with no sighting of this rare spectacle. I like to think our engagement got a special mention in the birdwatchers' logbook that night.

'And tell me this,' my father asked Hugh, after my parents had arrived to shake my fiancé's hand and hug me, 'how do you think you'll adjust to island life? I mean I know you've put in a few summers here, but it won't be the same in the winter. It's a whole different beast when the wind's stripping a few layers off you.'

'Oh . . . right,' Hugh answered, with trepidation. 'Well, actually, we thought, maybe that we'd give Dublin a go for a bit. See how we do there.'

I gave my father a small smile to reassure him that this was what I wanted, but I could see it there: the hint of sadness that what he had feared for the last few years since Hugh had arrived was coming to pass, that the life we shared was about to change. It was just Liam and me driving *Aoibhneas* at that stage: Dad had stepped away to let us young ones do the shifts while he took on a more managerial role. Now he would need to skipper with Liam again.

'Course you are, Hugh. I'm only kidding with you.' Dad gave Hugh a good slap to the knee, covering up his disappointment expertly, for which I was grateful. 'Why don't we get ourselves another pint and you can tell us about this family of yours up in Dublin that we're going to be marrying into, especially that wonderful millionaire granny of yours, Lord have mercy on her?'

Liam arrived soon after, only too delighted to raise a glass to my imminent departure. 'Well, I never thought I'd see the day,' he said, bringing over a full tray of drinks to lay beside the many others still undrunk for fear of liver failure. Teresa, who was studying in Limerick at the time and was down for the weekend, stood beside him, a little embarrassed, I suspected, by Liam's jubilance.

'That's mighty kind of you, Liam,' Dad said, nodding at the tray when I only managed a smile in response.

Liam shook Hugh's hand. Hugh knew our history well, having listened to me giving out enough over the years to understand its undercurrent. But they'd always gotten on this pair. I knew what Liam saw in Hugh from the minute our romance had become public six years prior: a man who might finally take me away. All my young life thus far, I'd been like a sticky back, the seed of the cleaver weed hooking onto him: he was unable to shake me off no matter how much he tried. But here before him was the solution to my irksomeness, one that I had produced all by myself without him even having to lift a finger.

He shook my hand too, but limply compared to the vigorous shake he'd given Hugh.

'Well, will you be settling in Dublin, then?' he asked Hugh, with not a hint of shame.

'That's the idea,' he replied, putting a calming hand to my knee under the table, pleading I not react.

'There are worse places you could live.' The man's lips must have been under some strain so wide was his smile. 'Teresa's always wanting to go up when we get the few days

together, aren't you?' The circumspect Teresa smiled dutifully but said nothing. 'She loves Grafton Street. We walk
the length and breadth of it ten times over in the one day.
I'm exhausted by the end of it.'

'Sure, they'll give it a go,' Dad interjected, standing up.
'Actually, as you're here, Liam, I thought I might bend your
ear about something.' Dad took Liam away from us, defus-
ing the situation with a grace that was so very him back
then, to stand at the bar as he, Liam and Michael-Fran
engaged in conversation.

'Well,' Teresa said shyly. 'I'll leave ye to it. Congratulations again.'

'It'll be you and himself soon,' I replied, a kind of peace
offering.

'Oh.' She laughed. 'We'll see.' She left us then to join
Dad and Liam at the counter.

Hugh took the last boat out the following day. Liam, who
was on duty, came down from the wheelhouse specifically to
talk to him. I watched them share a laugh at something. Liam
then checked his watch and turned to take the stairs two by
two before looking over at me, as I stood on the pier, and
giving me a wink. The man had never winked at me in his
life before. It was almost enough for me to change my mind.

The following day I dropped into Mammy in the library.
I was slumped on one of the two beanbags from 'Kids'
Korner' that had been repaired more times than I could
remember over the years, repackaged in new covers, more
beans added as the originals had flattened.

'What is it, my lovely?' Mammy asked, from behind her
librarian's desk. 'I thought you'd be full of the joys today.'

I sighed, utterly depressed, and watched Mammy as she sorted through all the islanders' loan cards. When I was much younger, I used to do it for her sometimes. I enjoyed making sure everything was alphabetical and behind the right divider and the figuring out of what was well over-due and who was committing such an offence, feeling that I was an essential assistant in the fight against such criminal goings-on as late loans.

'Patsy. AGAIN.' My poor bewildered mother. 'How many times have I told that woman? Two weeks, I say. And she leaves with that butter-wouldn't-melt-in-her-mouth smile. I'd never see the books again if I didn't call in to her and get them back myself.'

'Is that what librarians are supposed to do? I mean, I doubt they do it on the mainland.' As the years had gone on, I'd become less enthusiastic and more amused by my mother's policing of the islanders' book-borrowing habits.

'We're not on the mainland, Rosie, and neither am I your run-of-the-mill librarian.'

'No, you certainly are not.'

'And I don't take kindly to your implication that how I do things around here is in anyway misguided. Rules are rules. Two weeks. It isn't like they have to walk miles and miles to renew them now, is it? I mean, a simple phone call. These books are everyone's.'

'I know, I was just saying—'

'Well, don't, my darling girl.'

I grew serious again and finally said what had been lurk-ing in my mind all morning. 'It is the right choice, isn't it, going to Dublin?'

Mammy put down her precious cards for a moment and observed me with a smile that made me recall a time when

I was small, at midnight mass, and had snuggled under her arm, resting against her warm soft breast, and hearing the choir sing as my eyelids began to droop, no matter how hard I'd tried to stop them. A moment of complete love and safety.

'This is love, isn't it, Rosie? I mean you haven't been fooling us all these years?'

'Of course it is.' I felt slightly affronted that there should be any doubt.

'Well, that's it, then, I'm afraid. No matter how much you enjoy what you do and no matter how wonderful your parents are and how devastating it will be to leave us, you must follow what your heart is telling you. And, for what it's worth, I know Hugh is a good man and that's a wonderful thing for any mother to think about their daughter's intended.'

I looked at my knees pointing upwards to the Portakabin's ceiling, which my mother was sure still held rainwater from the last storm that one of these days would, apparently, find its way through, soaking all of her precious books if something wasn't done about it soon.

'And it's not like you can't come back for holidays. We're not going anywhere. I'll still be here trying to prise the books out of their arms.' She smiled, then got up to round her table and hunker in front of me, her knee bones clicking, to take my hands.

'I see it,' she said. 'I see that look in your eye when you're with Hugh. And I know it. I wore it often enough around your father. Your grandmother used to tease me about it. She said it would arrive on the morning of his coming to pick me up for a walk in the town, well before he'd knocked on our door and possibly before he'd even gotten onto the boat to travel over. I recognise where it comes from and to deny its pull is a waste of your time. You think I wanted to move here to this place from the town where I could get what I wanted when I wanted and didn't have to wait a week?'

'But what if Hugh moved here?' I asked, like that had been a true possibility and not a pipe dream.

'Does he want to?' She let go my hands to pull over the other beanbag so we two now faced each other, beanbag to beanbag, knees almost to knees, in the empty library, which would soon fill as the boat was due in.

'No,' I said, disappointed. 'He told me he wasn't sure he'd be able to make a living from designing the one house that someone might want to build here once every ten years.'

'Ah.'

'He doesn't have it anyway, that thing, that . . . *connection* with this place.'

'Well, it's not like I had it instantly. There were years when I first came when I'd look out at the mainland wanting nothing more than to go back to what I still considered my home. It's not for everyone, this life.'

'But you got it in the end, right?'

'Sure, but not everyone does. Anyway, I think a part of you is always back where you began, no matter where that is, and that's OK, you know, that's simply the natural way of things. It'll be that way for you too up there in Dublin. But, like me, you'll get used to it, and will grow to love it.'

I wanted that, wanted to find my place in that city just as easily as I had fallen in love.

'But . . .' I trailed off, too embarrassed to continue the sentence.

'But what, love? Come on, out with it. Now's the time to get this all sorted, not on the way down the aisle.'

'Ugh, it's, well, if I go, Liam gets it all, doesn't he? Just like he said he would when we were kids.'

'Liam? This is about Liam?'

Too shamefaced to look in her direction, I concentrated on a hardback on a shelf to Mammy's right that was jutting out, not neatly flush against the others and I had the urge to jump to its aid, pushing it back in safely. I didn't, but its skewed existence sat in my brain, as annoying as a piece of grit caught under a fingernail.

'Seriously, love. You have to stop letting that man dictate your life.'

'He's not dictating my life.' I was indignant that she would think he held such sway over me. 'It's just I can't stand the thought of him having *Aoibhneas* all on his own and treating her like crap. He doesn't give a shit really, you know. He only wants the power.'

'Listen, Rosie.' Mam leaned forward a little. 'You're forgetting your father is still here. He owns *Aoibhneas*.'

'But I love her, Mam. I really love her. It's what I was born to do. It hurts me so much even *thinking* of leaving her. How the hell am I going to feel when I have to go?'

Mam didn't reply straight away. We sat in silence, as I sniffled, and she rubbed at my knee, looking at me in such pity.

'I had a dog, you know, back at your granny's,' she said eventually. 'Sandy. God, I loved Sandy. She was beautiful, golden and happy. And, you know, she was my best friend, not that I told Nuala Doran that – if she'd known she'd never have spoken to me again – but she really was. I could spend hours tramping the fields with her. Even when I was seventeen and working away in O'Sullivan's, she'd be the thing I'd be thinking of getting home to after work.

Not even your granny's cooking and she was, as you well know, the best cook in all of Cork. But when I met your dad and fell in love with him and agreed to come to this place, I thought my heart would break. I considered asking if I could take Sandy with me, but she wasn't mine. She was your granny's and I couldn't do that because I knew she'd give her willingly and that wasn't fair. But I had to go. What choice did I have? I loved that man who'd drenched my cash-register belt with his stolen soggy daffodils, which, as you know, he still insists on bringing me every spring, waltzing me round the kitchen table like the lunatic he is. I knew if I stayed my heart would break into even bigger bits without your father and I worried that if I grew into an old unmarried, unloved spinster that my love for Sandy might lessen with resentment. So I did as I knew I would, despite all of my plan-hatching of how I could have both. I left her and made a life here with your father. I'd see her whenever I was back over and, you know, it was enough. I still had both things that I wanted in my life, her and your father, only not in the same amounts. What I'm saying is, you'll still have *Aoibhneas*, she'll still be here for you to skipper whenever you want, but the main thing is you'll have Hugh. And that, my lovely, is the most important bit.'

'Wow,' I said, thinking of the Sandy I had never met. And *Aoibhneas* – trying to come to terms with having a lot less of her, but never fully having to let go. 'I'm sorry about Sandy.' I sat forward a little to return the kindness of the knee rub from earlier. 'I never even knew you had a dog.'

'She died long before you were born.'

'And there we were thinking you just didn't like dogs and that's why you'd said no to Michael-Fran every time he suggested getting us one from the pound.'

'Sandy was irreplaceable. No other dog could live up to her. I'd have been too disappointed, you know, and that wouldn't have been fair on the pup at all. Besides, I was too busy with you lot.'

'No, I get that.' And I truly did: there would never be another boat like *Aoibhneas*, not for me.

'So,' Mam asked, after a second or two of silent contemplation had passed, 'where are you now with everything?'

I nodded half-heartedly. 'I'm OK. Or, at least, I think I will be.'

'Time,' Mammy said, with a groan, as she struggled to roll herself out of her beanbag. 'Give it time and all will be well. I promise you.'

I smiled, not yet fully consoled but with the feeling that I would be, eventually. I got up then to fix the book sticking out before hugging my mother and stepping out into the chill of the day in time to see *Aoibhneas* pull into the harbour with Liam at the helm. It still hurt that he was getting her, but I had to trust in all my mother had said. So I continued on my way, my eyes averted, back up home.

That evening we had my mother's signature shepherd's pie for dinner, my favourite – and indeed the island's. This famed dish was dropped in by Mammy to a house whenever there came word of an illness or death. Sometimes those conditions were even faked in order for people to get their hands on one; Críostóir of the goats had not corrected Mammy when she'd misunderstood him, thinking his most favoured goat, Geraldine, had died. He was about to, he claimed later, but on hearing her say she'd drop over a shepherd's pie he had suddenly lost his voice.

As Dad forked at his steaming plateful, he took quick glances up at me, then down again, like a man on the verge of an admission. Eventually, he cleared his throat, his first forkful held midway between plate and mouth, and began: 'I wanted to say, Rosie, even though you'll be heading off with Hugh, as is right, *Aoibhneas* will always be yours. She'll be here waiting for you whenever you get down to us. I know you love her, and that will never change, and neither will the fact that you are the greatest skipper she's ever known. We'll be sad to see you go now, but happy every time you come back, as will she. She's yours, Rosie. Nothing nor no one will ever change that. You have my word.'

Mammy smiled with only a tinge of embarrassment that I had figured out the meaning of their quiet mumblings earlier over the dinner preparations in the kitchen as I'd sat in the sitting room, staring at the fire. I rose to hug my father who had to delay his first mouthful a while longer, imparting my gratefulness that they, and she, would always be mine.

This is my father. And I'm Tara, the girl who had served her so often in Angelo's clothes shop in Dún Laoghaire said.

Oh, right, yes, I'm Saoirse.

I left Roaring Bay a couple of weeks later. Dad and Michael-Fran, who had travelled over with me on the ferry, argued over the best way to pack Hugh's car with all the stuff I was taking, towels and curtains and pillows and cushions and a kettle and a duvet and cutlery and a sweeping brush, all the spares of Mammy's life finally getting their chance to shine. Hugh and I stood against the pier wall allowing them at it. Hugh had to use his wing mirrors instead of his rear-view the entire journey to Dublin by the time everything was squashed in.

We drove straight to Hugh's granny's terraced house in Glasthule, the village next to Dún Laoghaire, which we were in the process of buying for an absolute steal with its two tiny bedrooms and a kitchen-cum-sitting room downstairs and a shower-room tacked on at the back. It was cute, but dark and in need of a lot of work. I never thought of myself as an interior designer but I let the painting, the upholstery, the soft furnishings, all the superficial things that we could do in the beginning to make it comfortable, distract me from my leaving the island, my mother and father and *Aoibhneas*. It was my self-made prescription, the very thing I needed to keep my brain occupied.

Within a week, I had also found the job at the ticket desk in the Dún Laoghaire ferry terminal. I liked it. The team. Roger, Billy, Dorothy and Dymphna were good people. There was chat and laughter enough to help me forget my separation from all I had known. After-work drinks in the Cavern, music gigs, Christmas parties and, as the years went on, engagement parties, weddings, christenings filled my life, allowing the quiet yearnings for home to slip away, exactly as Mammy had predicted.

I met the captains of the ferries and chatted with them, even getting, on the odd occasion, a tour of their wheelhouse when they discovered I had a nautical background. Yet I never hankered after it too much. I was like my mother refusing another dog, knowing there was only one ferry I really loved. But at night I'd dream of the water, its rolls of silk that could, in an instant, whip into a frothed fury. I'd be standing at *Aoibhneas*'s helm, my stomach churning in excitement, the power of my imagination allowing my fingertips to run along the line of the horizon, that smooth contentedness between the sea and sky far out beyond. On waking, I'd refuse to open my eyes, willing myself to retrieve that moment of pure happiness for one more second, but I never could. And yet its glow would linger through the push and pull of the subsequent hours, gifting me serenity even in the face of a long tailback of traffic, or a late ferry departure bringing more than one disgruntled customer to my hatch.

During my working morning, I would take my fifteen-minute break outside no matter what the weather. Whoever's shift I shared that morning might knock on the window and beckon me back in or laugh, in a kindly way, at my insanity when it was raining. But despite their entreaties, I'd keep sitting right where I was, wrapped up on the low wall with my mug in my hands and would inhale whatever the sea gave back to me. And before I left to perch once again on my swivel chair, I would thank it for its time, wish it well, and ask that it not take too many of those who rode her waves that day.

A year after I'd left Roaring Bay, we married, a small affair in a registry office with lunch for our immediate families in a restaurant in Glasthule. No honeymoon. Instead we put the money into the house, updating the kitchen and bathroom downstairs, while upstairs, we managed, through Hugh's clever design, to get the smallest of shower-rooms, leaving the spare room with enough space for a single bed, and also a cot because, aged twenty-three, I was pregnant.

We hadn't been trying but neither had we been taking precautions, simply allowing nature to take its course. The time that followed had been glorious, nine months of happy anticipation. I was excited about meeting her, not that I asked if she was a girl at any of the scans. I didn't need to: Patsy had already told me. I was curious about what she would look like, what bits of me I might see there, what bits of Hugh, and what bits would be all her very own.

When she finally screamed her way into our lives in 1992, I remember asking one of the midwives, 'Should she look that blue?' But no one answered as they whisked my baby to a table on my left where Hugh looked on, his back to me, blocking my view. There followed a second in which the tense silence invaded the room to the point of suffocation. And then I heard it, that first piercing cry, and I closed my eyes and smiled. They returned her to me. Wrapped in a blanket, she was whooshed up under my top where she nestled in against my chest and fell asleep, her bloodied head so very puffed and serious, her chubby eyelids closed tightly against the world that had so rudely dared to wake her. I looked up to see Hugh crying as he watched us both.

I winked at him, and he put his hand gently to her head and then bent to lay his against mine.

I cannot pinpoint the first realisation that darkness was descending. But perhaps it was there, from as early as when the epidural wore off. I cried desperately over Saoirse not latching on, then being too overwhelmed to see Ely, Hugh's brother, who'd travelled across the city to see his new niece, but that was normal, surely, I told myself. The day they told me we could go home, however, I found I didn't want to. I wanted to stay, in the comfort of their care, the experts who knew what to do. I felt a panic so deep and thick and clawing that I had to sit on the hospital bed after we were dressed and ready to go, Saoirse already in her car seat, as I convinced myself I could do this. I was scared, pure and simple, so very, very scared.

It continued at home, the constant panic that I was getting everything wrong. Out of my depth, alone, bewildered by the petite thing who cried. The living being whose demands only stopped when she was asleep. I would walk through Glasthule village and along by the sea from noon till two o'clock, pushing her in her pram, like the baby book that had become my Bible had told me. I'd dream of getting home and crawling to the couch, to fall into unconsciousness. But she would wake as soon as the movement stopped, exactly when we arrived at our front door, no matter how gently I came to a halt, and would want to feed again. At other times when she attempted to fall asleep on her play mat, I'd whisk her up because it wasn't sleep time, the book having warned that if she were to doze outside the allotted times she would never sleep through the night. I had visions of her at twelve years of age still refusing to go to bed at a reasonable hour if I didn't nip it in the bud right then and there.

And if she complied and happily kicked her feet and hands on that play mat, the arch of soft toys above her, their wings and noses crinkling and ringing, I would will my eyes to stay open in case some horrible accident occurred. Instead, I'd ask her not to cry or whimper so I could simply stare at nothing. A kind of rest, I told myself. At some stage, my eye would find the clock and I'd count down the hours and minutes until Hugh might arrive home. But I could never depend on when that would be, so erratic were his projects, his commitments, and so young were both he and the business that he had to do the work when it was there. It would be years before he had people around him whom he could depend on, defer to. And so there were days when that wishing he would put his key in the door early, that maybe today he would make it home by five, turned into desperation, panic and pure madness. When bedtime came, I'd lie on our bed by her Moses basket with weary tears wetting the pillow, singing some song out of tune, then fall into a type of delirious sleep from which I would wake to her protests at my silence or, if I was lucky, Hugh's hand on my shoulder, his voice whispering, 'Hi,' into my ear.

She was six weeks old when I sat on the kitchen floor one morning, and begged Hugh not to go to work – not demanding, not suggesting but begging, crying and begging. Hugh seemed scared, as if finally understanding there was something deeply wrong. He towered above me, Saoirse in his arms, not able to find the words to answer. He hunkered down, the three of us in a huddle on the floor, and put his hand to my head, patting down the wiry mess of pillow hair.

'I'll call Mum,' he said. Ursula, who lived not twenty minutes away.

But I shook and lowered my head and felt the tears come faster. I didn't want her. She'd only want to clean my house and tell me what tried and trusted methods she'd used to mind her boys when they were little. And while she would mean it kindly, I would have to endure the voice in my head that said, *See how you are so much worse at this than everyone else in the world.* I'd have to make her endless cups of tea and sandwiches as she did all I was unable to do, and I couldn't be sure that the bread knife might not end up in me or her by the end of the day. All I wanted was for my own mother to come and take Saoirse to feed, change, bathe and sing to her so I could sleep. But even if she got on the boat right at that moment and hitched a lift to Cork City and took the train – my mother not being the best at driving on the mainland – she wouldn't be here until evening, and right at that moment, it felt like a year away.

I shook and shook my head again until my hair fell forward to hide my shame.

'OK, look,' he said, checking his watch again. It was past seven thirty when he usually left. 'I have a meeting at nine thirty so I'll stay till nine, nine fifteen. Murray is always late anyway, OK? You can have a shower and maybe another half-hour in bed. Me and Saoirse will be fine.'

He helped walk me to the end of the stairs. I climbed each step slowly, leaning heavily on the banisters, not looking back once. I showered dutifully, desperately hoping that the fresh face and non-greasy hair would somehow make me a better mammy, one who wanted to be around her child. And when I laid my wet hair down on my towel-covered pillow, I pulled Hugh's over my head to block out his high, happy cooing from down the stairs.

He woke me later, when perhaps an hour had passed, whispering in my ear, 'I have to go, love. Saoirse's asleep.'

I didn't even turn my head to look at her Moses basket.

'I've called Maeve, the public-health nurse. She's going to come by today.' I was impressed that he had not only managed to remember her name and find a number but that she had answered before nine fifteen. What magic powers did he possess that I did not? 'And your mother too. She's going to come up tomorrow, OK? So the cavalry is on the way.'

I should have been happy on hearing that Mammy would be with me soon. Wasn't it all I'd wished for earlier? But now I panicked at how she would react to seeing that I didn't love Saoirse as I should, that I was an awful mother. What would she feel about her daughter then? I was sure, as I tried to smile for Hugh, as I closed my eyes and he kissed my forehead, that she would hate me as much as I hated myself.

The public-health nurse was quite severe, not in voice but look. Angular of nose and cheekbones. Cropped dark hair with a short grey cut jacket, black top and trousers, ankle boots with silver studs that I did not like. She was kind in her own way, weighing Saoirse, measuring her. I was unsure why – she'd only done it a few weeks prior.

'And now Mammy,' she cooed at Saoirse, whom she laid on her play mat, as if she was about to produce a larger scale and ask me to curl myself into its metal palm and wait until she got a read and checked against her chart to see if I was average or above or, good heavens, below, as I'm sure it most definitely would turn out to be.

'How are we doing?' A perfunctory question, I felt, given Hugh would have already told her I was losing it on the phone, or why would she be here so quickly?

'I . . . I'm not good.'

'Right. And tell me, has your period started to come in again?'

I looked at her, confused. I had forgotten all about them. Those horrors that would return later more vicious than ever before, clots the size of kidney beans that would flood me so at times I had to wear two sanitary towels and a tampon.

'No,' I said, but then thought better of it. 'Maybe, though. I don't know.'

'Well, have you bled yet?' she prompted, as I seemed to have lost all idea of what a period entailed.

'No.'

'They may be on their way. Your hormones are all over the place. Like pregnancy, it can be the trickiest of times for your body.'

But, I'd wanted to say, I was so happy when I was pregnant. No periods, no sickness, I loved it. I had never felt so healthy in my life. Everything was glorious. Even in the final trimester I was tired, yes, but not like other women talked about. In fact, it felt so odd, so unfair to those others that I should be so lucky in my contentedness that I felt the need to exaggerate some of the downsides and use all the beached-whale and exhaustion terms expected of a mother-to-be in that stage, so no one would hate me, especially the other women in the antenatal classes. Of course I was tired, but only just. And the thing was, I adored my little baby growing inside me, would cradle the bump, chatting to her out loud and in my head. Two bodies in one, in sync and very much in love. But then she left and all that changed. I mourned her leaving, would pat the now diminishing rise of my belly. When I felt the contents of my stomach or intestine shift, I'd lament that it was no longer her extending a leg or fist or pressing her back hard against the curve of my skin.

'Dad says you're not coping so well,' Maeve continued, finally acknowledging the obvious.

'No,' I agreed. 'I don't know how to make her happy.'

'Babies simply need food and love and sleep and cleaning. And the smiles will come.'

I looked over to Saoirse as she concentrated on all that lay above her, her little body jerking, her legs happily cycling away and her pink lips pursing.

'But the connection we had before,' I laid my hand on my stomach, distressed now, 'is gone. Or perhaps it was never there, and I just imagined it.'

'Are you getting sleep?'

'She feeds a lot at night.'

'So, you're still breastfeeding?'

'No.' I felt ashamed of that too. I'd managed two weeks, but the pain shot through me, curling my toes until I had to unlatch her and she wailed. 'But I'm pumping still.'

'Are you trying to keep her to a routine?'

'Yes. I have this book.' Having temporarily forgotten its name, I looked around for it. Its dog-eared presence was never that far from me.

'Don't worry about it.' She waved away my attempts at its retrieval. She leaned forward, her hands now clasped before her on her knees as if she was about to pray or at least impart something extremely significant that would sort me out once and for all. 'Look, I'm going to tell you something that I tell all young mothers: throw the bloody book away. You aren't perfect. I wasn't perfect. None of the mothers I meet are. And what we don't need is a book telling us where we are constantly getting it wrong.'

'But . . . it's all I have.'

'Rubbish. You have you. You are your greatest ally and her greatest hero.' She pointed at Saoirse, who had now drifted into another sleep, one that wasn't part of the timetable the very book in question had suggested. 'Look at her. She's thriving. She's contented. *You* are doing a great job.'

I wondered how she could have misread me. I clearly was no hero.

'What if I were to tell you that I was going to take her with me?' she continued. 'Walk out that door with her in my arms and not bring her back. How would that make you feel? Heartbroken, I bet. Am I wrong?'

She looked so confident that she had me now, having skilfully backed me into a corner from where I'd have to admit that I loved her with every breath in me.

'I'd say take her.'

I looked away to the 'Welcome Baby Girl' cards over our fireplace, in particular the one with the stork and the pink sling hanging from its beak. I had meant every word. And I'd held that woman's eye as I'd said it to let her know that she wasn't dealing with any ordinary case, no pushover exhausted new mammy. She was dealing with a demon, a cruel woman who had no idea how to love her child.

And it was there, there that the seeds of all that would happen to us seventeen years later were sown. Here it was, the nub, the little acorn, the beginning from which our future was written. There was no one else to blame. It was me. *I* had asked that she be taken away.

Maeve looked at me blankly, as I'd known she would, as was all I deserved. But she surprised me by saying: 'There's someone I would like you to meet. She's a nurse like me but she specialises in counselling mothers suffering from postpartum depression. We are very lucky to have her in this area – there's no one else in the country doing it and I think she's exactly what you need. Will you go and see her? Although if you do, you will have to find a babysitter for this one, I'm afraid. Have you anyone during the day who can take her?'

'My mother's coming from Cork tomorrow.'

'Well, good. I'll ring Helen the minute I get back to the office. Expect a call.'

With that she packed her bags and left. But not before telling me, as she stood at my door, that this was natural and nothing to be ashamed of. Our bodies, she said, had the power to hurt us, and sometimes be unkind, but in time they could also heal.

'Wait until you hit the menopause. That one's an absolute joy too,' she said, turning and finding her car parked further down the street.

My body took its bloody time.

I was a whole year like that during which I had several sessions with Helen. My mother stayed for two weeks that first time and returned on three different occasions to see me and my Saoirse through. But by the time Saoirse's teeth appeared and her first step was taken, I had fallen in love with her once more. When she started speaking my love burrowed deeper, curling itself around my veins and my capillaries, seeping into my bones, bedding down in the roots of my hair, never to forsake me again.

I didn't suffer with postpartum depression in quite the same way with Cullie. Its blackness lingered in the background but never became as overpowering. I was ready for it, as was Hugh, to fight it off, or, more, to nurse or cajole it away. And I was relieved that I could love that little man almost instantly.

And yet the dark place to which I'd gone with Saoirse has haunted me to this day. No matter how much I might tell myself I'd had no control back then, it was there in my head, lurking, and every now and then it would cause me to stop what I was doing and close my eyes as tightly as I could over how I had wished my daughter gone.

As they took off, she looked out of the back window to see her bike on the ground. She glanced towards the upstairs windows of her house and felt ill at ease.

Where did you say the accident had happened? she asked turning back to father and daughter.

When Saoirse and Cullie were little, we would visit the island each summer for a month, sometimes longer, and I loved it. In order to catch the afternoon ferry from Rossban, Hugh would be up at 6 a.m. packing us into the car alongside our luggage, the bags of shopping, presents I'd bought for Mam and Dad, buckets and spades, the kite that had survived the previous year ready for its outing above my parents' house on Mac's Hill. Hugh could only spare the week from work if there was no big job but we three would stay on for as much of the summer as possible.

The beach at Carhoona Beag featured large in our daily outings around Roaring Bay. Saoirse and Cullie liked to build sand forts there. They would race the sea, they told me, trying to get the fort built before the tide came to flood it, at which point they would scream and laugh and dance around, watching all of their hard work wash away. After, it was swimming and exploration time, the two of them scampering up on the high rocks that cupped the beach.

'Look how the water moves, Daddy,' Saoirse had shouted at Hugh, the first day she had noticed the small whirlpool form at the base from her perch higher up. She was maybe eight or nine by then and we were sitting on top of the rocks to the right of the beach looking out at the ocean.

'Why is it doing that?' She watched the little swirl of water below us as she lay flat on her stomach, her head leaning over. It had always been there, this little circle of magic where the sea was trying to invade a small opening between two boulders. I'd watched it often enough as a child, but I'd forgotten its existence.

'It's trying to get through the narrow opening. Can you see it?' She peered down following Hugh's pointing finger. 'Careful now.' He caught the back of her swimsuit as she leaned a little further out from the rock. 'The water's too fast and the opening is too narrow, so it starts to spin.'

Over the years I'd given up trying to stop my children climb those dark, slicked boulders, fearful that they would fall and there would be injuries, of which there had been plenty – grazed hands and knees, bumped heads, although thankfully no breakages. But none of those minor scuffs could stop my intrepid pair, so I gave up trying to curb them and instead joined in, in the hope that I might forestall any major disasters. Only by that point, they rarely fell any more.

'I want to come here every day,' Saoirse said, turning slightly towards me, swiping away the ribbons of her wet black hair from her face.

'So, what, you don't want to go over to Diarmuid's now?'

Diarmuid's was their favourite for early morning swims, and where sometimes, to their parents' amusement, at high tide, they would avoid the watery pools sprayed up on the slipway so as not to get their feet wet, before running on as fast as they could to the bottom, launching themselves into the sea, feet and all.

'Oh, no, I want to do that too. But I want to come here after.'

'And so do I. I want to come here every day as well.' That was Cullie, whose arrival in our family two years after

Saoirse had meant that we had needed to move from our tiny house in Glasthule. I was aware of our good fortune, a young couple not even in their thirties, me being twenty-eight and Hugh twenty-nine, with enough money to get a mortgage for a run-down, four-bedroomed detached house in Blackrock, while most of Hugh's friends were still renting one-bedroomed flats. But because Hugh's business was going so well and because our profit on the sale of the house in Glasthule had been so good, we had managed it.

'I want to put a stick in it,' Cullie shouted. He was on his tummy, too, by that stage, peering down at the whirlpool alongside his sister. Hugh and I both clung to our children's swimwear in case they should decide to shuffle further towards the edge.

'No, it's too far down, love. We can't get to it,' I explained.

'Awh.' Cullie looked so disappointed in his mother.

'The rocks are too high up and the water's too deep at that part,' Hugh said. 'Maybe another day we might take out the kayaks to see how close we can get to it. OK?' We kept a pair of two-man kayaks up above the beach in a metal shed Dad had erected the previous year.

'Yay! Now.'

'No, not today,' I interjected, like the mean mammy I really was. 'I have to help Granddad on the ferry this afternoon and, anyway, Granny wants to take you two to the library.'

'Canoe, Mummy, please.' Cullie was up again and had twisted his little head in under my arm and snuggled into my side. 'Daddy can do it.'

'Eh, when it comes to matters of the sea, son, I think it's best we wait for Mum.' Hugh, not being a natural when it came to water, always insisted that I was there on such outings.

'No, my chicklet,' I concluded, rubbing his hair. He knew that tone of voice, the one without the waver, which could not be convinced of just five minutes more. 'We haven't time.'

'You heard Mummy, Cullie. We can do it another day.' Saoirse had turned onto her side and was looking at us, adopting her bossy-sister voice. But it always struck me when I heard it that it never veered into the overly stern, keeping, I was proud to note, an edge of care. That day she got up to try to take his hand, which had defiantly curled itself against his stomach. 'I promise, OK?' she added, waiting for his reluctant nod and his palm in hers.

'And anyway,' she continued, 'Granny said she has some new books for us in the library. And I'm going to read them for you on the beanbag.'

He looked up at her, his eyes squinting in the sun. 'And after, will we get ice creams?'

'Let's go home and count our money and then we'll know, OK?'

And they were off, gone from us so fast as they wove and jumped their way down off the rocks and scrambled back up to the road to reach the jeep. They were friends, those two. Always had been, my perfect pair. And as the years went on, they remained perfect in their moods and their tantrums and their unwillingness to go to bed, which meant we couldn't, for one half-hour before we, too, fell asleep, breathe without the burden of their welfare. They were perfect in their hatred of vegetables, in their disorganisation, in their daydreaming, and their unique ability to sweep a kitchen floor half-heartedly. They were perfect in their door-slamming, their name-calling, their utter intolerance of their parents' opinions once they had passed the age of ten.

Hugh and I trailed behind them, no longer fearful of an imminent tragedy.

'They love it here,' Hugh said. A thing we repeated to each other summer in summer out.

'Yep, a child's paradise.'

'I never appreciated it, you know, as much as I should have all those years ago when I worked here. I never really understood the magic of it even when I'd come back down to keep you interested.'

'Keep me interested?' I laughed. 'You make me sound like a client you were trying to woo.'

'Well, you know, some other intriguing man could have arrived and whisked you off your feet.'

'Around here?'

'You found me here. What's to say another stunner couldn't have come along and charmed you?'

'You've upgraded yourself to a stunner now. Such a little cutie.' I took his cheek between my thumb and index finger and gave it a waggle. 'Anyway, I wouldn't worry about it. Not everyone falls under this place's spell. And, besides, you were dazzled by me and that, my handsome man, is all that matters.'

Hugh pulled me into him and smiled. 'Do you miss it? I mean, like, have you ever thought about coming back?'

'Well,' I laughed, amused at this topic, one we'd never, as surprising as it seems now, discussed before, 'you may have noticed I never took you up on your five-year deal to move here if things weren't working out up in Dublin.'

'True, but as I recall it wasn't easy for you to leave.'

I didn't answer immediately. Over the years, I'd never told Hugh when I had dreamed of the sea or being invited to the bridge of a ferry. It's not that I was deliberately keeping these things from him. It's simply that they weren't weighing me down, so I didn't feel the need to talk about them. They were my quiet, personal thoughts that didn't necessitate the interruption of the frantic life we, as a young family, were leading. But his enquiry had caught me now, making me remember back to when that parting had really hurt.

'No, no, I guess it wasn't,' I replied. 'But look at me now. I love Dublin – you couldn't get me back down here full time if you paid me. I mean, yeah, there are moments when I'm standing in line at a checkout and I think about the peace and silence of this place. But before I know it, I'm home or tramping through a forest in the Dublin Mountains with you guys and I'm over it. Forgotten, just like the washing-up.'

He let me go and we continued on.

'But *Aoibhneas*, don't you miss skippering her?'

'Yeah, I guess, sometimes, but it's enough to be with her a couple of times a year. I'm done then, my fill is had. I choose you guys any day of the week.'

Hugh looked a little dubious, like he didn't believe me.

'What?' I asked.

'I dunno. Sometimes I wonder if you gave up too much of yourself because I insisted.'

I stopped us in our progress again, laying a hand on his arm. 'Oh, my God, Hugh. I was happy to go – you do know that, don't you? It was the right decision. I love who I am now. I love who we are and I even love working that stupid counter in Dún Laoghaire and, yes, I love coming back here in the summer and working the ferry. But that doesn't mean I want it back *all* the time. I want you and I want them, and I want the overflowing washing basket and the downstairs loo that doesn't flush properly and even your sweaty cycling gear. You believe that, right?'

He laughed. 'You couldn't possibly love the sweaty cycling gear.'

'OK, well, maybe not that.'

'But what about a cottage? We could get a place for us all for the summer. And when I do retire you might be able to persuade me to come down for a couple of months here and there. I've always fancied a summer residence. Although, granted, I had been thinking of the Amalfi Coast but, you know, for you I'd sacrifice the Mediterranean sun.'

'Why, thank you.'

I looked out to the ruffle of the sea, its mild discontent despite the summer's day, as I considered his offer. 'No, I like coming home to Mam and Dad, and so do the kids. I want them to know them like this. In and out of their lives, annoying them, making nuisances of themselves and with plenty of times for cuddles and tickling and all that ordinary everyday stuff. No, who we are now is perfect, I want nothing to change. I want to grow old and incontinent right by your side in Blackrock.'

'Lucky me.'

I turned back to kiss him. By the time we reached the jeep, our pair were waiting patiently for us, Saoirse already suggesting which ice cream they would be purchasing later on with Mammy.

She saw her brother walking up the road as the car took a right out of her estate. She waved but he didn't see her. Looking back at him she wondered when he had gotten so tall.

When Saoirse was fifteen, she'd written down a list of Hugh's and my favourite films alongside those she'd read about with good or controversial reviews. She liked lists, keeping them in the notebooks she bought – leather, if she had enough money, or cloth-covered, such as the tartan one from our camping holiday in Scotland. Of course, there were also cheap ones bought in the Two Euro shop with her pocket money, or wages as we called it, as if our children were proper little workers – which they were, emptying the dishwasher and hoovering, although mainly when we reminded them. Santa was always good at making sure she got a nice one among the bigger gifts she'd asked for. She'd examine it, front and back, running her hand over the material, undoing the lock or the button or the long elastic strip, then finally allowing herself to open it, to flick the pages and smell them before carefully closing it again and smiling.

Saoirse was working her way through watching all of the movies on her lists, sometimes on her own, sometimes with us. They were the best of moments, the four of us, when her brother could be persuaded, in the sitting room, Hugh in his swanky swivel chair, made by a young Dublin furniture designer, that he'd spent a fortune on, Cullie and me on the couch, listening to Saoirse as she stood in front of the freeze frame of the opening credits with the controller in her hand, giving us the usual instructions before the show began:

'No asking questions as the movie plays.' That she directed at me in particular, as I wasn't always the best at keeping up. 'If you have lost track, you have to ask me to stop the movie and then we can discuss your issues.' I nodded my *mea culpa* head, while Hugh smirked in my direction, usually giving me a wink to save me from the severity of my admonishment.

'Toilet breaks are permitted but let's all try to do it at the same time.' We had three toilets in the house so how did she suggest we were going to manage that?

'No looking at phones.' That was most definitely meant for Hugh, who would salute and get up and put his phone on the hall table. My hand often brushed against his in solidarity as he passed. I knew how hard that was for him. Having his own business was a full-time job, and I loved him for giving up his phone regardless, for our very amazing girl. Sometimes he'd kiss my head on the way back in before retaking his seat.

'We can stop halfway through the movie for more refreshments but again could we do this when we're taking the toilet break?

'And no sighing.' That was for Cullie, who had an excellent range in that area which he would showcase when he realised he had made a big mistake in agreeing to watch a movie that was 'totally lame'. 'If you don't like the movie, then leave.

'And if the doorbell rings, we don't answer it. No getting up off these seats outside of those rules.'

We all agreed readily on that one. Any disturbance at that time of night was generally Nancy Littleton looking for Raymond, her cat, which, as we had come to learn would mean, taking our lead from Nancy, an hour of us calling, 'Puss-puss,' in high-pitched voices around the gardens of the neighbourhood, until she rushed back to tell us that Raymond, 'the little scamp', had been in the airing cupboard all along.

Of course, those rules got broken every time and we would bicker affably until the movie was eventually done and it was time for our eldest child to give her summation of the 'arc' of the movie, the camera work and the character development. When she was finished and had left the room, her bedraggled brother behind her (if Cullie had stayed for that bit: normally he'd have scarpered once the closing credits had begun), Hugh would come and sit beside me, pull me into his arms and say, 'Wow, we made that.'

Where did the accident happen? she asked again when they hadn't replied, as they took another right-hand turn.

The last time I saw Saoirse was at 2.20 p.m., Thursday, 16 July 2009. I'd seen her from Cullie's bedroom window cycle up the road of our estate. I'd glanced at his alarm clock, and chuckled to myself, thinking she'd certainly made sure she was home well in time for her dinner, mac and cheese, her favourite. I hadn't expected her back till much later. I thought nothing further of it and went on gathering up the washing from each of our rooms, fully expecting to see her when I eventually got down the stairs with a full load finally in hand.

I called hello as I made my way along the hallway and into the kitchen, but there was no reply. In the utility room, loading the machine, I was curious that I couldn't hear her outside, putting her bike away. By the time the wash had started, the front door had at last opened.

'How's the head?' I said, going to greet her – she'd had a headache before she'd left for Dún Laoghaire earlier.

But it was Cullie.

'My head is perfect, Mother. How is yours?'

'Sorry.' I laughed. 'I thought you were your sister. Your head is indeed beautiful as always.' I reached out to tousle his hair and then to steal a cheeky hug, a thing fifteen-year-old boys weren't always up for. 'Did you see herself out there?'

'Saoirse? No. But her bike's there, *just* lying on the ground,' he said, good-humouredly, as if he'd found the perfect evidence of how irresponsible his big sister really was.

'Really?'

I opened the front door and looked out but couldn't see it.

'It's behind the hedge on the path.' He gestured with his phone.

I walked out to find it where he'd said it would be. Lying abandoned on its side.

'Strange,' I said, loud enough for Cullie, who was still in the hallway now texting, to hear. 'Maybe she's called into the Cassidys.' Although it wasn't something she normally did. 'I suppose I should take it in.'

'Hmm? What?' Cullie finally raised his head.

'I said, I suppose I should take it in.'

'Oh, right, yeah.'

'No, darling, don't you worry, your mother can manage despite her decrepitude.' I'd already picked up the bike and was wheeling it up the driveway.

'Mother, please allow me.' Cullie put his phone into his pocket and came out to take the bike from me with great exaggeration and wheeled it through the back gate.

I looked back at the estate, expecting to hear her voice, but all was silent save for the sound of cars passing on the main road to Blackrock.

By four o'clock, my concern began to niggle. I texted her but received no reply. Rang her phone but it told me she had either switched it off or she was out of coverage. I knocked on Cullie's door.

'Has Saoirse been in touch?'

'No.' He didn't even bother looking around, just kept concentrating on the Xbox.

'Weird. Can you try ringing her? It keeps telling me she's out of coverage.'

'Well, it's hardly going to tell me any different.' He'd finally turned to give me his full attention as he called her. 'See?' He shrugged and hung up. 'Same.'

'Were you talking to her at all? This morning maybe before she left. She didn't say what she was up to today other than going to Dún Laoghaire, did she?'

'Nope. I didn't even know she was doing that. The house was empty when I got up.'

It was a rare day off for me from the ferry port. By then I had gone to get my hair done. I hardly ever went, my long straight hair needing such little attention, but Hugh had given me a voucher for my birthday and it was in danger of running out.

'I just thought she might have gone into you before she left. She wasn't quite herself. We kind of had a bit of a row before she stormed off.'

'Oh?'

'It was nothing, stupid stuff. I wasn't able to give her a lift to Dún Laoghaire, that's all, and she wasn't best pleased.'

'Well, I wouldn't worry. I'm sure she's perfectly fine. Maybe the light was at its "optimum" and she had to just "grasp the moment".' His slagging of Saoirse and her ways brought a reluctant smile to my lips.

'No, it's not that. Her camera is still here. I checked.' I cocked my head in the direction of her room. 'I think I might just go and see if she's next door.'

'Sure thing, Mom.' His exaggerated American accent was accompanied by a bright, unconcerned smile before his feet propelled him and his chair around again to his screen.

Our house is the third in a cul-de-sac of five, us sitting right in the middle, two neighbours either side. Think of a thermometer and you can imagine the long, houseless, tree-lined road leading up to a bulbous round of our detached homes, each spaced out from the other. A line of oak trees in full summer foliage, and blossoms on grass verges at the footpath's edge. A small, private place where we neighbours mostly left each other alone, except at Christmas time when we took turns in throwing a small party to catch up on all that'd happened in the year. At least, that was how it used to be. It stopped in 2009. There have been no Christmas parties since.

The neighbours hadn't seen her. The Cassidys, the Littletons, the O'Hagans and the Rices all reported that she hadn't called in as I'd hoped. They hadn't even noticed her cycling up the road. I was mad at Nancy Littleton for that, in particular. The woman usually knew everything that moved in the place, a hand constantly pulling back that lace curtain of hers. That one time, that one bloody time when she could have been useful, could she not have looked out of her window? But she just stared at me and said, 'I'm sorry, pet.'

'No worries,' I told them all, trying not to let my growing anxiety show.

But Nora Cassidy sensed it. She even walked me out to the end of her driveway where I pointed to where the bike had been that Cullie and I had innocently taken in, not realising that later, the where of its position and how it had lain, would be needed as evidence.

Nora had squeezed my shoulder and she promised to check with her Emelda and Louise, her two grown-up, college-going, summer-job-working daughters, who were due home in an hour or so. It was the first time that day that I felt it, the lurch of real, visceral panic in my stomach.

'You're very good,' I said, forcing a smile, wanting to get away as fast as I could to try Saoirse's phone again.

By five o'clock I texted Hugh, wondering if she'd been in touch. I didn't elaborate on the bike situation, just a breezy 'Hey, how are you' kind of thing. I wasn't quite ready to upset his hectic day needlessly, because I was thinking that maybe she might still have been peeved with me and had chosen to communicate with her father instead about her whereabouts. No, he'd replied, a single word, a sure sign that he was in some meeting or other, too busy to type anything further.

I told Cullie I was going to walk the block, maybe even as far as Blackrock village, just to see if she was around. I asked him to keep trying her phone and maybe to give Aimee a call, Saoirse's friend, just in case she was with her.

He'd turned around immediately on hearing that. 'Mum, are you, like, really worried about her?'

'It just doesn't feel right, Cullie. I mean, I'm possibly just jumping the gun here, but she's never done something like this before.'

He shrugged his shoulders not wholly convinced I wasn't overreacting – and yet still I could see the small seed of doubt that had been planted.

'All right, I'll keep trying her. I'll give her another fifteen minutes and if she isn't back by then I'll call Aimee. OK?'

I nodded and closed his door again, and headed off.

Saoirse wasn't with Aimee. When I returned from my fruitless tour of the village and the seafront, I found Cullie on the stairs waiting for me.

'She has no idea where she is, either,' he confirmed. 'She did meet her earlier in Dún Laoghaire, though. They'd gone for a coffee, walked around the shops for like an hour and then Aimee had to go 'cause her mother phoned her to say the neighbour she babysits for came looking for her to mind the twins.'

'Right, that's it,' I said. 'I think we need to ring your dad.'

'Take a breath and slow down,' Hugh told me, when he eventually answered. It was now six thirty. He'd asked me to repeat what I had just said. Her bike was where?

'On the ground, lying there, right outside the gate.' I was walking up and down our hallway while Cullie was still on the stairs, texting as many people as he could think of who might know something. She was gone four hours.

'And she'd cycled it up the hill right before, is that what you're saying?'

'*Yes*. Well, no, not quite that.' I felt guilty as I admitted the part about my delay with the washing. I stopped pacing as I explained it was Cullie who had come across her bike.

'And he hadn't bothered to pick it up?'

'Oh, for God's sake, Hugh, that's not the bloody point.'

Cullie looked up from his perch, intuitively aware, it seemed, that he was being accused of something.

'So, he hadn't seen her at all on his way up from Black-rock?'

'No. I told you already. And you know her, she usually gets in touch. I even called to the neighbours. But no one's seen her, Hugh. She's disappeared.'

'What about Saoirse's mates, Theo and Aimee? And what's the other one's name, the one with the hair?'

'Cullie? The guy with the hair, did you text him?' I made a circular motion above my head trying to indicate the curly mop that the guy constantly wore in a high ponytail.

'Ross? Yeah. Nothing.' Cullie offered up his phone like it was useless.

'None of them know a thing, Hugh. Although Aimee says she met Saoirse in Dún Laoghaire, but she was fine. Nothing unusual, nothing out of the ordinary.'

'And she saw her get on her bike and cycle home?'

'Cull? Did Aimee say she actually saw her cycle home?'

'Oh, right, hang on.'

'Why don't you people phone each other? What is it with all the texting? He's texting her now. Wait, hold on, Hugh, do you think I didn't see her on the bike? Is that what you're saying? Because I did. It was definitely her.'

'No, Rosie. I'm not . . . Look, I don't know what's going on either. I'm simply asking questions, even stupid ones.' And as if to prove his point perfectly, added: 'Have you tried her phone?'

'A thousand times. She's switched if off or, I dunno, maybe the battery's dead now.'

'Right, that's it,' he said. 'I'm coming home.'

It was unusual for Hugh to leave his desk at Dunne Architects before 8 p.m. The kids and I were long used to eating dinner without him. A part of me had wanted him to tell me not to worry, as if hearing *him* say it would somehow be enough to make it all right and for Saoirse to appear at the door. But his saying he was leaving the office early weakened me, and before I knew it, I was sitting on the bottom step of the stairs asking him the unthinkable.

'Hugh, should I call the guards?'

'The guards? Jesus. Just . . . just let me get home and we'll figure it out then, OK? I'm on the way.'

Hugh called to the neighbours again and, with those who were free, had gone out to walk the roads. As I waited at home, pacing the hallway still hoping her key would turn in the door at any minute, I imagined him running down streets, calling her name, grabbing elbows of those he passed to ask had they seen her as he frantically pointed to the screen on his phone. Cullie had gone with Nora and Declan Cassidy in their car, circling the wider territories of Booterstown, Stillorgan and Leopardstown.

Both arrived home empty-handed within minutes of each other around 8.30 p.m., our agreed cut-off point after which the phone call had to be made. Cullie was crouched to the hallway floor and I was leaning against the wall, allowing it to hold me up as Hugh dialled the number.

'Hello, yes, I'd like to report a missing person.'

Inspector Mick Malone arrived at ten o'clock with a female guard, whose name I can't remember now and who I never saw again after that night. She was in uniform; he was in civvies, dark grey suit, white shirt, navy tie. He was tall, solidly built, like nothing or no man could knock him down. About ten years older than us. Fifties, I guessed. The woman, late twenties.

'So,' he said, after he sat in Hugh's swivel chair at the window, taking out a black notebook from his breast pocket, the female guard taking the seat that Saoirse usually commandeered when she watched a movie. 'Your daughter, Saoirse, she's causing you a bit of worry.'

I hadn't liked the insinuation that this was simply a case of overprotective parents and neither, it seemed, had Hugh.

'It's more than a bit of worry. She's been missing eight hours now. I think that gives us the right to be *enormously* worried, don't you?'

'My apologies, wrong choice of words.' The inspector grunted then, as if trying to clear his throat of any more annoying turns of phrase. 'I wouldn't be here if we weren't taking this seriously, Mr Dunne, I can assure you of that.'

Hugh and I said nothing as we sat opposite him on the couch. Cullie was on a small stool at our coffee table, our now fearful boy whose leg bounced and whose thumb was gnawed to bright red. Hugh and I had wondered if we should have seen the police on our own first but then decided it was important that we three were there, in case one of us forgot something, the others could jump in.

'And she's never done anything like this before? Upped and left for a few hours without telling you? It's more common than people sometimes let on.'

'No,' Hugh and I said in unison. 'She always texts or rings if she's going to be late,' I carried on. 'Always. That's why this is so unusual. I mean, I know there is a first for everything, but this . . . this really is out of character.'

'OK, let's start with what we know.' Mick was quite businesslike at this point, not allowing too much space for any emotional displays, although that would change in later years when there would be countless occasions on which he would give us his time if things got too much. 'According to what you said on the phone, Saoirse was last seen at two twenty p.m. today.'

'Yes, that's right,' I said. 'I saw her cycling up the road here. She'd been in Dún Laoghaire earlier, shopping.'

'And it was definitely her? It couldn't have been a friend of hers? Young girls can look the same, these days.'

'No,' I retorted, looking at the dried red skin around his eyes and nose.

There was no possible doubt in my mind that it was not my daughter. All girls of a certain age are not alike, you stupid man, I had wanted to add. But I held back, knowing that we needed him.

'We have to be certain, Mrs Dunne, that we aren't starting from the wrong place. You say it was her but what if someone else, say a friend of hers, had cycled the bike home for whatever reason and she was still in Dún Laoghaire all along?'

'Most of my daughter's friends are boys. If it was a girl, it would have been Aimee, and she has blond hair.' I was growing more impatient by the second. 'And it's not Mrs Dunne, it's Rosie.' His referring to me so formally made this awfulness feel so very real.

We weren't getting off to the best of starts, Mick and me, but all of that would change, in time.

'Rosie,' he stated, with a nod and a smile. Mick has the nicest of smiles, unshakeable even in hostile territory, kindly and slow to leave. 'I don't mean to offend you, or doubt what it is you're telling me. We simply have to get this as right as we can. For Saoirse, you understand.'

I felt ashamed then of those inner thoughts about his stupidity and his arid skin. Did he have a wife, I wondered, children he hugged tighter than they wanted when he returned home at night? Perhaps I, too, would look drained if I was presented, day in, day out, with desperate, broken parents wanting me and me alone to find their child. As I was to find out, Mick was the expert in this line of work, carrying in his wallet the photographs of those children still missing and whose cases he managed.

'Of course,' I replied, looking at Hugh. Hugh, who seemed paler than his now-cold milky tea.

'You're OK, love, you're doing great,' he reassured me, taking my hand in his. 'We know it was her you saw on the bike. We believe you.'

'Perhaps,' the woman interjected, 'you could start on a list of contact details of everyone who knows her, people she'd be in regular contact with?' She looked at Mick for approval.

He gave a little nod, took a moment then started again. 'It's important to say at this point that these questions we're asking and lists we'd like you to make are just for our records. In most cases, the person walks back through the door. So, we're asking you to just bear with us as we run through what we have to do so we're ahead of the curve, if things turn out to be more than just a misunderstanding or the likes. Is that OK?'

His words calmed me, suggesting as they did the real possibility of a speedy return.

Cullie immediately set to work, taking out his phone and then getting up to look for a piece of paper to write down the names and numbers he had.

'And can you put her mobile number, if she has one, at the top there?' Mick again. 'And also add the shops you think she may have gone into in Dún Laoghaire? If circumstances haven't changed we'll do a round of all the retailers and offices over the next few days but it's good to know which ones might have been definites.'

Cullie nodded uncertainly at that final instruction as he sat back to the coffee table.

'Here, I'll do the shops bit, love.' I indicated for him to pass over the pen and paper. 'I know most of them from all the bags she leaves lying around.'

'Can you tell me what she was wearing?' Mick held his pen ready to take down every detail in his book.

'Black leggings and hoodie, no insignia,' I began, peering up from the list I had already started. 'White Adidas runners and her necklace, her silver smiley-face necklace.'

We had given it to her as part of her seventeenth birthday present back in March. It was a family joke – from about age two onwards Saoirse had taken to smiling so much we called her Smiler: 'Here comes Smiler'; 'Where's Smiler?' Hugh would call when he came through the door of an evening if she hadn't already been put to bed. We'd thought she'd think the present funny, but never imagined she would love it as she had, and would wear it all the time.

'OK. And from what you told us on the phone earlier she has long black hair, blue eyes. Any birth marks?'

'No, but she has a little scar, tiny one, right here.' I pointed with the pen to the top and centre of my forehead at the hairline. 'She fell when she was little but I . . . I can't . . . I can't remember when.' My eyes welled in the knowledge that I had long since forgotten how she had fallen. It had never bothered me before, but now it did. 'Hugh, can you remember, can you?' I asked, my panic rising.

'Rosie, it's OK, I don't think they need to know—'

'No, no absolutely, that doesn't really matter to us,' Mick interjected. 'It's simply to know so if we ever need to—'

'Monica might know,' I said, ignoring them, as if they hadn't spoken at all. Monica, the woman who ran the mother and toddler group I'd attended when Saoirse was little.

'Rosie, seriously, love.' Hugh consoled me, placing an arm around my shoulders, encouraging me to steady myself. 'It's OK, now. Come on, it's OK.'

I nestled in against him trying to return to that moment of sheer fright when I must have realised she'd fallen, when I would have bent to pick her up and hugged her, saying, my baby, my poor, poor baby. I wanted to remember kissing her and soothing her till she ran out of steam. I wanted to recall her little head lying on my shoulder, but it didn't come. I noticed Cullie watching me then, pale-faced and frightened. It was enough to make me pull away from Hugh, wipe at my eyes and nose and issue a weak apology before attempting to resume the list of shops.

'Nothing to apologise for, Rosie,' Mick said.

'A cup of tea,' the woman suggested, with great enthusiasm, attempting another distraction, already getting up and making her way into the kitchen.

Mick smiled again. 'I know this is hard, but if it's OK with you both, I'll press on. I just have a few more questions. The more we get now the better. We'll wrap this up as quickly as we can.'

'Of course,' Hugh answered.

'Was she wearing her hair up or down?'

'Down.' I gave a sniffle. 'It was easier, em, with the helmet on the bike.'

'And did you see any cars, unusual cars, or vans? Maybe at the time you saw her out the window, Rosie?'

I looked up from writing 'Angelo's', a clothes shop in the Dún Laoghaire Shopping Centre that Saoirse loved. 'No, I didn't see anything. Cullie, what about when you were walking up from Blackrock?'

'I wasn't really minding.' Cullie glanced at Mick, like he had done something wrong by not taking account of every vehicle and driver and licence plate that had passed him on the road up from the village earlier.

'Don't worry, the neighbours might have seen something.'

'They didn't, I'm afraid,' Hugh replied. 'Both Rosie and I have spoken to them.'

'I'd still like to talk to them, anyway. No harm in introducing myself.'

As I handed the piece of paper back to Cullie so he could begin on the phone numbers, I wondered if, despite all his previous assurances that Saoirse could well be home soon, Mick didn't believe that at all, and that was why he wanted to meet the neighbours – so they would know him, as he was going to be around a lot more. It was enough to unnerve me again.

'Tea,' the woman announced, bringing in a tray with a teapot, pulled from the depths of a cupboard, mugs, sugar bowl and a milk jug that must have barely known its purpose, given I'd never used it. She poured five mugs and passed them around. I don't think I touched mine after the first obligatory sip.

'Look,' Mick continued, as if reading my very thoughts, 'this could be as innocent as a friend that you weren't aware of swinging by and making her an offer she couldn't refuse.' Mick's eyebrows rose encouragingly, a suggestion of hope, which I grasped with both hands and clung to even though I knew none of her friends had ever driven a car, let alone owned one. And yet wasn't there a chance that one of them had just learned to drive and had borrowed their father's car? Yes, it was all so very possible, and I needed that life raft. As did Hugh, who took my hand and squeezed and nodded in hopeful agreement with Mick Malone.

'But the bike,' Hugh said then, 'I mean, leaving it on its side like that. It's like she rushed away to something, didn't even have time to lean it against the hedge or put it into the driveway against the wall or anything. Who does that unless something unusual happened?'

'Or someone.' Cullie looked up from the coffee table, appearing surprised by himself for saying such a thing. 'Well, it's like the inspector says, someone might have come to surprise her.'

'Was she seeing anyone?' Mick asked, leaning over to look at the list. 'Any of these guys, Taylor or Ross – or what's that name there, son?'

'Darren.'

'Right. Any of them?'

'Well,' I began looking dubiously from Hugh to Cullie, 'not as far as we know. But maybe Aimee could confirm that. I'm sure there was stuff we didn't know, although we were close. Cull, she didn't mention anything to you, did she?'

'No, nothing.'

'And there was no trouble with any of these friends. No fight that she was upset about?'

No, we each replied, in our own despondent ways, wishing there was something, anything we could give this man that would mean he'd know exactly what to do and where to start in bringing her back to us.

'Except,' I began nervously, repeating what I'd admitted to Hugh when he'd returned home earlier that evening, 'we'd rowed, Saoirse and me, before she left for Dún Laoghaire.'

All four turned to me with Mick and the woman giving me those now-we're-getting-somewhere looks.

'It wasn't a big row,' my husband defended, even though he hadn't been there and had to take my word for it from all I'd told him.

'It can often be the simplest, most innocent of things that can cause a chain reaction,' Malone said. 'It's important you tell us everything. Go on, Rosie.'

'She'd wanted a lift, that's all.' I shifted in my chair, my eyes closing on the memory of what had happened earlier.

It wasn't like her to want a lift. She, like Hugh, cycled everywhere.

'But I have a headache,' she'd said, to my amused suggestion that she was perhaps turning into her brother who preferred sitting in traffic in a car.

Truth was, I thought she was exaggerating the headache. I'd heard her mooching about downstairs the previous night having watched another film into the early hours of the morning.

'Perhaps not going to bed so late might help,' I'd said, in the way only mothers can, the way that makes you want to stamp on their toes. 'Besides, a bit of fresh air on the bike is the best thing for headaches.' How I've hated myself for those words every day of my life since, and how I will go on hating myself until I am buried in the earth and the worms can feast on the voice-box and tongue that gave them life.

'Fine,' she'd said, 'fine. Don't then, I'll cycle, but if I'm coming down with something you're to blame.'

She'd stormed out to the utility room, opening the back door, with me following her, telling her, 'It's mac and cheese tonight, your favourite, so don't be late.'

I'd watched as she banged and crashed her way through the back gate with her bike, my determination relenting with every grunt she made.

'Oh, leave it there,' I'd said eventually, fully realising the extent of her annoyance. I could be a bit late for the hair appointment, I thought. Annie'd forgive me this one time. 'I'll give you a lift.'

I'd left the back door, followed her into the passageway. But either she didn't hear me or chose not to, because off she went, the back gate still open, one foot on the pedal as her other leg swung over the bike frame and she was gone down our driveway onto the road, our lives changed for ever.

I hadn't realised, but all that time I was explaining what had happened to Mick, my tears had flowed steadily and dripped onto the collar of my T-shirt. Feeling the dampness on my skin was the first time I became conscious of their existence.

'I'm sorry,' I whispered to them, but to her most of all. I bowed my head and felt Hugh's hand rescue mine.

'And you think it was just the headache that had her so on edge, Rosie?' Mick asked, pushing me on, not wasting a second. 'There's nothing else you can think of that meant she *needed* to get to Dún Laoghaire today?'

'Well, no. There was nothing as far as I know that was bothering her.'

'And that goes for all of you?' He looked from one to the other. Each of us, I suspected, burning with guilt for not having something more to offer. We shook our heads.

The inspector examined his notebook before reaching for Cullie's list on the coffee table in front of him. He checked it, folded it over before putting it and the book in his inner breast pocket.

'I'll need photographs. As many as you can find.'

Hugh and Cullie began to search for what we had, coming back with the photo albums and some envelopes still full from the developers.

'It's best we have a few with different expressions. We need to get a sense of her,' he said. I stared at him as he resumed scanning through her life. 'And, of course, we need to choose one to circulate if we end up going down that route. One with that necklace, if possible.'

As the lads searched their phones and mine for the most recent pictures, I wondered if we were becoming *that* family now, whose daughter's face would appear on leaflets and milk cartons and buses and bus-stop shelters. Hugh halted his scrolling, perhaps thinking the same thing.

'Can I take these?' Mick held up a bundle of photos.

'Of course,' Hugh replied, having to grunt a little to get his voice to work again.

'But do we have copies, Hugh?' I panicked, my hand held out, ready to grab Saoirse back in case he answered no.

'Don't worry, love, I can get some.'

I lowered my hand reluctantly but still I considered the pile Mick had made, feeling like she was disappearing all over again. He perused the photos Cullie and Hugh had found on their phones and told them which ones to send to his number.

'OK. I think I have all I need for now.' He tapped the hard-copy photos off the coffee table like a pack of playing cards. I watched him put them into his inner pocket alongside the contacts list. 'I'm going to call to the neighbours. The more information we can get now while it's fresh in everyone's minds, the better.'

'I'll go with you, to introduce you,' Hugh said.

'No, no, it's OK. You stay. We have this covered now.'

The young guard stood to follow Mick to the sitting-room door where he stopped, turning back to us and reaching into his trouser pocket for his wallet.

'I'll be in touch with you first thing tomorrow. And any news, don't hesitate to call us. Here's my card. That's my direct line. If you can't get me there, try the mobile. If I don't pick up, leave a message. And remember,' he concluded, 'people come home more often than not.'

After the front door had closed and it was just us three again, we returned to checking our phones, watching from windows and listening for the opening of the front door. All I wanted was to hold her and say I was sorry for so many things: for the time when she was six weeks old and I had asked that she be taken from me, for not giving her a lift as she had wanted earlier that day, and to tell her that I would bring her anywhere, any time for the rest of her life, always and for ever ready, never questioning a bloody thing she said, ever again.

Not far now, the girl replied.
Just up here.

From then on Hugh's days were fuelled by sheer determination and utter desperation. Working closely with the guards to organise groups of volunteers to comb every bit of land between Blackrock and Dún Laoghaire and beyond for anything, her phone, her bag, something to push the case on.

They all came: Mammy and Daddy, Michael-Fran, Hugh's parents, his brother Ely, uncles and work colleagues, Cullie's friends, pupils and teachers from the school, our neighbours, Billy and Roger from my job, friends I'd made at the school gate, their families, their neighbours, strangers who came from as far afield as Wicklow, and one man who had come all the way from Belfast. They walked every road, every laneway, every cul-de-sac in the area. They spilled out of the Presbyterian church hall, not five hundred metres from our door, which became our HQ, wearing walking boots and runners and shorts and T-shirts and sometimes windcheaters when the forecast turned bad. They listened as Ely told them what locations they were covering that day. It was better to let his brother take the lead, Hugh said. Someone who was one step removed was always more level-headed, less emotional. Hugh's colleagues in the architect business had made large-scale maps, so he could point out the areas. Each person was assigned a group: A, B, C, D, E, et cetera.

I think one day they actually got to O. Ten people in each. One leader apiece, usually a family member or someone we knew well.

Hugh was better with the volunteers than I was. He could talk to them, whereas I was the silent mother, too shocked to speak. Some would come to say hello and commiserate, while others would avoid me. And who could blame them? I could barely raise a smile, let alone an encouraging word. But I did try. Every day, Hugh and I would stand hand in hand beside the map right before the briefing and I might say something like: You have no idea what this means, the time you're giving us to help bring her home. At least, that's what I always planned to say because often I would get half-way and stop, sometimes because of tears and sometimes because there was nothing left in me, no energy to finish it off. I'd feel Hugh's arm tighten around my waist then and I would drop my head and let him finish.

How much they gave. How much those strangers gave.

I'd stand back, watching this machine in full flow, wishing with every cell of me that I was them, an outsider, someone there to help, someone who would do their utmost, upturning every discarded Tesco bag, poking through the empty crisps packets and Club Orange bottles in a lane, leafleting every door, doing my best, my very heartfelt best, to find some clue about this girl whose name I knew was Saoirse.

I didn't want to be me.

They left in swarms, murmurations of searchers, with lunch packs handed to them as each exited the hallway. Someone who worked for SuperValu, who I can't now remember, donated bottles of water and heavy cardboard boxes of fruit. The sickening smell of bananas wafted around the room on those hot summer mornings. I can't eat them to this day. Sandwiches were made if nothing free could be blagged from any of the local businesses. That was my job, me and Mammy up at the crack of dawn buttering bread. We paid for it all, Hugh and I. Those volunteers followed their leaders in graceful flows as they crossed roads, got into vans and cars, letting the hall fall into a riotous silence.

On the fifth morning of their departure, following four days of empty-handed returns, I found I couldn't breathe. Bent double, I heaved violently as if I had run a marathon, Mammy catching me before I collapsed fully to the ground.

'Oh, my lovely,' she'd said, as she pulled me up to a seat. She rubbed my back in a rhythm I didn't want to end, before coaxing me up into their car and driving me that short distance home, in her nervous stop-start way, to where someone was always waiting, one of the neighbours usually, someone Saoirse would know should she arrive. I'd insisted on that.

I couldn't bear it, the anxious wait in the hall, wondering if there would be some success this time, then watching team after team come through those double mahogany doors with nothing and feeling something way beyond disappointment – it was a withering of my heart, a sucking away of its blood and its ability to beat.

Nathan and Daniel, my brothers, came home from the States in those early weeks. They brought their grown-up sons and daughters to help. It's funny which moments of that time remain so very clear when others don't, like Daniel's dry hands when he returned from a leaflet drop in Dublin's city centre one night. He'd always suffered with them: hot weather, cold weather, the very air it seemed, especially if it was windy, turned his skin raw and cracked.

'Jesus, Daniel,' I said, reaching for them, feeling their roughness.

'Sis, I've worked on building sites my whole life. I know how to handle it. I'm grand.' He tried to pull away, but I held firm to their hard crustiness.

'Do you have stuff with you?'

'No, I—'

'I have some hand cream.' I indicated the stairs. Somewhere up there I knew there was something that could help.

'Ah, don't be bothering. I've seen them a lot worse.' But I didn't listen and climbed those stairs to find a jar I rarely opened on my dressing-table. Back in the hallway, despite his continued protests, I took his hands and rubbed the yellow substance all over the tender cracks, as carefully as I possibly could, until it seeped into those red fingers that now shone.

'It'll dry, I promise, Daniel. And there's no perfume or anything in it. It's all-natural stuff, beeswax.'

'Beeswax, really?' He held up his glowing hands and I thought he might wipe them against the raincoat that Hugh had loaned him in case the threatened thunderstorm had reached our eastern shores.

'I can put the heat on if you want.'

'The heating, in August? The saints and all the angels couldn't be dealing with that kind of blasphemy. Nah, I think I'm good now. How about I make both of us a cup of tea instead?'

But before we headed for the kitchen, I took his invitation of a tight bear hug, reassuring me I'd done just fine. 'We will find her, you know that,' he whispered in my ear, as I laid my hand against his chest feeling the beat of his heart.

When darkness fell and another search came to an end, with still no trace of bag or phone, Hugh and I would find ourselves in our sitting room wondering all over again why she might have chosen to leave. Why had we lost our girl? We'd begin mid-sentence on some theory that had been knocking round our heads, inner thoughts spilling out into the air as if it was all perfectly normal: Could she really have been that angry with us? I'd ask. Or we'd wake after a few hours' precious sleep wondering aloud at changes that had happened in our lives, like Hugh taking on a major redesign of a building on Dame Street. Was it those longer hours, and my narkiness at his being more married to his job than to me, that might have caused her to leave? Or had it been the exams, that bloody Leaving Certificate – had the pressure been too much? Or was it a relationship problem? Even though we knew of none . . . But teenagers are secretive, aren't they, and rightly so, trying to carve out their lives away from the gaze of their parents. All of these things repeating over and over in our heads, in our conversations, hounding us for what we had done or not done, asked and not asked. The decisions we had made for our child that might have sent her down the wrong path.

Hugh kept lists of everyone involved. He had a book. Black hardback with a red spine in which he kept it all. Every volunteer in case we needed them in a hurry. Every guard, their number, rank and station. Every journalist willing to talk to us. Every missing-persons group we were told of. Every volunteer who'd come to play their part. At night, he'd flick through it when he came home, reviewing all he had learned that day, and he would write himself a note on another slip of paper of things still left undone. On its inside cover, he listed the important phone numbers, Mick's at the top. And, near it, the number: 730. A heavy blue ink surrounded it, forcing the paper to rise slightly in a little mound. How he must have lingered over it, darkening that circumference with every tracing of his pen.

'What's that, Hugh?' I asked, one evening, as he sat in his swivel chair, staring at the TV, shattered from another day of organising and walking the roads.

He reached for his glasses from the mantel over the fireplace and regarded it for longer than I had expected. 'It's nothing.'

He handed back the book and took off his glasses again.

'Well, it has to be something. You've circled it enough.'

'I'm telling you it's nothing.' His voice grew annoyed, and then, almost as quickly, softened again. 'At least, nothing that's of any use to us.'

'Oh, come on, Hugh.'

He didn't reply, pretending to find whatever it was he was watching extremely interesting.

'Please, Hugh.' I said it quietly, gently trying to coax the answer from him. He peered over, but not at me. It was the red-spined book where he lingered for a moment.

'It's . . . it's the number of people who've gone missing in Ireland since 1950 who they've never been able to find.'

It was a second before I fully comprehended what he'd said. A second in which I had felt the heat rise and my eyes sting.

'Oh, I see. That many?' My finger traced the indentation on the page. 'Is she in there? Saoirse? Is that what they think, that she's one of those now?'

'Don't, Rosie. Don't torture yourself.'

'Well, you must've done. Look how you circled it.' I held up the book as evidence. I waited for something further from him, but when nothing came, I asked the unaskable: 'Do you think that too, Hugh, that she's not coming back?'

'Rosie, please. This isn't doing us any good. It's only a number, for God's sake. I'm not even sure if it's true. It might be half that for all I know.' And there it was, his avoidance of my question, damning evidence of the first thread of doubt entering our lives that she might ever come home.

'And they've never found them?'

'Rosie,' he sighed in exasperation.

I got up then, dropping the book onto the floor. Unable to look at him I left the room and climbed the stairs to open Saoirse's door. There I stood among her things, which for eight years thereafter I would allow no one to touch, not even Hugh, who every now and again wondered if we might simply put some of them in the attic, to beseech her over and over, to stop being one of those 730 lost souls, to please, please be the one who came home.

A month after those first enthusiastic searches, the hall became the church's again and the crowds that had helped had disappeared. It wasn't that they wouldn't have done more, it was that, by then, they had searched it all, anywhere that the guards had thought a possibility. And there were simply no more leads to follow.

Officially, the guards confirmed that she had never left the country. Her passport still sat in her room. CCTV cameras at airports and seaports had produced nothing. When shown her picture, staff, exactly like me, sitting at ferry desks, had shaken their heads, shrugged their shoulders saying she could have been one of the many thousands who passed their way every day.

'But people still manage to cross to other countries without being seen, we all know that,' I'd said, when Mick had sat with us thirty days after Saoirse had gone missing to update us on his progress. 'And what about forgeries? Isn't that a possibility?'

'Anything is possible, Rosie,' he had replied. 'But what was Saoirse running from that would cause her to go to such lengths?'

I had no answer to give.

We had officially run out of road, it seemed.

Over the coming months, Hugh and I went on *Crimecall*, *Ireland AM*, and countless radio shows: Ray Darcy, Joe Duffy, Pat Kenny, appealing once again for her to come home and for information, for anyone to get in touch, even the smallest thing Hugh said that might help reignite the case. I was still so quiet, though, letting Hugh take the lead, speaking only when the interviewer addressed me directly and even then I couldn't be sure my low voice could possibly be heard over the airwaves.

After, we received hundreds of letters from people in support of us. Envelopes making it to our door with only the simplest of addresses:

The parents of Saoirse Dunne, Dublin.

People we did not know wrote that they were praying for us, wishing us well. Some even pretended to be Saoirse. She'd written to us from Carlow and Russia and Heaven, would you believe, despite the Dublin postmark, telling us she was happily working for Jesus.

But from all of those letters, and the five hundred questionnaires the guards filled out there had been nothing. Not a whisper, a breadcrumb, an upturned stone pointing out the direction in which my daughter had gone.

Dad knows the way. He'll have us there in a jiffy, the girl said. But you *saw* Aimee, right? Is she OK?

Around August, two months after she'd disappeared, Hugh, Cullie and I were alone in the house. We were getting used to that again, Mick not being around as much, family not being there constantly. It was just us three now. It was morning, early, well before the traffic had started to build on the Blackrock Road.

'Saoirse and I had a row too, you know,' Cullie announced, from the kitchen counter. 'I never told you.'

'What row?' I turned quickly from the patio doors, where I had been staring at the garden with a cup of tea in my hands, not taking in any detail – it could have been a safari park and it would have made no impact on me.

Hugh stopped his perusal of the *Daily Mirror* – he liked to scan each of the tabloids every day to make sure there was no news of anything, something leaked by the guards that we did not yet know – to look at Cullie, with a quizzical frown.

'No, no,' Cullie said, raising a hand to ward off the thoughts he realised were now going through our heads – here was the missing piece of the puzzle. 'It honestly was nothing major – we made up, like. See, we'd decided to have a movie day and we'd gone down to Xtra-vision in Blackrock to get a DVD each and popcorn and shit. I'd picked *Runaway Jury*, like, in five seconds but she took for ever reading the back of every box and checking for the producer, director and writer – you know what she's like. So, eventually she picked *Lost In Translation*. But when we got home she insisted that she would be playing her movie first, like after taking half the bloody day, so I just lost it and hurled my DVD box at her. If she hadn't bent down at that moment to press the open button on the machine, I'd have got her head. She was fuming. I mean, I said sorry. And she was fine again by the time I said she could play hers first. But imagine if I'd gotten her. That might've been the thing that changed what happened.'

'What do you mean?' Hugh asked.

'Well, you know I've been thinking about how life is all about chance. I mean what if the box had made a gash that meant she had to go and sit in A and E and maybe get stitches? It would have changed things, wouldn't it? Like, maybe she'd've been too wrecked from waiting all day in A and E to go anywhere for the rest of the week. Or maybe she'd've been too sore or too embarrassed if she'd had a big plaster on her head to go to Dún Laoghaire. Don't you see? Each thing we did in those days leading up to it had an effect.'

'Oh, come on.' Hugh closed the paper and threw its ruffled pages on top of the others, still neatly folded, awaiting their perusal. 'That kind of talk is ridiculous. You had no power over what happened.' He leaned on the marble countertop, palms face down either side of his broadsheet bundle. 'I really don't want you thinking that way. It doesn't help anyone.'

'OK, but,' Cullie shrugged defensively, 'it's just, I dunno, cause and effect.'

'Yeah, well, don't go there, Cullie.'

It was Hugh's dismissive tone that made me step in. 'But isn't he kind of right, Hugh? Not about *their* argument,

I don't mean that. I mean about mine. Let's face it, if I'd given her a lift none of this would have happened.'

'Not this again. Do you not know your daughter at all?'

My annoyance rose to match Hugh's. 'Of course I know my daughter, Hugh.' I stepped towards him away from the door.

'Really? Well, then, you'd know she wouldn't be doing any of this to us just because you two had an argument. And it wasn't even a big one. Look, how many times have there been rows and she just got on with things? Like we all do.'

This was new. Hugh had never said this before, never shut me down when we talked like this, wondering at why she might have left. Something had changed.

'But what if this time she—'

'If she what? Ran away because you wouldn't give her a lift?'

'But—'

'No, enough, Rosie, you know that doesn't make sense. That appealing to her to come home in interviews is just *bullshit.*'

Hugh shook his head, exasperated, taking up the perfect bundle of papers and slamming them back down onto the counter, making Cullie and me jump. 'It wasn't because we didn't turn around three times before opening the front door that morning or because we put on the wrong socks or because we weren't particularly nice to each other for one bloody minute in the day. It's ridiculous. Those things had nothing to do with what happened. And do you know why I know that so clearly? Because it's Saoirse we're talking about here. And the more this goes on the more time that passes and she hasn't come home I just . . . well,

I just know this wasn't her. No one's seen her, for Christ's sake. Not one person she trusts has even heard from her. That makes no sense. Somebody,' he said, looking up at me with those sad, tired blue eyes, 'has stopped her getting back here.'

I put my hands over my ears and shook my head. 'No,' I said. 'No.' I turned towards the patio doors again. It was too much for me, I still needed to believe that she had simply chosen this.

'But it could be someone she loves,' Cullie suggested, a slight desperation in his voice, trying to quell the fire he had unintentionally lit, trying to bring his parents back together to solid ground where he desperately needed us to be. I turned back to look at him, to show willing.

'You guys said it yourself, we don't really know if there was anything going on with anyone.'

'I really want to believe that, Cull, I do.' Hugh's annoyance at us had dissipated, his voice more level now, I was happy to note. 'But Aimee would know if there was the slightest bit of romance involving Saoirse. She told her everything and Aimee's already told us there was nothing going on.'

'Not as far as she knew, sure. But, Dad, we all have secrets, don't we? I dunno, I'm just saying we can't fully rule it out yet.'

'He's right, Hugh. He's totally right.' I gave an encouraging smile, a call to arms not to give up.

'Fine, fine, you guys keep believing in your love story then.' His hands were in his pockets now, his head bent as if looking at the headlines of the paper. It was a second before I realised that he'd started to cry, the little spasm in his slouched shoulders giving the game away.

'Oh, Hugh, it's OK.' I rushed to hug him, but he didn't let his head dip to my shoulder as I'd thought he might.

'She's not coming back, Rosie,' he said quietly. 'She's never coming back.'

'It's all right, Hugh.' I glanced towards Cullie to see if he had heard his father's words but of course he had. 'You're just exhausted. You need to sleep now. Come on,' I said, turning him, my arm around his waist, bringing him towards the door. We made it up the stairs and to our bedroom slowly, and there I laid him down and took off his shoes, and pulled the duvet up around him. 'Rest now,' I said. 'That's all you need to do.'

When I got back downstairs, Cullie was still at the counter, his head in his hands.

'Fuck, I'm sorry, Mum,' he said, looking up at me. 'I honestly didn't mean to upset anyone.'

'It's OK, love, I know that. We're all just on edge.' I crossed the room and gathered my son in to me, kissing the crown of his head. 'It's all going to be OK.' But I knew the shift had come. And the fissure that had crept between Hugh and me without us even noticing, would keep expanding and growing until one day we were staring into a canyon.

Saoirse's Leaving Certificate exam results arrived a couple of weeks later. She'd done it: she'd gotten the film-production course she had worked so hard for. All of those weekends working on those short films, *Bank* and *This Edible Life*, had paid off.

I accepted her place in college when the offer dropped into her inbox.

'Why, Rosie?' Hugh asked.

'What do you mean, why?' I was incredulous that he would even ask. It was late, we were in bed, my laptop balanced on my thighs. 'Hugh,' I sighed. 'I know right now you aren't coping very well, and that's OK. Look how you held me up in these last months. Maybe it's my turn, you know. I'm able now. I'll keep this ship afloat. You don't have to worry. Let me take the lead and you rest,' I tried, hoping it was enough to end this conversation, because I knew where it was going.

'Rosie, you need to understand—'

'No, Hugh,' I said pointedly, but with a smile. 'I don't. I'm not giving up on her coming home. Now, maybe you're right about someone keeping her away from us, but I know she is still alive. And it's not just because Patsy said it—'

At that he tutted.

By then Patsy had made her pronouncement that she felt Saoirse was close by, somewhere out there, finding her way back.

'Listen. I feel it so completely in here,' I placed my hand against my heart, 'right in here. I can feel her and she's breathing. And I won't have you saying anything different, not around me and not around Cullie. OK? I just won't. I can't.'

I wiped an unbidden tear from my cheek.

'I can't stop you thinking what you want, Hugh, but I *can* accept this place in college for her. And I *can* keep looking for her. And I *will* keep asking her to come home.'

My determination relented slightly then. And I began to regret the sharpness of my words.

'Please, Hugh, please just let me do this. Let me prove to you that there is hope. Can you do that?'

I took his hand, beseeching him. But his face gave me nothing. His forehead bore no frown, his lips were flat, his eyes concentrating on the hand I held.

Eventually I felt it squeeze mine.

'OK,' he said, with the effort of a small smile. 'OK.'

The following year when she still hadn't returned, I visited the college president to ask they hold her place one more time, bringing with me her sketchpads and notebooks, pushing things out of the way on his desk so he could see what she had achieved. He had agreed, rescuing a glass paperweight from where it sat precariously at the table's edge. I returned the year after and the year after that. Each time he assured me her place was safe, but who am I to know if he kept his word? Perhaps he said it simply to get the pleading woman, whose tormented face he could no longer look at, out of his office. When year three rolled around, Hugh asked me to stop but I couldn't. Four years in total I went, and each time that man smiled, gave me his word, I chose to believe him.

Mick Malone had told us about a group called the Families of the Disappeared when, after a week or so following Saoirse going missing, he began to suspect we were in this for the long haul.

Hugh had contacted them immediately. Gerry Conroy, their volunteer coordinator, husband of Fidelma and father to Tadhg who had disappeared twenty years prior, had been invaluable, advising him on how to deal with the guards – keep pushing them, he'd said, be a nuisance as much as you like. He'd put up Saoirse's picture on their media platforms and their website, had sent it on to their international connections. You might come and meet us, he suggested. We have a gathering once a year. It's always a good day out, never a bad thing to be around people who know exactly what you're going through.

In the October, when we were back at work and Cullie back to school, I suggested we take Gerry up on his invitation to join them at their event that year in Carlow. Hugh had been reticent, but we had all gone, Nina, Cullie's new girlfriend, now an almost constant presence in our lives, included.

Maggie, mother of the disappeared Claire, was the first one to see us standing in the doorway looking a little overwhelmed at the packed function room in the Killeeney Castle Court Hotel. 'You are most welcome,' she said, throwing her arms around me as if we were old friends.

'Thank you,' I replied, to this colossus of a woman. She was so tall my head had to stretch up so that it wasn't buried in her armpit. When she let me go I thought I'd better qualify exactly who we were in case she had mistaken us for some others, a family she actually knew. 'I'm Rosie Dunne, and this is—'

'Hugh.' She had gotten there before me, had begun to hug him already. 'And you must be Colmán. Handsome man.' Another hug, another slightly confused Dunne.

'And I'm Nina.' Nina had immediately thrown her arms around Maggie enthusiastically. 'Thank you for letting me be here.'

'Oh, my goodness, but of course.' Maggie, finished with the embracing, stood in front of us, smiling from one to another until she focused on Hugh and me. 'We hoped you might come. Gerry told me to wait right here and watch out for you in case. I'm Maggie.'

'Gerry's been a great support,' Hugh said.

'Well, that's our job, being there for each other. Our unwritten motto: just be there. That's it, plain and simple. Now, I know this can be overwhelming but this is us, the families of those who are missing. Parents, children, uncles,

aunties, grandparents, cousins, friends, we're all here.' Her
hand stretched out to explain the crowd, a cheerful bustle
of people catching up with each other.

'And this is Ultan.' She plucked a man from a nearby
group. 'My other half, God love him. Don't ask me why I
ended up with a Kerry man.'

'Pure luck,' Ultan replied, and shook our hands, welcoming us to the mayhem.

From the hotel bar, I watched Hugh that day, looking so
lost among the group that I had thought would help him
out of his stupor. Would give him hope again, at least.
He was standing across the room trying hard to have a
conversation with Ultan, two other men and a woman. His
face was empty of emotion, and he spoke only when asked
a question, trying at a half-hearted smile. By then I had no
clue where Cullie and Nina were – the last I'd seen of them,
they were laughing with a group of young ones over in the
corner. But they weren't there now.

'Is he OK?' Maggie asked, jutting her chin towards Hugh.

'He's, well . . . We're struggling, to be honest.'

'Of course you are. How could you not be?'

'Maggie?' I asked, deciding to put faith in this woman
who was being so kind to me that day, hardly leaving my
side as she'd introduced me to as many people as she could.
'How are you so sure your Claire is . . . well, dead?'

She'd already told me how she firmly believed her daughter had been murdered by a man nearly twice her age, who
had been infatuated with her.

'I knew it from the get-go. Mother's intuition. Ultan
couldn't bear to hear me say it, but as the evidence grew, he
came around to my thinking.'

'We've nothing, no proof of what has happened at all, zilch. But I just know she's still out there, breathing.'

'Hold on to that.' She half turned to me, the index finger of the hand clasping her gin and tonic pointed at me. 'Keep listening to your instinct. Let that be your faith, let it guide you through this crap. Listen, the road ahead doesn't get any easier, believe me, so you'll need it.'

'You don't think I'm wrong believing she's still alive?'

'Unless Mick Malone can walk in here with absolute evidence that she isn't, then of course it's possible.'

'And that's what he has for your Claire.'

'Pretty much. We just have to nail the fucker now.' She took a mouthful of her drink. 'So, I'm guessing he's not on board with this?' Again, she's looked in Hugh's direction.

'Not any more, no. He can barely listen to me talk about the case these days. But you should have seen him at the start. Such a warrior. Don't know what I would have done without him.'

'Yep, role reversal, I know it well. And the arguments – don't talk to me. But as long as Ultan's still there with me somewhere in the house, even if he is sleeping on the couch, I know we'll be OK.'

'Hugh's in the spare room now.'

'Ugh. Life, it's mostly just one big bag of rocks. But we'll get through it, missus. I promise you. Do you need more proof than this lot?'

We looked around at them, the people in that room, leaning into each other, imparting their wisdom, allowing a tear, laughing at something remembered about their amazing missing people, and for the first time in four months I truly felt it – even Hugh must have, I was sure: something close to hope.

But when we left he seemed more sullen than he had been before we had arrived.

In the car on the way home we were tired. Even Nina, the girl we were only getting to know, with her ability to be enthusiastic about the most boring of things, was quiet. But Cullie was restless – I could see it in the rear-view mirror as I drove. I knew the signs of old: a hand constantly running over the cowlick on the left-hand side of his hairline.

'You know,' he said, right when my curiosity was about to give in and ask, 'one of the girls, Sandy – was that her name?' He looked to Nina for confirmation.

'Blue-dyed hair? Yeah, that's her.'

'She said that this guy, David Walsh, I think his name was, his body just washed up down the coastline in Wexford. He'd been missing for like a couple of months.'

He said nothing more, but I could sense he was looking at me, waiting for a reaction.

'Right.' I nodded, keeping my eyes firmly on the road. I sensed Hugh turn to me from the passenger seat, but I kept looking forward. When it grew time for me either to respond or for Cullie to elaborate, I said: 'That's very sad for David's family.'

'Yeah, but they have him now, right? I mean, they know what happened. They aren't worrying any more about where he is. Like, that has to be better than this waiting.'

'Look, Cullie,' I began, then hesitated, digging deep to draw strength from all Maggie and I had discussed earlier. 'We want this to be over, but we have to keep the faith in her that's she still out there, alive. We've discussed this. We *are* going to get her back.'

My eyes shifted left to the rear-view to gauge Cullie's reaction. He said nothing and chose instead to stare out of his window, his teeth gnawing at his poor thumb again. I watched Nina's hand creep quickly to his knee, to rub at it in kindness. It seemed my son, too, was coming around to his father's way of thinking, that Saoirse was now dead.

Several times over the following years Mick tried to reignite interest in the case by asking me to do more interviews. Hugh was no longer interested in such things. Unlike my earlier quiet, shy beginnings, I had grown confident, unwavering.

'I mean, are you telling me,' I demanded of Miriam O'Callaghan on *Prime Time Investigates*, 'that no one saw her? It's simply ridiculous. Somebody somewhere knows something.' By then such emotional displays mattered nothing to Rosie Dunne.

A man called the Garda Confidential Line straight after to say he had given Saoirse a lift from Dún Laoghaire to Wexford Town on the day she'd gone missing. As we waited for the guards to follow this up, I bit my finger-nails, moved things pointlessly on the mantelpiece and boiled the kettle for no reason at all. But it had been a lie. The man's wife had confirmed that he was nowhere near Dublin on that day. He'd been at home with her. They'd lost a daughter in a car accident when she was seven and since then he hadn't been so well, she'd said, but that he'd meant no harm. And then there was the woman who'd seen a car pull up to the abandoned house next door to her in Enniskerry around the time of Saoirse's disappearance. The driver had carried something bulky inside but had come out without it after a while. The guards searched that house thoroughly. Mick even told Hugh they were getting sonar equipment to make sure nothing was buried under the cement floor. But it was fruitless. Hugh seemed more defeated than ever at that dead end, locked himself into the spare room, wouldn't even go to work the following Monday, until Ely came and knocked on his door and was allowed inside.

In the November of the year after Cullie had started in Maynooth College and moved into digs in town with Nina, Mick had rung our doorbell. It was late when Hugh and I sat across from him to hear talk of a man, a sexual predator, he said, who had tried and failed to pull a twelve-year-old boy into his car some months prior to Saoirse going missing, and a thirteen-year-old girl some months after. These incidents had only just come to light, following a review of reports around the summer of 2009, as being possibly connected to our case.

'But Saoirse was seventeen. An adult, not a child – well, not like that,' I said, confused at the association.

Hugh stayed silent as he'd listened to Mick, his right leg bouncing up and down.

'These guys,' Mick said, 'don't always have a type. Some go for whoever's there and vulnerable, someone they can take quickly.'

'But no one reported seeing a car in the cul-de-sac that day, as I recall.'

'No, although that doesn't mean it wasn't there, Rosie.'

'And there was the bike,' Hugh said, 'being left like that.'

'But Howth, Malahide?' I said, ignoring their interventions, 'I mean they're on the other side of Dublin.'

'It's still worth examining the possibility,' Mick said. 'People such as these throw their nets wide. We already have the names of one or two suspects who fit the profile. We're following them up. I know this is hard but

I wanted to give you both fair warning in case it gets into the papers.'

'No.' I shook my head. 'This doesn't feel like it has anything to do with Saoirse's case.'

'Jesus, Rosie, he's not asking for our permission here,' Hugh said, in exasperation, running his hands down his face. 'Let them just get on with it. OK?'

'All right,' I relented, taken aback by the vehemence of his reaction.

Thereafter the nights stretched out long and sleepless. I walked our downstairs hallway, in and out of the kitchen, blocking my ears as if I was being told it all again. Let her be dead, I whispered to the walls I passed, and into the empty spaces through which I waded, please let her be dead, one of the only times I ever asked that of the universe. If this is what has happened, let that monster have put her out of her misery. PLEASE. I watched and listened and smelt the air, waiting for it, a confirmation of my request, but nothing came.

Mick couldn't connect anything to either of the suspects he had mentioned, each having an alibi.

'Thank God,' I'd cried into Hugh's neck as I clung to him the evening Mick had rung with the news. 'I told you, haven't I always said she's still out there?'

But he said nothing when I emerged from my place of safety in the curve of his neck. How far we had drifted from each other, I thought sadly, looking at his profile, our beliefs now so very much at odds.

Knocked down, yeah.
She was knocked down,
the girl said, distractedly.

Right before Saoirse's seventh anniversary, Hugh knocked on our sitting-room door. By then the piano had been bought and he had, as ever, headed to it straight after eating the dinner I had left when he got in from work, so I was surprised to see him standing there, unsure, it seemed, as to whether he was allowed in or not.

'What?' I'd said, in worry that something had happened, and he was coming to break it to me gently.

'No, it's nothing. Can I join you?'

'Of course.'

I put down the papers I was riffling through and muted the TV. When I wasn't knee-deep in something new to do with the case or with the Families of the Disappeared, I would watch nature documentaries. It was all that I could stomach.

'Do you want to sit here?' I had, over the years, comman-deered his swivel chair. I was half out of it already, holding those pages to my chest lest they fell.

'Not at all. I'll be grand here on the couch.'

There he sat, glancing surreptitiously at me every second or so.

'H-u-u-u-g-h?' I asked eventually, putting the papers back down. 'Come on, what's going on?'

'Can a man not just come and sit with his wife for a bit?'

'Of course he can.' I smiled kindly. 'And the wife is glad. But the man hasn't wanted to sit in here for a very long time so it's making her a tad nervous.'

It was only having him there that made me realise how much my heart had missed him. His quiet, stable presence. A man who in the past, on an advert break, might have gone out for a moment only to reappear with a glass of wine or a cup of tea without his wife having even hinted at it.

'Well, if you have nothing in particular you want to talk about, I have bad news for you: there's nothing on. At least, nothing I want to watch. But here, have a look for yourself.' I passed over the TV guide. 'But the *Doc on One* is on the radio shortly if you want to have a listen. Or you can help me figure out where this year's gathering's going to be.'

I'd attended the annual event of the Families of the Disappeared every year since that first time. Sometimes with Hugh and Cullie but sometimes on my own. The previous year the president had invited us all to the Áras. We had sat with Michael D and Sabina, his wife. They were kind and thoughtful, as we'd known they would be, listening to our stories as if their aides had never briefed them. We ate canapés and, after, planted a tree in the garden, right outside their front door for those so clearly absent. Michael D said he wanted it there so he could see it when he walked the dogs so that there would be another soul remembering them and willing them to find their way home. Otherwise, we took turns in organising our get-togethers. That year was my turn.

Hugh took the magazine and started flicking through it, but not really focusing on anything. 'What about the Royal Marine?' he suggested.

'Bit pricey?'

'Well, the Architects Association have held a few gigs there and those boys don't like spending money so I'm guessing perhaps not as much as you might think.'

'OK. Well, I'll ring them tomorrow,' I paused. 'Oh, wait, though, how's the parking?'

He looked up, squinting one eye, trying to remember. 'Actually, no idea. I usually walk down.'

'You know how the Conroys are. If there isn't easy parking, they mightn't come. Fidelma's hip isn't so good, these days. And I really want them to be there. They deserve a nice day out. Everyone does. Could we stretch to paying for it, Hugh, do you think?'

I thought for a minute he hadn't heard me, so long did it take him to reply. Or perhaps he thought I was delusional, given we were flat broke from everything. Our bank accounts had whittled down as our credit cards expanded, so much over the years that all our money was gone, save for the house, which we had remortgaged, and Hugh's business, which his faithful workers had kept going throughout – and still did, he maintained. 'I'm not the man I once was,' he regularly announced.

'Rosie, I don't think it's a good idea to be setting a precedent with one family paying for everything because the next lot who are organising it will think they have to do the same. Besides the last thing these people want is pity. We have to contend with enough of that out there.' He pointed the magazine towards the window, to the world of others who could never, nor wanted to, fathom what it was we went through. 'Let's get a nice function room and people can pay for themselves, like we always do.'

He'd said it almost reluctantly, no doubt knowing how happy it would have made me to gift something to these

people. But he was right. We families had enough to concern ourselves, without keeping up with the Joneses.

But he had been wrong about the other thing.

'It's not pity, Hugh. It's a way of thanking them: Maggie,
Gerry, Ultan, everyone, for their kindness, their understanding. Just being with them makes me feel that I'm not
some freak. I can talk about anything I like with them, and
they get it. They're all we have.'

He didn't look up immediately, but I could see his nod
before he replied: 'I know.'

I added calling the Royal Marine to my to-do list the
next day, which also included ringing the president's sec-
retary, the taoiseach's office and the minister for justice. It
had been a while since I had called them. It helped to keep
letting people know we hadn't gone away.

'Listen, Rosie . . .' And there it was, the change of tone,
the one that signified I'd been right all along, that there was
a reason for his being there. He put the magazine down
carefully beside him on the couch, giving it a little pat, like
he might damage it if he rushed. 'I was chatting to Mick
about something and I thought I'd mention it to you.'

We regarded each other for a moment.

'And?' I encouraged, a little suspiciously.

'Do you remember Gerry Conroy telling us a while back –
God, it must've been very early on – that after seven years of
being missing, a person can be, em . . . declared, well, dead?
If the family want it, that is. Now, I'm not saying we should
do that. I wanted to know if you remembered, that's all.'

Of course I remembered. All the families knew about it.
But we also knew its main use was if a family needed to
access the relative's estate or make a life-insurance claim or
something along those lines.

'Why?' I began. 'Why would you want to know if I remembered it? What possible reason have you to ask me that?'

'Please, Rosie. I've already said I don't want to do it—'

'But why bring it up? It's not like we need to look at this for legal reasons. It's not like she has some stash of money we need to get our hands on. She's seventeen, Hugh. *Seventeen*.'

And there it was, my big glaring mistake bouncing around the room like a powerful echo, so loud in its blunder that I'm sure the Cassidys heard it as it rushed over the hedge and through their walls. For Saoirse was no longer seventeen. She was coming up to being twenty-four.

'You know what I mean.' I shook my head and closed my eyes, frustrated with myself.

'I don't want to do it, Rosie. I . . . I'm just finding this so hard. I mean, would it be so wrong to accept that she is gone now?' His voice had strained in its appeal, and perhaps a little in shame at hearing the words out loud.

'I know she's *gone*, Hugh. I'm simply trying to get her back.' My voice, on the other hand, was steady and calm. Reasoned, I thought, if not perhaps a little frosty.

'Yes, but you think she's alive.' He stood up, one hand out, pleading his case. 'You won't see what's so bloody obvious.'

'Hugh, please.' I couldn't bear to look at him like that, couldn't bear to hear it. We both knew which side we stood on. Could he not let us be, entrenched, quietly believing what we wanted to, like we had managed for so long?

'No,' he replied, almost whispering it. I had expected a host of protestations. But not that simple, quiet, to-the-point no. I stared at him as he slumped back to the couch. 'It's so hard, Rosie. Watching your delusion.'

'My *delusion*.'

His bent head shook from side to side as he stared at the sitting-room rug we'd had for years – everything in the house still the same for when she walked back in the door. 'It hurts too much. You being this way pulls me back into that awful place where maybe you're right and all of this will be OK. Until I wake myself up and see that's never going to happen. I won't – no, I *can't* keep going this way. And I honestly believe you know it too, despite all you peddle to the world, that wherever Saoirse is right now, right this bloody minute, she isn't breathing. There is only one ending here, Rosie, that I really need you to accept because . . . I'm not sure how I'll manage to do this any more.'

He cried then, big full tears that hit the rug, and then a keening that tore at me but at which I closed my eyes, unable to bear it. His demand had shocked me into silence. I was at a loss with what he was asking of me. To do anything to comfort him might suggest that he had convinced me. If I showed the slightest bit of give, he could dig and dig until I crumbled and called her dead. For seven years, we two had clung to whatever managed to keep us upright as we sat tensed in our separate corners of that house, and my defences, like his, were flimsy. I had never thought for a second that he would ask this of me. Neither had I imagined that my stance was hurting him to the point he needed me to stop.

But I could not.

I stood up and walked towards the sitting-room door. In my periphery, as I passed him, I could see his head hadn't risen, no protest made at my leaving. Long after I had closed my bedroom door and curled into a ball, my tears soaking the duvet, I imagined him still sitting on that couch, wondering what would happen now.

The following day he watched me over breakfast, but I would not turn his way. We ate and drank in silence.

And when he was finally ready to go to work, panniers packed and cycling gear on, he leaned against the utility-room door frame.

'Rosie, you've got to understand.'

I wanted not to answer, not to have to entertain this again, so I shut it down. 'I'm thinking chicken for dinner tonight. Does that suit you?' I said it as brightly as I could, not turning in his direction, instead opening the fridge door and staring in at the contents with intention.

From the corner of my eye I could see that he was looking at me. I imagined his incredulous face, a slight gape to his mouth, a closing of his eyes as he let out a sigh or a running of his tongue over his lower lip. A moment passed and then another, in which I willed him to leave it be. To go and never mention this topic again.

'Sure, chicken,' he finally replied, with an air that seemed a cross between despondent and sarcastic. I dared to glance his way, to see his eyes now fixed firmly on his cycling shoes. And then, without another word or a raising of his eyes, he turned to click-clack his way out through the back door.

A long and ragged breath escaped me and I found myself on my hunkers, a hand reaching out spider-like to the floor saving me from a fall.

The days that followed, I spoke to Hugh as if that evening had never happened. I shut it down. Rambled on and on, filling every space that sat between us so that he would never find an opening again. Mick this, Mick that, interview this, interview that, posters, websites, forums, help lines, I jammed them all in. Filled the air with everything I was doing, would be doing, planned on doing. But in front of me, I made sure he never said the words that she was dead again.

And then one day, a week, maybe two, after we had spoken, my son arrived.

'Cullie, the very man. I've just been on to that guy in RTÉ, what's his name, ugh, you know the one. . . sounds like caravan.' I clicked my fingers at him two or three times trying to remember the name of the reporter I had literally hung up from as my son had turned his key and stood half in, half out of our front door. 'Garvin, that's the one.'

'Nice to see you too, Mum.'

'Yes, yes, sorry, come in, come in.' I beckoned him in fully and kissed his cheek. 'Tea, will you have one? I had a pot on there, although that was possibly hours ago. What time is it now? Why aren't you at work?'

'Eh, because there's no club tonight, just like every other Tuesday,' he seemed mildly exasperated. 'It's six thirty.'

Tuesday, right, yes, it was a Tuesday, wasn't it? Every other weekday night, bar Fridays, there was a youth club but not Tuesday. Why did he always have to remind me? And why did I always let my brain forget these details?

'Six thirty? Sure it can't be. It was only one o'clock the last time I looked. I'll put a fresh pot on. But wait, dinner. I'll make something. Pasta and a bit of Parmesan? Won't take me a second. You love the plain pasta and Parmesan,

don't you? At least, I think I have Parmesan. Me and shopping, these days.'

I'd already scurried my way back into the kitchen with
him following.

'Yes, I liked it when I was four, Mum. But you don't need
to be making me anything. I've eaten already.'

'You're sure? I can make you something and you can
bring it with you in a Tupperware box for you and Nina.'

'Mum, seriously, leave it. Can you stop with the . . .' he
twirled his hand in my direction, '. . . moving.'

I put my hands down by my sides on his command, as if
I was a child being given out to by the teacher.

'Sorry, Mum, but it's like you have no off button sometimes.'

He took off his jacket and put it on one of the stools at
the island and sat down.

I'd never seen a person look so immediately tired. As if
a make-up artist had slipped in without my noticing and
brushed a grey tint from hairline to chin, then dabbed an
extra layer of darkness under those big eyes of his. It was
me, I was exhausting him.

Not for the first time I saw Hugh in him. With every passing year Cullie grew more like his father. And now he gave
me that smile, Hugh's speciality, the pulled-in lips that said,
I'm trying here, and perhaps I'm doing a shit job, but I still
mean no harm.

'Listen, Mum, I was chatting to Dad and . . .' I lolled in
my reverie, wondering if Saoirse had morphed more and
more into me over time too. I'd heard his words, and was
trying to turn my attention away from them, because in
truth I didn't want to hear the rest, but out they came nevertheless. '. . . well, you know he's sorry about the seven-year

thing. He was never going to do it. He handled it badly, that's all. He just wants you guys on the same page.'

'Please, Cullie, I think it's best we don't do this.' I had moved again, despite his request and was now filling the kettle because we would have tea or coffee or whatever it was he drank these days, rather than this conversation, which I wasn't able for again and certainly not with him. 'How's Nina?' I segued, above the rush of water.

'Mum.'

'Wasn't she changing roles again? Is she doing the publicity now or something?'

'Mum, can we not talk about Nina?'

'Huh, she wouldn't like to hear you say that. She's so bright, though, isn't she? I don't just mean intellectually, I mean in her whole being. She's ethereal, is that the word? She'd know – she has lovely vocabulary, hasn't she? We should get her on the radio more for us.' I was by now tapping the word 'ethereal' into my phone.

'Mum, seriously.'

'Ah, yes, lightness, see. Oh wait, fluffy, airiness. Perhaps not exactly what I—'

'Jesus, Mum.'

But I didn't look up at him, despite the exasperation in his voice. My efforts at distraction had failed, so I left down my phone on the counter and turned back to the kettle to make him tea, to pass the mug and milk and sugar his way without looking at him once.

I sat silently to his left, twirling the teabag in my own mug, watching the liquid darken, knowing I would never drink it now, I was a weak-tea drinker, hardly Irish at all. It was the drag and swirl of the bag that was holding my attention, not the taste.

'You know things can't go on like this, Mum. All this non-stop nervous energy.'

'I'm not giving up on her, Cullie, if that's what this is about.' My words were determined, perhaps a little too much so.

'Who's asking you to give up on her?'

'Your father. And you, by the sound of it.'

'Really? *That*'s what you think we're doing? Every time I update the website, is that what I'm doing? Every time I retweet another missing-person message, is that what I'm doing? Every time I take a day off to meet up with the Conroys and the Bellows, is that me giving up? What – so we all have to be going around telling the world she's still alive? Is that the only way we can fight for Saoirse? Is it Rosie Dunne's way or no way at all? Is that what you're saying?'

I didn't answer, keeping my eyes fixed on his untouched tea.

'I want her to be alive, Mum. I so bloody want that. Don't you think Dad wants that too?'

Still I would not look at him and ran the teabag around my mug again. And then he bowed his head right down to the countertop, his forehead rolling a little from side to side as he sighed. Only then did I give in slightly, imagining my hand touching the soft darkness of his hair. He sat up so quickly that I wondered had he sensed it.

'We're worried about you, Mum. We can't suggest another possible outcome here or you freak. We have to watch what we say. Editing ourselves around you. It's getting harder to come over. Each passing year you dig yourself deeper into this one answer. And I know you know, don't you? That that isn't how it's going to end and yet . . .' he stopped for a second, blinked, then considered the counter, maybe wondering if he could lay his head down to rest one more time, but he didn't, and from somewhere found the will to finish what he had started, '. . . something in you won't let go.' He paused for a second, his face softening, losing some of the mounting exasperation. 'And, Mum, I do get it, I really do, but please stop expecting us to play this game, as well.'

'Game? It's not a *game*, Cullie.'

'No, I know.' He sighed, ashamed at his own misstep, a hand rising to rub his tired eyes. 'Of course it's not a game, Mum. I didn't mean it like that. Stupid choice of word.'

I felt ashamed, for the obvious error I had pounced on, like he had meant it. I stretched out my hand for his, and when he gave it, I felt the warmth of his fingers curling around mine. We exchanged the saddest of smiles as we squeezed our forgiveness into that touch.

It was that moment shared, the closeness to him, the vulnerability that allowed, for the first time ever, a momentary loosening of the reins on my determination that Saoirse was still alive.

'I keep thinking, you know, that time will make it easier. I really do. That with each passing day, I will grow to accept this. But it isn't how it works, is it? I hate the desperation, don't you? How useless you feel. You want something to give or to shift or to move. But the days and months and years go by and nothing. Nothing that brings you any closer. And closer to what? The . . . the . . .' And I couldn't even do it, say the words, the reality of what might have befallen her, the cruelty she might have felt, the indignity, the injustice, the barbarity. No, they would not come, and neither would I let them. Instead, the tears fell so fast and furious that I had to take back my hand to hide my face. He pushed away his stool and came to gather me up. I allowed my body to collapse against his chest while I keened as Hugh had done days before without the slightest comfort from me.

'I can't, Cullie, I can't.'

'Ssh, Mum. It's OK.'

'Don't make me. Please don't make me say those things.'

'I'm sorry. I'm sorry.'

And I cried and moaned, and he apologised and rocked me for a period of time I can no longer quantify. Until, like an ebbing tide, my anguish and my tears receded, and we were left with a silence so consuming, so comforting that I willed his arms to keep me in their protection for ever, for him to remain right by my side for always.

But his kiss to my head broke the spell and he loosened his grip enough so he could look down at me. And I knew, despite my instinct to grab at those arms and wrap them around me again, that I needed to smile, to wipe at my eyes, to tell him I was fine now.

'I shouldn't have come and I shouldn't have asked—'

I shook my head and raised a finger for him to stop. 'No,' I finally managed, wanting to tell him that he had nothing to apologise for. Name one possible thing that you have ever done wrong, I wanted to say. And yet no further words would come because I crumpled again, lost in a grief for both of my children that I felt was drowning me. He attempted to cradle me once more, but this time I found the will, the strength to push him away.

'Nina will be worried about you, Cullie. You should get back.'

'But, Mum, I can't leave you like this.'

'I'll be fine. And, what's more, your father and I will be OK. I'll talk to him. I promise. We'll figure this out.' I wiped at my tears and smiled. Or gave my best attempt, wanting so desperately to reassure him that I'd find a way to face the reality that he and his father believed to be true. That we would all go forward on the same page.

I got off my stool and began to tidy. And there I was back to the busy mother he had so earnestly asked me to stop being not five minutes before.

'You know, you coming here has helped me,' I said. 'I know it doesn't look like it now but, honestly, love, it's done me the world of good. Now unless you want me to start putting a dinner on for you, I suggest you get back to that wonderful girl of yours.'

I knew without looking at him that he was unconvinced, yet I wouldn't stop with the wiping down of the counter and the clearing away of our mugs.

He finally took his jacket and swung it around so his arms slid back into its sleeves, and I remembered the years of him being unable to put on his coat when he was little. In the end we had come up with a system where I laid his jacket upside down on the hall floor, the hood tipping his toes, and he would bend to put his arms in, to swing his coat over his head. And as he left, he looked at me with such sadness – the look of a boy who didn't really want to leave at all. But he pulled the door closed anyway, as I stood in that very spot in the hallway, shy of the swing of the door, where I had, eighteen years prior, laid down his coat on the floor for the first time and he had laughed when I'd told him what to do, and laughed again when he saw his arms were indeed in his sleeves without any pulling and tugging and pushing. I had told him he wouldn't be able to do it in school, though, as I didn't think the teacher would want a whole class of five-year-olds bending down and knocking heads together, swinging coats high with zips and buttons catching in eyes. It was our secret. Our very own game that we would only play here, at home, alone.

But Aimee was going home to Dalkey. Why would she be out this side of Dún Laoghaire?

My mother died the following October, three months after my husband and son had asked me to consider Saoirse as dead. I think it was a broken heart. I think she could no longer bear the strain of her missing See-see – that's what she'd called Saoirse from the minute she was born. Her heart, having filled with so much sadness, had overflowed, finally breaching its banks in the library as she bent to sort out the picture books for the last time. Darcy, the librarian, said she had *Can't You Sleep, Little Bear?* in her hand. It had been Saoirse's favourite when she was little, the one she would always find among the messy debris of other children's busy rooting and sit to read. Sometimes she and Cullie would huddle up together in the one beanbag, her rhyming off every word, remembered rather than read, with Mammy looking on from her desk, proud as ever a grandmother could be.

'She was sitting in the beanbag,' Darcy said, her voice strained and panicked, when she phoned me. 'I thought she was asleep. And I let her be. If I'd only gone over to her. But she looked so peaceful. And I didn't want to disturb her. Oh, Rosie, I'm so sorry.'

I was at a conference with Maggie in Liverpool. By that stage, I was speaking more and more at conferences both national and international. Conventions of the missing, spreading word of her. I wore a badge with her face on it, so even if there was a language barrier, they'd know her. I stood on podiums and pointed to the screen where her picture, as she might have been then, appeared. I was good at it, holding the attention, talking not only about her but also about Ireland's other missing children, comparing ours with the struggle of the country in which I stood. Encouraging the joining of forces to find our disappeared.

When the library number had come up on my phone, I had ignored it, thinking it was Mammy ringing to tell me that a new book had come in that she thought I might like and that she was going to send up. Books were her way of trying to save me. To rest my mind, she'd say. To help me escape. What's the point? I'd reply. I only have to come back to this world, I may as well stay right where I am. Even still, I would try to read it. But it was useless and my thoughts would drift back to where I wanted them to be, with Saoirse. So, I'd rejected the call that day standing in the hotel lobby only for it to ring a second time. I'd excused myself and stepped away from chatting with a family of a ten-year-old boy called Lenny, who had been missing for a year and three months.

'Mammy, I'm in the UK, can I call you back?' I'd said.

But the voice that replied was not the one I'd been expecting, the one that might easily have ignored my request and continued anyway. It was cowed.

'No, it's me, Darcy.'

Poor Darcy. I don't think she ever got over having to deliver such news.

I'd left Liverpool as soon as I'd hung up the phone. Maggie had insisted that she come too. She wouldn't hear of me going back to Dublin alone. She'd negotiated our change in plane tickets as I sat waiting, staring at the silver poles from which those black belts were pulled to create queues in airports. I witnessed the swift closing off of one line and the opening of another with such ease. I was mesmerised, lost in the immense importance of those bollards and how they created order out of what might have been chaos if they had not been there. When Maggie came to get me, I didn't move, despite her coaxing. I wanted to stay lost in their simplicity for ever, it felt. But eventually, after a second or two, I let her take my hand to lead me through the security gates.

Dad was home from the ferry by the time I landed in Dublin and I'd finally gotten him on the phone. 'She's gone,' he repeated, between gulped breath and tears. 'Are you coming?' he'd asked.

'I am,' I said. 'I am.'

Hugh drove us down. Me in the passenger seat, Cullie to our rear. None of us saying much of anything beyond comments on traffic and traffic lights and traffic cops. We stopped in Mossfield Shopping Centre on the Cork City ring road. We watched shoppers in our silence as we ate in the food court. I don't think we even knew what we had ordered. By the time we stepped off the ferry there was no energy left to me at all. Liam must have been skippering that day – who else would it have been? – but I don't remember it. I let people take my hand to shake it, managing a nod as we got into Michael-Fran's Land Rover.

I found Dad in his chair, as unable for words as I was. I hunkered beside him and laid my head in his lap. He patted it as he might have done Ergo, now asleep on the floor by his side, as Hugh and Cullie and Michael-Fran dealt with anyone who called. We sat together in a corner, huddled like children, simply nodding our hellos and goodbyes when the door once again opened. The next morning I managed to get up to decide the ceremony with Dad and Father Michael from Rossban, the island chaplain, the one who came over on the ferry every Sunday evening to say the mass, and later to choose the coffin with Ignatius Cullen, the funeral director from Clonkill. But I couldn't speak as Dad pointed to the mahogany casket, managing only a nod.

And when four days later we buried her – we'd had to wait for the boys, Mammy's beautiful sons, to return from the States – all I seemed capable of was the act of breathing through the mass and at the grave, with Hugh and Cullie either side of me, their arms tight around my waist, holding me up. Daniel and Nathan had left this island as boys, and now they came back with shoulders as wide as Michael-Fran's bar counter and hair flecked with grey. They hugged and squeezed their grief into me. And Dad, they shook his hand and pulled him in and bowed their heads so the wisps of his white hair brushed their foreheads, and there he heaved against those walls of muscle and let them hold him upright. Later, they took out wallets and phones to show us pictures of grown children and grandchildren, most of whom we had met and loved and sent presents to on every birthday. How Mammy would have loved us all together again in one room.

When we sat to the buffet dinner that Diarmuid had cooked for the whole island in Páidíns later, there was barely any standing room. The place was packed with the islanders and mainlanders who had travelled over. Even the head librarian from Cork County Libraries had come, a coup if ever there was one that Mammy would have appreciated. The place was so packed that people sat on the harbour walls and all the way down to Diarmuid's benches, and Diarmuid and his helpers were so run off their feet that at one stage Hugh joked that he'd have to jump in and help. Diarmuid took it as an offer and told him to go to the shop to get the packets of paper plates that he kept there to sell for emergencies as he'd run out of china. He'd even resorted to side plates.

It meant something, having those people there. Although I was struggling, I knew my future self would appreciate it. On the day, however, I wanted it to be nothing more than us, the immediate family. We had a table to ourselves, but only Dad and I kept to it: the men were up and doing and greeting and laughing one minute and being solemn the next. As I sat watching them, I considered how far I seemed to have travelled from similarly working a room not one week ago in Liverpool. Every now and again, I'd hold Dad's hand and ask was he OK. And he would lift his head a little and say, 'Ah, you know yourself.'

Later, the place did empty, and all that was left behind were the close blood relations and those who couldn't resist the pull of an open pub. The lads were back at the table now, running hands down tired faces, yawning, drinking in pure exhaustion. I'd had one or two myself at some stage during the day, but my glass now sat empty beside me.

My brothers looked old.

At some stage, I don't know exactly when, Daniel leaned over the table with swimming drunk eyes and reached his hand across to me. I gave him mine. His felt softer than it had that Dublin night he came home to search for Saoirse, but still the threat of chafed skin seemed only a light breeze away.

'What, Daniel?' I asked, trying to raise a smile, rubbing the precious hand that had built so many things in its lifetime.

'How have things *really* been, Sis?'

'Oh, you know, busy.'

'Still walking the streets at night looking for her?'

'I'm still appealing to her to come home if that's what you mean.'

'Really, Rosie? After all this time, you think she's coming home?'

I could see he was far too drunk to understand exactly what he was saying, taking on a bravery that was unwise. But even so, I could not let it go as I should have, perhaps, in the circumstances: Mammy dying, the long journey they'd had, the day of raising toasts, and slapping backs, and jokes and memories shared.

I took my hand back.

'Rosie, I'm thinking of you here. You've got to face reality. We all know it. Even Mammy knew that that little girl isn't alive any more.'

I squinted. 'What do you mean, "Mammy knew"?'

'Rosie, ugh, look, don't go—'

'I said, what do you mean "Mammy knew"?'

'Rosie?' Dad asked, leaning into our conversation, concerned at his daughter's sudden animation. I could feel my heart had rallied from its slow, sleepy pace of grief to the roaring engine of a furious mother in a blink of an eye.

'Dad, did Mammy think Saoirse was dead?'

'Now, Rosie, don't be upsetting yourself, not today. This is hard enough.' I ignored his plea and forged ahead.

'Daniel said she did, Dad, so did she?'

'Sis, I didn't mean to upset you,' Daniel said kindly, trying to placate me.

Hugh, sitting to my right, had stopped talking to Nathan and turned to place a hand on my arm.

'Don't,' I barked, before returning my attention to my brother. 'I don't believe you.' I stared him down, defying him to protest, which he didn't. 'And I think it's unfair of you to put lies in her mouth when she isn't here to defend herself. Mammy would never have said that about Saoirse. Never. She believed she's still out there. Do you hear me, Daniel? Does everyone hear me?' I raised my voice so that I addressed all of them sitting at the table, all of these men surrounding me. Husband, son, brothers, father, uncle.

I stood up, my arms strained in their straightness, my fingers tucked into tight fists, taking in their faces, one by one. Scared – or was it more shocked? – their eyes shifted to someone else or to the floor, anywhere away from me.

'Let me just tell every one of you once and for all so that there is never a fucking question about it ever again. My daughter *is* alive. ALIVE.' I took in each turncoat, making sure they knew never to speak of this ever again.

'I'm the only one who has faith in her. How do you think she'll feel when she hears that you all had her buried, like her grandmother?' The anger of seven years spilled forth and with it came these words: 'And this one here wants us to get a judge to rule she's dead.'

I pointed at Hugh, who was by now also standing, his hand at my back.

'Rosie, come on. Let's not do this.'

'Leave me alone.' I slapped his hand away. 'You of all people, how could you do that to her?'

'Ah, now, Rosie.' My father, to my left, looked up with tear-filled eyes but even that could not dissuade me.

'Rosie, this has been a long, hard day.' Hugh, trying his best to calm me. 'Maybe we need to go up to the house now.'

'I'm fine, for fuck's sake, Hugh. I'm bloody fine. Left here with all of you men, how would I not be? The two women I had, gone. Robbed from me. Left with all this bloody male weakness. You know why women are stronger? Because we have belief and grit and staying power. You lot should be ashamed, giving up on her.'

My body had strained over the table, my accusatory finger stabbing at them, even my son.

'Let me out. God almighty, let me the fuck out of here.' I turned left then right then left again. Seeing my father and his inability to move quickly on one side and Hugh blocking my way on the other, I got up onto the table, plates and glasses falling as I let my feet find their way through, not caring for the damage. Daniel was out of his seat, but I knew he wouldn't stop me, could see it in his eyes. He stumbled to one side as I put my hand to his shoulder to swing myself down, nearly falling. Then I ran the length of the pub, but as I got to the door, I looked back at them in their suits.

'Traitors,' I called, my eye lingering on Hugh for a second longer than all the rest before I hastened out into the drizzle of the night.

At first light the following morning they found me on Carhoona Beag beach, huddled in against the rocks. They hadn't discovered me the previous night with their torchlights, they said. I'd nestled right in and covered myself in seaweed, apparently. I don't remember it. Can't even imagine having gone to such lengths. Somewhere between the pub and there, I had truly lost my mind. I wanted only to be beside her, beside where she had played when she was young, imagining her still throwing stones into the water and examining rock pools for any sign of life, and where once she had stood with her hands cupped in a summer shower and told me with great anguish that she was losing the rain she was so desperately trying to save.

They say I wasn't conscious. That I was cold. That people had run for blankets to the priest's house, it was the closest, wrapping me up and trying to force me to drink water. Father Michael had apparently said prayers over me, even though I was breathing. The nurse had been called, woken from her bed. Enduring a hangover, she had still managed to come, take my pulse and have the wherewithal to ring the lifeboat.

There are whole days afterwards that are blank to me now. The first thing I can remember was waking in Clonkill hospital with a drip in my arm and Cullie holding my hand. I should have spoken to him, should have told him that I was sorry to have called him and his father weak, but on seeing him, all I did was close my eyes again, not able to say a word. I didn't speak for three weeks.

I was transferred to Saint Pat's Mental Health Hospital in Dublin where I had a room to myself and into which the winter sun shone brightly every morning. Normally that glorious display would have made me smile, but I turned my back on it. Hugh visited most days and sat silently by my bed for a half-hour before getting up and walking out and coming back the next day to do it all again. Cullie and Nina came too and carried on a conversation as if I was a willing participant, both talking about their work but never Saoirse. Not the thing that might set me off again, climbing tables and calling people traitors. Nina brought me flowers and sometimes played me music, like I was in a coma. But I was there, living, breathing, hearing but wanting none of it. I closed my eyes on a piece that featured only a cello and let the tears stream down my cheeks unchecked. It reminded me of when I was training for my ticket in Galway and had shared a house with a musician who had escaped London and ended up as far away as her money could get her to find empty beaches on which she would play her instrument. When I was at home she never played: she was petrified of an audience. Except this one time, before I left to go home with my licence in tow, she obliged after my consistent begging. And there in our horrible kitchen she had sat herself in a chair with the cello between her legs and had begun. And, oh, my word, I thought someone had split open my heart and that I must be crying, even though I couldn't feel any moisture on my cheeks. I'd pulled in a breath that normally comes with fright, my hand rising to my heart so sure was I that I was mourning some great loss in my life because those deep, resonant notes had dived into my soul and weakened its very core. I had never heard something so moving, so vulnerable before. When she finished, that woman shook visibly, so much that I could see her hands tremble. Observing them herself as if they were not of her at all, she swore she would never play a chord in front of anyone again. Matilde, that was her name. Matilde. I never heard from her after. She disappeared from my life as if I had never met her. And there in that room, with Nina and her music, I had felt that sorrow again, the splitting of my heart, not moving one finger to stop the tears that fell.

Hugh brought me home, to put me in our bed. Three days in a row he'd had to come home early, phoned at the office by Nora Cassidy, who had tried to coax me from the pathway where she had found me sitting, where Saoirse's bike had been. Each time he'd picked me up gently and brought me back to our bed where I turned my head to the window looking out, imagining myself there where she had once been. I tried reliving that day all over again. I would start in Cullie's empty bedroom, seeing her cycling up the road to our cul-de-sac then doing as I should have done, back on that day our lives had changed, charging down our stairs, throwing wide our front door and running to the footpath, to sit exactly where her bike had lain. Timing it. Thirty seconds, then twenty-eight until finally my record of twenty-five. Twenty-five seconds to have saved her. Twenty-five seconds to have saved us all.

On the third occasion of finding me there Hugh didn't bring me upstairs to the bed but sat me on a stool in the kitchen where he told me it had to stop. He was not angry. There was no scowl or scrunched crow's feet. The life had simply left him, and he was now reading from a script he had been given, so deadpan, so not-there did he seem. He told me there wasn't much more he could take. That this was killing him, even more than losing her, and he never thought that anything could manage that. That if I didn't stop, he'd end up there, too, in his pyjamas out on that spot from which she'd disappeared. He'd left the room then. Gone to his piano. I'd expected to hear his music straightaway, but when I didn't, I'd crept to the door, putting my ear up against it and hearing the effort of silent tears: the gulping, the sniffles. But instead of opening the door and begging his forgiveness, I slumped to the floor, pleaded with myself to try.

I was mostly bed-bound thereafter and certainly silent, but at least not sitting outside. For the rest of the time, Hugh left me food either by the bed or later, when he realised I had actually gotten up, out on the counter in the kitchen. He brought home takeaways, or made scrambled egg or pasta for dinner and I would pick at it. But I continued not to speak until one day he left a single daisy by the sandwich he had made for me, which I had found in the late evening.

I was still sitting looking at it when he came home, my sandwich uneaten on the plate. 'Thank you.' I'd said. Two simple words that caused him to cautiously approach and kiss my cheek. He leaned his head against mine for a moment then, and I knew that he was crying. And even though I believe that that kiss was given with love, it felt like a goodbye. That while he was happy that I had somehow returned, he had nothing left. That the effort it had taken to coax me back to the living had finally drained him of everything, including his once unconditional love.

I was never quite the same thereafter, even when I was, ostensibly, back to full health. Walking, talking, cooking dinners. But I had lost the mania of the fight. As if that molecule had somehow been removed by the doctors at night when I was sleeping in the hospital, so I didn't know. My conviction never changed, though. I still believed she was alive, but I never talked about it with Hugh or Cullie. Instead, Hugh and I retreated to our corners of the house, polite strangers who discussed the ongoing campaigns, but nothing more. Living in separate rooms, yet feeling the other's presence, like a heat source, knowing when they moved or shifted, listening for an opening of a door, wondering where they were going, what it was they were looking for in the press, and yet unable, unwilling, to connect.

By the time those men who loved me most, father, husband, son, had contrived to bring me home to the island and Hugh told me to go, I knew that he was right. We had hit a corner around which we could not manoeuvre. We were stuck, one behind the other, facing into the blankness of a wall that was immovable, impenetrable, our lives worn so thin and flimsy that we could hardly sustain ourselves, let alone the other.

PART 3

I dunno. I'm just telling you what we saw.

When I arrived home to my father's house last September, the day I left Hugh for the second time, I rattled the door handle loudly, gave a good thump of my shoes on the mat and shouted hello before opening the inner door. My father looked up from his seat, frozen for a moment in confusion, not quite believing it was me, before quickly shoving the pages he was reading onto the step of the stairs beside his mug of tea. He got up slowly but without too much strain, I was glad to see, and uttered my name in surprise as he crossed the room.

'What has you back?' he asked quietly, as I opened my arms to lay my head on his shoulder and cry.

'There now,' he said, 'there now.'

We stood entwined as Ergo came up alongside to sit panting by my father's leg, looking up every now and again, wondering when he'd be let in on the secret that we two were sharing.

'I just need a bit longer,' I said, when I finally managed to find my voice.

'Well, of course you do. And don't you know *Aoibhneas* will be glad to have you. Glad to have you is right.'

We stayed that way in the stillness of the room for a little while. Lulled by his gentle rocking, I was sorry when he stopped to lead me to the couch, where I tried to stifle my tears. I reached into my pocket for a bunch of tissues I had used continuously as I drove those roads to the ferry.

'Ugh,' I said, 'the state of me, you'd never know I wanted to be back, would you?'

'Now, now,' he replied, patting my knee. 'You are as beautiful to me as the day Patsy Regan came to tell me I had a baby girl. You were divine then. You are divine now.'

'Would you stop.' I smiled in spite of myself.

Ergo nuzzled his way in to sit between our legs, happy now to be a part of this exchange.

'I wish your mother was here. She'd know how to make this all better.'

I leaned my head against his shoulder.

'I wish she were here too, but, Dad, there's no making this all better. You know that, I know that. We're simply getting through.'

'But she had a way of saying something right, didn't she? Me, I avoid it. Can never find the words. Too afraid of the consequences.'

I lifted my head.

'What do you mean, Dad?'

'Ah, perhaps it's too late now.'

'Too late for what?'

'To clear the air.'

'I'm not following.'

'Well, to be honest I should have said it a long time ago. Even before you came back this summer, but do you think I had the bravery? Divil a bit.'

He shifted on the couch trying somehow to find it now, the courage to say whatever it was that had scared him into silence.

'I'm sorry for not supporting you about Saoirse back at the funeral. Your mother would have been ashamed. It was just losing her like that, it put a stopper in me somehow and I couldn't see how you were hurting.'

'Ah, Dad.' I grabbed for his hand. 'There's no need to go there. We're OK. You and me. Always have been. What you've done for me, making me come back here, is exactly what I needed. You, this place, that boat, you've saved me.'

His eyes, shy and uncertain, flickered towards mine.

'And what about you and Hugh?'

'Me and Hugh?' I looked to the ceiling, searching for an answer to that one. 'We . . . well, we're tired. Dad. We're so very bloody tired.'

From outside the familiar sound of the wind getting in under the tarpaulin that covered the winter firewood ready for this year's burning, ruffled and rumbled. I could see it, my mind's eye puckering and ballooning before finally calming again. I wiped at my nose and gave a conciliatory smile.

'I'll be OK, Dad. Honestly, here with you, with *Aoibhneas*, I'm doing good.'

The tarpaulin unsettled a second time, uneasy in itself.

'You are, love, you are that,' Dad agreed, squeezing my shoulder in support.

Ergo gave a sharp whimper before sitting to attention, his ear pricked at the wind's restlessness.

'What it is?' My father asked him, the look of a man expecting an answer. Ergo gave a half bark and got up to stand expectantly at the door. 'Do you want out to see what's going on, is that it?'

Dad gave a soft pat to my knee as he rose to open the door.

'And don't be chasing those rabbits,' he told Ergo, letting him free, 'that brother of mine will report me.'

When he came back, he stayed standing, unsure what it was he should do next, but as if Mammy was prompting him from above, he said: 'But, you know, Daniel was wrong, your mother never stopped believing that Saoirse would come home and neither have I.'

Outside, Ergo yelped, and I imagined a rabbit caught in his sight. I felt its vulnerability. I swallowed hard before nodding my head.

'Thank you,' I said, my words muffled and weak but there, out in the open, nevertheless.

A moment lapsed before my father clapped his hands and said: 'Tea. I think we might have one.'

The eternal, and in that moment, welcome, answer to everything.

'Sure.' I complied. But if I were being honest, I had no more thirst for such a thing, a drink of water would have suited me better, but we both needed the ceremony of it, the feeling that we were succeeding at the ordinary at least.

He shuffled towards the kitchen and soon I could hear the kettle being filled. 'You have a new crew member, by the way,' he shouted back to me.

'I do?' I wiped my face and walked over to lean at the doorway.

'Phelan's gone. Fjord-spotting, as we speak. It was looking a bit desperate, actually. I was thinking I'd have to call in Michael-Fran to give me a hand and we all know how well that would've gone down. But this young lassie turned up last Saturday looking for work. You'd only just left. Éilísh. Course Liam wanted her. Told me he'd swap up Éamon or Séamus for her.'

'Does that man have no shame, his own family, like?'

'It doesn't look that way, no.' Dad placed the kettle on its perch for boiling. 'Mind you, he hadn't much of a beginning with them, that's for sure. But he's a man now. Well able to make his own choices and demands.' Dad leaned snugly into the right angle of the countertop, arms folding in defiance against anyone who might argue otherwise.

I decided it was time.

'What's happened there, Dad? You used to be killed defending him when I was younger, and now it's as if you don't even like him any more.' Finally, I had found the bravery to ask the reason for my father's change of heart about Liam.

Dad pushed away from the counter to retrieve two mugs, which he placed on the table, then made a huge thing of looking for the milk in the fridge. 'Where to blazes . . .'

'It's there.' I pointed to the table, where the blue and cream striped jug sat as obvious as the discomfort in the room. 'Come on, Dad,' I encouraged, not letting him off the hook with his distracting.

The kettle clicked itself off and he retrieved the teapot, popping in the teabag, buying himself as much time as possible. 'It's the summer bloody timetable.' He threw it out as he'd turned back to the table, like it was the first thing off the top of his head.

'Really? He's started to complain about the rota, the same one he's been working for years?'

Dad poured my mug of tea.

'Lord Ó fucking Kiersey, thinks the world owes him a favour. Here.' He turned the mug handle towards me, sitting, with a sigh, in his chair. 'Now, if you don't mind, that's enough talk about the man for one day.'

'All right, all right.' I held up a hand in surrender and sat across from him, with no intention of saying another word.

'Is she good, this new crew member?' I asked after a bit, bringing us back to safer ground.

'She says she is. Has some of the exams already. Got a ferrying background. Tarryfore, up north Kerry way.' Dad took a slurp of his tea and looked out of that window again towards the mainland.

'I see,' I said, impressed, then yawned instantly, feeling a world of tiredness weighing me down from all that had transpired with Hugh and Cullie in Dublin, making me unable to ask what would have been the thing at this point: which family is she from, whose daughter, which boats has she been working. I followed his eyes to see the clouds that had spread themselves across the sky now merging rapidly, small white independent entities annexed into one great mass. Once I had finished my tea, I decided, I would take those stairs to close my eyes on all that had returned me here and once more sleep the deepest of sleeps in my child-hood bed.

Éilísh could not contain her excitement when I arrived at the ferry the next morning. She was there waiting for me when I pulled up in the jeep.

'Oh, my God,' she said, shaking my hand as soon as I was out of it. 'I came all the way especially to work with you. You're a legend in our house. My dad's Mac Finnerty, he sails out of Tarryfore, and when I was little, he talked about this girl he knew up in Galway who had studied for her ticket just like him but had given up ferrying years and years ago. And then we heard you were back, and I changed all my plans to come here instead.'

'Mac?' I said, crossing towards *Aoibhneas*, amused by this woman and the memories she had evoked. 'Well, my goodness, you'll be a joy to work with if you're anything like your father. He was the only one who didn't slag me for wanting to be a skipper when I was training. Mind you, he was possibly too terrified to say anything. Those men were something fierce.'

We headed down the steps to open up *Aoibhneas*.

'I was so disappointed when I realised I'd missed you.' Éilísh was so close at my heels she was in danger of tripping us both. 'You'd literally left the day I arrived, can you believe that? But your dad was so good and promised he'd train me well. "Sure who do you think made her so brilliant? 'Twas me," he said.' She could do a fairly good impression of Dad, much to my amusement. 'So I agreed to stay for a few weeks anyway. But here you are.' She stood there with the widest of smiles that was instantly infectious.

'Yes,' I replied, looking up at the bridge, closing my eyes, and sighing. 'Here I am.'

'And you're staying this time for good, like?'

'Éilísh,' I said, opening the hatch to the engine room, 'I learned a long time ago that nothing is certain in this world. But, unless some kind of miracle occurs, I believe I will be here for the foreseeable.'

'Phew.' She laughed, wiping her brow exaggeratedly.

'And tell me, have you met Fergal?'

'No, not yet.'

'Well, you'll have a bit of a wait. Fergal, unlike you, it seems, likes to cut it fine. Right so, engine check. Shall we?'

I motioned towards the opening into which she practically dived, as I followed with a smirk.

Later, that lunchtime, I found myself at Mammy's grave. It had been a while since I'd sat there. By rights, I should have been down on the pier wall with Éilísh and Fergal, and for half a minute I felt bad not to be, especially on Éilísh's first day. But I had noticed something between that pair from the minute Fergal had screeched to a halt on the pier, some shyness. For the entire journey, Fergal had barely left her side. And I thought, Why interrupt what did not wish to be? It took me way back to Hugh and me, sitting on the pier wall wanting only ourselves, and no one else diluting what felt magical.

I sat in front of Mammy's grave on the bench that Michael-Fran had put in after Mammy died so Dad could spend time with her. The graveyard is situated above the library and the pier, and from which, on the right day, you can not only hear the birdsong but the hum of chatter of those milling about below. I took in the older pockmarked headstones and the new, smoother ones, like the small one we'd erected for Mammy in the shape of an opened book.

'Back again, Mam,' I told her, feeling an ease in my bones, not wishing to move an inch in case I lost it. From my left I heard someone approach and looked over to see Iggy.

I bumped my shoulder against his in greeting when he sat down.

'You're back,' he said.

'I am.'

'I was expecting you this morning.' He motioned towards the sea.

'Is that so?'

'I got over it, though. But you missed the best swim and the best coffee *ever*.'

I smiled. 'Tomorrow, I promise.'

'Coffee *and* swim?'

'Yeah, maybe.'

Down below, I watched a small sailboat dock at the moorings that had been put in three years earlier for the mainland day trippers rich enough to have their own boats. A young lad hopped off, grabbed the rope thrown up and tied her securely.

'There's one man I'd say isn't too happy to see you again.' Iggy nudged me as his foot swung left in the direction to where Liam was filling his truck at the petrol pump outside Páidíns.

'No, I suppose not.'

'Actually, do you know, Teresa asked if I'd mind teaching the lads swimming in the pool in Clonkill during the winter months, said she'd pay me. They can swim all right but not brilliantly. She'd told them if they were determined to take after their father and work the sea they'd have to get better. They refused the pool swimming lessons, saying they'd look like right eejits among the nine-year-olds. It was Lar who suggested me. We agreed we'd do pool in the winter and sea come the summer again.'

Lar and Paul, Liam's sons, were good kids. They had no fear of me, or in-built resentment, more Teresa than Liam, it seemed. Confident lads, no longer shy, who had sometimes approached me over the summer, when I sat on the wall, to ask how the ferrying was that day. I wouldn't object to having them as summer crew when they turned sixteen, I thought, after they had left, to carry on with their day, and I had never thought I'd say that about an Ó Kiersey.

'Nice.'

'And Páidín is thinking of taking a bit of time off this winter to go to his daughter in Limerick so he's asked me to work the bar at the weekends when it's open. So, between that and the swimming and a few shifts with Diarmuid, I shall not starve.'

'Good to know.'

Another pause in which we watched Críostóir arrive at Diarmuid's with a new batch of ice cream. It was coming to the end of the season: soon there would be no more to be had until the following May.

'The winter months aren't going to be easy, sea-swimming wise,' Iggy said.

I rolled my eyes. 'Honestly, you'd think I never lived here the way you go on with me sometimes.'

'Just takes a bit of getting used to that's all,' he continued, as if I'd never said a word. 'A quick dip. Does the immune system a world of good.'

'Well, thank you for that expert advice.'

'So are you staying for a while this time or . . .?'

'I'm staying until I know it's time to go. And right now I haven't a clue when that might be.'

He nodded in agreement, like that was his exact strategy also. I liked that Iggy's own brokenness allowed me to be broken too, without having to explain, to justify my actions.

'There's Danny.' Iggy's foot pointing again to the top of the pier. I saw my father, looking around, then going over to Fergal to have a word.

'He's looking for me. Bet he's checking up to see if I'm OK.'

'And are you?'

'I'm fine.' Iggy lingered on me a little while before turning back to the scene below.

'Uh-oh, he's been spotted. Liam.'

Iggy sank down in his seat as if he was an undercover operative.

I smirked at his theatrics, then watched as Liam beckoned Dad over to where he stood at the pump. Dad moved reluctantly, checking around him, possibly still trying to find me. I could have called him. He might have heard me from there, but I was curious.

For a while nothing much passed between the pair, Dad standing a foot or so away from Liam, chatting, until suddenly he took a step forward, pointing a finger at Liam. Liam moved in further too, straightening himself as tall as possible, both hands jammed into his pockets, his head tilting with the sharpness of the words he was spouting at my father.

'Jesus,' I said, 'maybe I should go down there.'

'Hold on, wait a minute.'

'But they look as if they could swing for one another.'

Iggy held me back. 'I'm guessing you going down there, Rosie, isn't going to make it any better.'

'But what if he hits him?'

'Liam isn't going to hit your father.'

'I meant the other way round.'

'Really?' Iggy seemed surprised.

'The way he was going on yesterday I wouldn't be so sure.'

'Wait, though, look, Liam's going.'

The sound of a car door slam rose into the air. We watched Dad eyeballing Liam as he drove past the top of the pier and up by Diarmuid's.

'What in God's name was that all about?' I asked, already rising to go down to Dad, but as I did, Críostóir pulled up alongside him. He opened the passenger door and in my father got. I slumped back to sitting, totally flummoxed.

'I tell you, this island is better than Netflix any day.' Iggy said.

'Netflix? How the hell do you have Netflix? You barely have the price of a pint.'

'I'm Diarmuid's guest user. Although he doesn't know it. I may have been watching over his shoulder in the shop when he logged in on a break one day.'

'Well, whatever that was down there was serious. There's something not right going on. Dad is pissed off with Liam about something, but he won't tell me what.'

'Would Michael-Fran know?'

'Maybe. I bet Phelan does.'

'Ah, yes, the fjord-hunter. Actually, I'm watching this Norwegian YouTuber at the mo. Annika Lund. Or, wait, maybe she's Swedish. I can't really tell.'

'Right,' I said, only half listening.

'I'm not sure what it's about actually. I don't speak Swedish or Norwegian but I love the way she sounds. It's so up and downy, very sexy altogether.'

He'd got my full attention now, distracting me from my worries about Dad. 'You should've moved there then instead of here, I bet *they* all swim.' I realised I was the tiniest bit jealous that Iggy had another woman who intrigued him, however far away she might be.

'What – and miss peeling spuds for a living? Speaking of which,' He nodded in the direction of the shop door where Diarmuid was standing, checking his watch. 'Besides,' Iggy said, getting up, 'I have this dream that someday Annika is going to come and find me.'

'Of course she will,' I said, joining him to return to *Aoibhneas* for our next sailing. 'I only hope we have enough room in the harbour for her Viking longboat when she does.'

That evening, when my shift was over, I was through our front door quicker than Iggy and his butterfly stroke, turning the volume down on the TV, much to Dad's disgust, about to launch into how I wouldn't be taking any more of his avoidance, that I wanted to know everything that was going on between him and Liam, when we heard a car rumble over the cattle grid at the entrance to our driveway.

I looked out of the sitting-room window. 'Fuck, it's Liam.'

An efficient knock came to the porch door, which neither of us responded to. Before my father had even stood up, Liam was in the room, loitering in the doorway.

Clearly uncomfortable, and with one good eye on our unexpected visitor, my father told me to go and stick the kettle on.

'No, Danny, I'm grand now.' Liam stepped in a little further. 'It's not just you I've come to see this time so it's best she stays. She has a right to know.' Liam looked in my direction for the first time, and I sat up straight.

'*She* has a right to know *what*?' I asked.

'Jesus, Liam, you have some cheek landing in like this now.' Dad shook his head in disbelief and sat again. 'I suppose your uncle knows you're here?'

'He does.'

'Well, by Christ, but that man is some traitor.' Dad spat on the wooden floor. Dad never spat. Never. And certainly not in the house. I stood in fright, staring at the frothing white spittle six feet away from me. 'No. You're both traitors. You *and* Tommy. I've done nothing but give you both livelihoods that put bread on your tables for years and now here you are trying to steal mine.' Dad's bony finger stabbed in Liam's direction.

'What's going on, Dad?' But I may as well have asked an empty room because no reply came.

'Now, Dan, what we're offering is fair.'

'Fair? Is that what you call it?'

My father laughed in mock-disgust and shook his head. I got up to cross the floor and hunker down in front of him so I could see into those eyes that were, to my horror, welling up.

'Dad. Tell me what he's talking about.' I laid a hand to his knee. 'You can tell me. Whatever this is, we'll sort it. *I'll* sort it.'

'Not unless you have a couple of hundred grand sitting around you won't.' Liam's words snuck quietly across the room.

I felt my heart quicken. I leaned in against my father's ear and whispered, 'Tell me, Dad, please just tell me.'

But he would not be budged.

'The boat's been failing these last few years,' Liam continued. 'This place, every bit of land he has, is mortgaged to the hilt to keep it going, but there's only so long that will last. And if my calculations aren't wrong, time is running out.'

I did not move, not one muscle. He would not manage to entice me to face him, no matter what he said. I kept my eyes firmly on my father, at the sinews of his neck, at the collar of his shirt, noticing the missing button on the left-hand side. He used to sew them on himself. My head dropped at the memory of him, sitting in that very chair with the lamp beside him, concentrating on the pull and dive of the needle. I took those hands that had once been so deft in mine and kissed them, kissed those worn-out joints that could no longer close those small buttons let alone pick them from the floor to stitch them back on.

'Leave, Liam,' I said.

'Rosie, you should know that me and Tommy and another investor are willing to take it all on. Your father will have enough to pay his debts.'

I lifted my head to see Dad give a smile that begged my forgiveness. I squeezed his hands harder, perhaps hurting him in the process but it was all I could think of to let him know there was nothing to forgive.

'I said go.'

'It's fair, Rosie. We aren't trying to con anyone here. I've given Danny the figures. You should look at them.'

I remembered the papers my father was reading when I'd arrived the previous day that he'd put on the stairs but that weren't there now, currently hidden away, no doubt, in my father's room, way out of my reach.

Liam took a step towards me. 'And, Rosie, we'll always need crew. We'd be happy for you to work for us.'

'Ha.' I laughed, couldn't stop myself. 'I thought you said that you'd never employ me. Do you not remember? The schoolyard and your stupid Ferry game?'

'Rosie, we were seven.'

'Yep, and look at you now, all mature. So grown-up and reasonable. But you could never let go of your want of all we Driscolls had, could you? Offering me a job?' I scoffed. 'God, you would so love that, wouldn't you?'

Liam refused to be baited, curling his lips in against his teeth in case something unsavoury managed to escape. I had to hand it to him, such restraint was out of character, a sure sign that he needed me on board. One nod from me and my father would surely sell.

'Go now, Liam.' I said, 'If you don't, I'll call Michael-Fran and tell him to get Diarmuid and the lads to carry you out of here if they have to.'

'But—'

'The boat is ours. The Driscolls' not the Ó Kierseys'. Now leave.'

I stood up to face him, turned fully to that man who had always wanted what was ours, to let him know I would not be backing down, that nothing he had to say to me that night would be of any use to his plans.

He took an A4 rolled-up brown envelope out of his inner pocket, which he tapped against the palm of his hand, then held up in the air. 'Look at it, Rosie. That's all I ask.'

He tentatively placed the document on the arm of the couch, then left, without looking at either of us. I waited, listening for the outer door to shut, his engine to start and the rattle of the cattle grid, before finally addressing my father. 'Dad?'

Those fearful eyes of his couldn't linger on me for very long and they dropped to consider his hands. 'It's nothing, Rosie. Don't be minding him.'

'Right. So, if I go over and look at what's in that envelope, all I'll see is a pack of lies, is that it?'

He stared over at the couch. 'No, it's not quite that either.'

'So *Aoibhneas is* in trouble, then?'

'There's a bit of debt, yes.'

'And the house? Did you remortgage it? Is he right about that?'

He considered my question. 'I took some leverage, yes.'

'How much *leverage*? Are we talking quarter, half its value?'

He didn't answer but his hand ran over his mouth then down under his chin, his head stretching up, his neck turning left then right.

'Jesus, Dad. Please tell me it's not the whole fecking lot?'

'The engine was fucked, Rosie.' He finally admitted in frustration. 'And the winter months are lean, as you well know. And the government subsidy only covers so much. And these last few years those tourists haven't been coming like they used to, the divil knows why.'

'What's owing, Dad?'

Again, he refused to answer.

'Dad?'

'Three hundred.' Despite the almost whisper of a reply, I caught it.

'*Grand?*'

'No, three hundred euro. Of course grand.'

'But this place isn't even worth that. Two hundred at most.'

'It's the land too.'

'They gave you three hundred grand for these stony fields. Holy God, Dad, who do you know in there?'

'Just leave it now.'

I turned away, my hand covering my mouth. Everything, everything I had come back for was about to be taken. Almost as quickly, I spun back to ask another question.

'What's left on it?'

'What do you mean, "what's left on it"?'

'On the loan, how much is left?'

He had this astonished look to him, like he was wondering if I'd been paying attention at all.

'All of it.'

'You've paid back *nothing?*'

'The interest. I've been paying the interest.'

I stumbled my way back to the couch, unable for this news. The envelope sat to my right as my shoulders slumped, my elbows on my knees. I wondered how I had managed to miss all of this over the summer.

'But why didn't you tell me?' My voice, high in disbelief, felt almost out of air.

He shook his head, then let it fall into his hands. His fingers ran through his thinning white hair, tossing those wisps about, rubbing at the scalp. 'You'd other things on your mind, love.' When he finally raised his head again, his cheeks were wet. 'I was just so happy you were here. I didn't want to burden you. And, besides, I thought it would all be OK. The payments seemed doable. But the storms have been something rotten and, what with the tourist numbers dropping, things weren't going my way.'

'Oh, Dad.' It was my turn to feel that I had let him down, this man who had loved and cared for me my entire life. I made my way to kneel beside him once more. 'I should have noticed or, at the very least, asked. I don't know why I didn't.'

'I do.' He patted my hand and smiled. It was as if she was there in the room with us.

'So, what is the bank saying? Are they letting this arrangement go on indefinitely?'

'Not exactly. They've sent me a few love letters suggesting I call in.'

'OK, and when's that happening?'

'I haven't got around to organising it yet.'

'Well, I'll ring them. We'll both go. We'll explain the situation and we'll agree a revised repayment.'

Dad didn't answer, only looked at me with worried eyes.

'There are things we can do, Dad,' I reassured him, standing again, buoyed by the solutions swimming around in my head. 'Didn't I say we should start doing trips out to Shelley Island for the birdwatchers? And what about Bay Landing and Farnroe Lighthouse? We could run another out there to see the seals and the dolphins. The families would love it. There's loads of stuff we should've been doing long before now, but that fecker would hear none of it with his "I'm here to skipper this boat over to Rossban and back, that's all". The cheek of him. Refusing to do anything I suggested, then standing here, offering to get us out of debt like he's some big hero or something. Course you know what he'll do if he gets his hands on her,' I pointed my finger at him as if he was the very man in question, 'apart from wrecking her that is. He'll take all my ideas that will suddenly be his and make a mint. I've some mind to get in the car now and tell him to shove it all up his arse.'

Dad chuckled, the first bit of mirth that evening. 'I think you managed to do that already, love. I don't know how you do it, but you scare the bejesus out of that man.'

I laughed, too, but I could feel it, despite the momentary levity, the giving way inside me, the collapse of brick upon brick that for the last few months had held me upright.

'Rosie, don't be getting yourself upset now, all right? That's the last thing I want.'

'He's not getting her, Dad.' The tears began. Down they fell as I reached for the couch arm, crumpling the envelope Liam had left. 'I can't lose her.' I whispered, as I collapsed to the floor. 'I need her, Dad. I . . . I just—'

'Ssh, now, Rosie.' He was beside me then, voice cracking as he bent, despite the discomfort it must have caused him, to surround me in his arms. 'I never meant this to happen. I tried so hard to put it right. But it kept getting worse, and I . . .'

I shook my head, trying to tell him that it wasn't his fault. I'd loved this man so very much from the moment I'd toddled my way to running after him, when I'd first turned on the boat's engine and when, years later, he'd asked me one day, as we sat in our small fishing boat on an afternoon off – I was maybe eighteen at the time – and the clouds had morphed from white to grey far off to the west, a wind beginning to stir around us, if we should perhaps head for home. It was my opinion he had wanted that day, someone he respected and whose word mattered. Yes, I'd said, and he did not ask another thing, no debate, no quandary, he had simply turned our boat back towards shore. I would never place one grain of blame at his door.

'We'll figure this out,' he said, crying as he rocked me back and forth. 'We won't let him take her.'

The father did not speak. But every now and again he would look at her in his rear-view mirror.

My father wore a suit the day we sat in the bank's offices in Clonkill. The same one he'd had for years, pulled out and brushed down for weddings, christenings and funerals. He tugged at his shirt collar every second or so as we waited in that glass-surrounded cubicle.

'My neck has shrunk.'

'Your neck hasn't shrunk, Dad.' I rubbed my sweating palms down the leg of my black slacks, slightly annoyed at his foostering when I was trying to compose myself and embody the persona of an entrepreneur.

'I'm telling you it's not half as long as it used to be. It's all squashed down into one big rugby-player block. I used to be a fifteen-inch neck. I'm at least a seventeen now.'

'Open the top button then.'

'I can't. I'll look like I couldn't've been arsed, and that isn't the impression we want to give, is it?'

'Well, I'd rather you could breathe, as I'm sure will the manager.'

'All right, but if they turn us down, me and my open collar will not be held responsible.'

'I don't think they can say no based on your attire, Dad.'

'How innocent you are.'

He coughed, then tilted his head back, grimacing as he tried to open the button.

'Here.' I reached across, finally releasing him.

'Thanks, love.' He pushed his tie up higher in an effort to cover the gap, moving his head from side to side and sighing heavily.

The manager arrived soon after, a woman in her forties. We both rose, him slower than me, to shake her hand.

'What a beautiful day.' She beamed. 'The journey over must've been glorious.'

She seemed nice, I thought. Someone you might trust, if she wasn't working for a bank.

We want to restructure the business, I began when she asked, all bright and breezy, what had brought us there. We want to try out new routes for the tourists. I produced my business plan and my financial projections. An extension on the loan was what we were asking for so we could lower the repayments and begin, thanks to the new ventures, to repay it in full, not only the interest. She flicked through what I had given her, so briefly that she couldn't have taken anything in, then set it down and turned instead to our files on screen, perusing what appeared to be a lengthy history as Dad and I sat in a silence so thick that I could have reached out my finger and spelled my name in it, watching her eyes scan left to right.

'Look,' she said, eventually, 'obviously this proposal will go up the line for consideration, but I'll be honest, they're reluctant to extend business loans and certainly not one where there have been only partial repayments.'

'But it's a change of financial management now. I'm coming on board. Getting totally involved. You have my word that we will make every monthly instalment. All we are asking for is a couple of months' breathing space as we build up the new trips.'

For a moment we locked eyes, the pleading versus the pitying. Then she picked up my nicely bound A4 pages again to hold them in both hands, like an altar-offering.

'As I say, this will go up the line. But I'm not going to raise your hopes here. That isn't what I do. If I were you, I'd get on with these proposals as fast as possible and try to start making full repayments as soon as you can. Meanwhile, this will get logged in the system and so will buy you the few weeks it takes them to look over everything. That's as much as I can do.'

I didn't react immediately. I'd fallen into a type of daze where it felt my voice wouldn't have worked even if I had tried. It was Dad who moved first, standing, his hand already across the desk, thanking her for her time. Having been on the inside seat, he was unable to leave without me moving, so he tapped my shoulder. 'Rosie,' he said, very quietly.

'So that's it?' I asked. 'We've come all this way to try to negotiate the survival of our business, and after one quick search, you're saying no. You haven't even actually read the plan.'

'No,' she said, a tad indignant at the slight, 'but I will. I give you my word. I'll give it close consideration and I will make a recommendation. But the final decision isn't mine. I'm simply trying to be honest here. Not build up any false hopes.'

'Is that in the training manual? The "Don't Build Up Hopes" section?'

'Rosie,' Dad interjected, having sat down again. 'I don't think there is any—'

'No, Dad, we have a right to know what we're dealing with here. And I for one am *really* not impressed. I worked days and nights at that, you know.' I pointed at the plan.

'And it's good. It's realistic, achievable. Aren't they your buzz words? I've worked in ferrying all of my life, even in Dublin, and in one second, you tell me I haven't a clue.'

'That isn't what I—'

'You think you can play God with our lives, don't you? Bet you really like that too. Get your kicks from it. Denying us a chance.'

'Listen, Mrs Dunne—'

'No, you listen. If we have to go to loan sharks we will, because we aren't losing our boat, the one bloody good thing we have. The one thing that gets us up and out in the morning. The one thing that keeps a smile on my face.' I looked at her and the calm exterior she was keeping up. Sitting back in her chair, my proposal abandoned once again, watching me carefully. Wondering, I suppose, when she'd have to hit the panic button under her desk. 'Would you like that?' I continued. 'For your customers to put themselves in more debt? Is that it? Are ye all in cahoots – the banks, the loan sharks? Bet ye are. All mates together. Keeping the big boys rich.'

'Now, Rosie.' Dad's garda hand was out, slicing through the air, trying to stop me, trying to call a halt to this, demanding I get a bloody grip.

'Well, no one is going to touch her. You and your boyos up there in Dublin aren't getting her. Do you hear me?' My finger tapped at the desk, as I considered my next move. 'Do you know who I am?'

She looked confused.

'*Rosie*.' Once again, I ignored Dad's intervention.

'Rosie Dunne, mother of Saoirse Dunne. Ringing any bells now?' I felt it, the shame of using my daughter on this woman. But I would have done anything right then to save the last place where I could feel her close to me. 'Yes, that's right, you've got it. Mother of the daughter who disappeared. Thought you'd like to add that to your file. That your recommendation is to shit even harder on me. The whole lot of you can have a great laugh then, can't you?'

'That's it, Rosie. Up. Get up out of that chair.'

Dad rose to yank me out of my seat with a strength I had thought had long since left him and for which he would pay heavily for the rest of the week, having to lie on the flat of his back.

'I'm sorry now for this.' His eyes were too embarrassed to fully meet hers.

'No, it's—'

'It's what? What is it?' I shouted back at her, as my father's hand pushed me forcibly out of that glass-covered cubicle, to where there was a queue for the in-store machines and the one counter teller. Those waiting pretended they hadn't heard my raised voice, the admission of who I was, the choice language I had used. They, at least, had a bit of decency.

'It's criminal is what it is, criminal.' I kept at it all the way down the length of the bank. I'd seen the security guard arrive, looking at his boss, wanting to know if he should intervene. But she had held up her hand to stop him, to tell him that this was all in hand: the old man with a walking stick was quite successfully man-handling his crazy daughter out of the building. All was fine here. Everything was just dandy.

Her last words as we hit the exit were: 'Safe journey home.'

My father attempted to turn to her, but I was rearing again, so he simply lifted his stick aloft to acknowledge her wishes and forced me down the steps.

It must have been a slow week in banking high command because not seven days had passed before Dad received a letter telling him his contract as it currently stood would not be altered and that repayments in their fullest would be expected forthwith. They didn't use the word 'forthwith' but it felt as if they'd missed an opportunity to do so.

Dad had called me with the news on my last journey back from Rossban that day. As I drove up home, the brambles and briars on the glen road, to which, in my distracted state, I had veered too close, creaked and thrashed against the jeep's door without a care from me. The back of my hand was moist with tears wiped quickly from my checks. Passing the Wagtail, I did not beep the horn as I usually would have for those sitting on the low wall. Instead I rounded that last bend, failing to turn sharply enough, so that the oncoming car had to swing away from me, its tyres screeching to avoid the boundary fence narrowly and a dip down into the hollow of the glen.

The dust from our abrupt halt rose around both cars as Liam knocked ferociously on my window.

'What in God's name are you at? You nearly ran me off the road.'

His face seemed as pink as the island's fuchsia, now long dead since the summer had ebbed away.

'*Rosie*. Did you hear me? I said you—'

The rest of what he had to say I drowned out, as I looked beyond him at the last of the dust swirling around the wheels of his car before it slowly and gracefully settled on the ground. It was only then I opened my window. 'Yes, Liam. I heard you.'

'Well?'

'Well, what?' I asked wearily.

'What were you doing?'

'Nothing, Liam, I was doing nothing.'

'Except coming over my side of the road.' Now that my window was fully down, he had placed his hand on my door, his grip emphasising his annoyance.

'You're right,' I relented. 'I'm sorry.' What was the point in arguing with this man? What was the bloody point?

'I could have been down in that glen overturned—'

'*All right.*' My exasperation, never far away when it came to Liam, even when I was the guilty party, was not ready to give up just yet. 'I said I was sorry. No one was actually injured here so can we just, you know, get on with what we were doing?'

He took his hand away, but he was still watching me, distrustful, like I might at any minute start up my engine and launch at him again.

'Actually,' he said, changing his mind and leaning in for a nice cosy chat, 'perhaps your nearly running me off the road was divine intervention.'

'I doubt it. If it was, I might have succeeded.' I gave him my best sarcastic smile.

'You're not answering my calls, Rosie.'

'God, Liam, could you not give it a rest, just this one time? Would that be so hard?'

'If you'd only pick up your phone or your father would answer the door—'

'Have you been up hassling him again?' I was losing control of whatever slivers of cool I had been clinging to. 'Listen.' I pointed my finger to within inches of his nose. In truth, I had the urge to poke his eye and watch the ridiculous dance that would ensue. 'Stop hassling my father. It's not OK to shove your buy-out plans in an old man's face whenever you get the chance. Actually, I'm surprised Teresa lets you away with that.'

He stood up all of a sudden, flinching a little, as if I had caught him in the act of something he wasn't supposed to be doing.

'Oh, my God!' I laughed incredulously, 'She doesn't know what you're up to, does she?'

'Of course she knows.' He was indignant, overly and exaggeratedly so.

'But she doesn't approve, I can see by you. Un-bloody-believable.' I shook my head with a wry smile, amazed at this man's willingness to cause discord in his own house just to get his hands on *Aoibhneas*.

'And anyway,' I continued, making the most of the ball finally being on my side of the court for once, 'correct me if I'm wrong here, Liam, but I understood that what you were doing was *offering* us something, not compelling us to do it or to work to your timetable.'

'Rosie. I have investors waiting. There's only so long they'll hang around.'

'Aw, really? Poor Liam. You should have said. Then I'd have told those big nasty bank managers to hurry up with their decision.'

How I wanted to kick myself for handing him such information on a plate. It was none of his business that we'd gone begging to anyone, and especially that they had said no.

'Oh, yeah, like that's going to happen.' He snorted. 'There's no way on this earth that the bank is going to extend Danny's loan. I know how bad things are, Rosie, remember.'

'Is that so? And tell me, when did you become a financial whizz, Liam? As I recall you spent most of business class in secondary school with your finger either up your nose or down your trousers.'

For one beautiful moment, I had stunned him into silence. It was heavenly. I rubbed my tongue along the inside of my top teeth as I gave a small laugh.

'Do you know what?' he said, stepping back towards my door, his defiance refusing to be defeated, it seemed. 'I've had it with you and your higher-than-mighty attitude. All our lives you've treated me like I'm nothing. Well, who's standing in a whole heap of shite now, Rosie? Tell me that.'

A car pulled up to my rear and idled, the driver, reading the signs, wisely deciding not to get out to see if they could assist, instead waiting patiently for this situation to sort itself out.

'*I've* treated *you* like shite? Are you deluded, Liam? It was you who started this. You told me I'd never be able to skipper a boat. And when I did it, you couldn't bring yourself to say you were wrong. Instead, you've spent the rest of your life picking at every little thing I say and do.' My voice lowered to an almost whisper. 'But I'm telling you now, you will never get her. You will not take her away from me. I have the bloody money, Liam. So you can go and tell your investors your little scheme is over.' I did not drop my eyes from his. I would not be the first to avert.

I wasn't entirely lying. I had had an offer, even before we'd gone cap in hand to the bank. But I'd turned it down. I'd rung Hugh in a panic to get his help on drawing up my business proposal that I presented to them. Who else did I know with such financial acumen? We were still able for those transactional conversations, and I was, let's face it, desperate. In the course of his advice he'd offered the money: not him personally, given our financial precariousness, but the company. A loan, he'd said. Help us get started on the repayments and set up the new ferry tours. I'd said no, but not strongly enough, because he had persisted. But what if we can't pay it back? I'd argued, feeling unworthy of such generosity. You will, he'd said. You will. Where had that confidence in me come from? Did he not recognise the wife who had left? The wife who had organized our lives into a kind of strategic warfare for nearly seven years before finally losing it and having to be banished? The wife who had hidden from the world ever since? Why had he any faith in me? What evidence had I given?

I still hadn't changed my mind. I would not be taking the loan, but I could use it as a threat – perhaps I should have wrong-footed the bank manager when I was leaving her the previous week, telling her she could shove her 'close consideration' of our business plan right up her jacksy, but instead I had stored it up for this more glorious moment with Liam.

He squinted as he tried to comprehend this defeat. Victory, it seemed, was in my grasp and I could feel its warmth course through my body, so much so that I had the urge to stretch out my fingers and toes and sigh in pure delight.

But almost instantly everything changed, Liam's face transforming, a massive grin morphing quickly into laughter, a hearty bellow rising from his chest out into that space between us.

'Oh, Rosie, you nearly had me there. Honestly, that was so good.' What was it he had seen in my face to make him realise I was lying. Was there a twitch, a tugging at my ear, a pulling in of my lips? Or had I simply been too cocky? My mother had always said I couldn't lie to save my life.

He leaned into my car again, like he was about to impart a secret.

'Listen, here's what I know. *You* haven't got the money and *I*'m your one great hope. It's so marvellous, isn't it?' He clapped his hands together and rubbed them, like he had just gotten a sure-fire tip on the Grand National. 'But just to be clear, Rosie, I will need an answer by Monday, the latest, yeah? You make sure you call me or I will be back knocking on Danny's door, all right?' The fucker winked at me, then gave a double tap to my door in cheery good-bye, before saluting whoever had waited patiently behind us and hopping into his car. He reversed a bit, then drove on by me with a joyous rev to his engine.

'Fuck,' I said, dropping my head after he had finally disappeared around the corner. I grasped the steering wheel, trying to steady my shaking hands.

From behind me came a little friendly toot from the waiting car, I waved in apology in the rear-view mirror before turning on the engine and carrying on home.

Dad and I sat despondently by the fire he had insisted on building that evening, as if somehow its glow might bring some solace, saying little or nothing, both feeling we had let the other down. Bedtime came early for us. With no answers as to what we would do by the time Friday came, we lugged our disappointed selves to our rooms where I lay staring at the ceiling, knowing the little life raft of the bank I had been clinging to had been plucked from my hands and now I had no choice but to drown.

Sleep had come eventually, but sometime after midnight, I woke with a start. Drawn to the window, God knew why, I saw Patsy Regan, of all people, staring at the house, her eyes searching it, like a painting she was trying to understand. And when I was about to raise the net curtain, which for years my mother had bleached white but had now taken on a yellow hue, she turned and took the road back down Mac's Hill, rounding the first bend so that I could no longer see her white hair caught in the moonlight.

She'd come to tell me something, to impart some vision that would help me save *Aoibhneas*, I was sure of it.

I pounded down the wooden stairs. Ergo stood with his wagging tail in front of the dying grate, ready for the adventure. My father shouted from his bedroom, demanding to know what the racket was about. But I continued out through the front porch as if he hadn't said a word, raising the latch and running barefoot on the road, following her lead, Ergo by my side, sure that I still had time to catch her on the straight stretch. 'Patsy,' I called. 'Patsy, wait. Is it *Aoibhneas*? Is there a way to save her?'

But there was no one there. No Patsy turning in her tracks, startled by my panic. No voice coming back in answer, save for the lowing of one of Michael-Fran's cows. She was not there. And despite Patsy's sprightliness at eighty, there was still no way she could have hurdled a hedgerow or walked the length of that road by then. And yet I'd run to its end, right on down by the glen path, arriving at the harbour, but she was not there. I stood outside her darkened house, which looked out onto the sea, and lifted my hand to knock at her door but stopped, so sure was I that I must have dreamed it all. Ergo sat watching me expectantly, our breath heavy, feeling the coldness for the first time as a southerly wind circled us, seeping into the gaps of my pyjamas. I took a step backwards, seeing how pathetic I must look.

In the distance, the familiar foghorn of my father's ailing exhaust pipe howled down the hill. I turned to see his lights come and go through the hedging, the twists and turns of the road, until his Ford Cortina stopped outside the long path of Patsy's garden. He wound down the passenger window to beckon me to him.

'Get in, love,' he encouraged, his voice as quiet as possible over the rumble of his car. 'You'll have the whole place awake and you know how we like our lie-ins on a Saturday.'

His smile was kind as Ergo and I complied. I wondered if my face appeared as lost as I felt. 'You're grand now.' He let down the handbrake and checked his rear-view mirror, as if we were pulling out onto a busy mainland road in rush hour. Ergo panted hard on the back seat. And despite believing by then that Patsy had been an apparition, I still checked every ditch we passed on the way back in case she might have fallen in.

'Go back up to bed now, Rosie,' Dad said, when we got home. It must have been one or two in the morning by that point, but instead of heading up, I'd sat to the couch beside the fire. Ergo had already lain down on the mat and gone back to sleep. 'I'm not leaving you there. Your mother would have me mithered if she knew I'd left you without even a dressing-gown.'

'Dad, I'm grand.' I wrapped the woollen blanket that lay at the end of the couch around my knees. 'See?'

Accepting defeat, he took refuge in his armchair.

'What happened to you, at all?'

'Ah, you know,' I said, as if everyone was at it on the island, seeing things that were not there and running barefoot at one in the morning on roads that'd take the skin off our feet in a whip of a second without a hint of regret.

'"Ah, you know", what?' At that hour, Dad had no truck with answers that made no sense.

'Nothing, Dad. Can people not do a bit of sleepwalking these days without being hounded for it?'

'Not when they've never been known to do it before, no, and not when it involves nearly a mile.'

I looked at the blanket, running my finger over its thread for a second before answering, embarrassed, 'I thought Patsy was on the road, that's all. I must've been dreaming. We can all have a bad night's sleep, can't we, and be a little confused when we wake up suddenly like that? I'm grand now, honestly. You go on to bed. I'm going to stay here for a little bit.'

He considered me with the look he'd often used with Mammy, when he was up against it trying to persuade her into or out of a thing, like when she'd first suggested she might like to apply for the job in the library. Not that he hadn't wanted her to be a librarian, he simply felt that working in a Portakabin with the wind blowing in off the harbour would not be the warmest place for her to do it.

'And what kind of boat owner would I be to let you sit up the night? I've the health and safety of those passengers to think of. I can't have you half dead with exhaustion taking their lives into those hands.' He gestured towards said articles, and I looked at them, realising that although he hadn't managed to dissuade my mother from her dream of filling the island's little library with great works of literary escapes, he'd certainly gotten me.

'Right,' I said, with not a little exasperation. 'I'm going, OK?'

'Good.' He rose from his chair with some effort.

'Do you need a hand there?' Not that I'd leaped to his aid.

'I'm grand, now. Don't you be worrying. Get up them stairs and sleep.'

'Isn't it about time you got one of those remote-control recliner chairs that go up and down rather than all those cushions, Dad?'

'Rosie,' he began, having finally righted himself and now shuffling across the hardwood floor to his bedroom, 'if you think for one minute I'm having this discussion again in the middle of the night, you don't know me at all. Bed.'

'What am I, five?'

'Go.'

His door shut as I finally began to make my way reluctantly up the stairs.

I slept, after a while, though not before I'd gone over everything again. How my mind had tricked itself into following a phantom, and what it was that had woken me in the first place. What had I been dreaming that stirred me with such suddenness, certain that I was needed urgently, that there was something of great importance I had to know? But I couldn't remember. No matter how much I twisted and turned and put my head under the covers to try to pull it from the furthest reaches of the darkness, it would not come. In time, I drifted into a fretful sleep, one in which I seemed constantly on the edge of waking, yet that dream-like state had enough strength in it to pull me back.

Oh, great, you have a phone, the girl said, on seeing her about to text her mother. The girl reached around and grabbed it. Thanks, she said. I need to let my mum know we're going to be late and my phone's just died.

The following morning, I stood in the kitchen. I had gone through my usual breakfast routine, buttering every crust and corner of a piece of toast that I knew my stomach, after my disturbed night, would not allow me to eat. I carried it across the lino floor and opened the back door.

'Erg,' I called, into the clear blue morning, but all was still, no sign of my night-time escapade companion. He'd left the house as soon as I'd come down earlier to let him out. 'Erg,' I tried again. Nowhere to be seen, but I knew he'd arrive. I wondered what that day had in store. The quiet of its appearance, the calmness of its temperament, belied the awful sadness in my bones.

At the bottom of the garden – truly more field, in which seeds from a passing bird or the droppings of a rabbit grew – I saw the hedgerow shake.

'Come on, Erg,' I encouraged.

Soon enough his black and white snout appeared at its base. He watched me as he lay like a squaddie in training – his tongue hanging out, paws spread, ready for the charge.

'Come on.' I waved the toast. And he was off, bounding through the green until he stopped at my feet, perfectly poised, looking up at me in wait.

I held the toast straight out, between thumb and finger. 'Go,' I commanded. He leaped, catching it perfectly in his teeth before landing as daintily as a ballerina and, as noisily as any car on the island, attacking it, shaking his head ferociously, growling until he gave up and dropped it. His happy doggy slurps made me smile as he chewed at the buttery edges.

'Good boy.' I gave him a quick pet on the head, then went back inside.

I hadn't woken Dad. After my earlier adventure I thought it only fair that I left him. He still liked getting up to see me off, telling me the things that I already knew, like to mind the stone jutting out from Rossban pier that the harbour master had still to fix. He liked to repeat those warnings as if they were good-luck charms, ensuring that I and *Aoibhneas* and all her travellers would be safe. There were mornings when it exasperated me, and then there were others when I said, understandingly, Yes, Dad, ever the child putting up with the fears that hounded the parent.

As I set out, I took one final look back at the house to make sure he wasn't there, that I hadn't missed the opportunity to wave back to him. I'd left a note apologising for the previous night but, still, a wave was important. As I drove slowly out of our gate, I kept an eye on the door and the curtained windows through my rear-view mirror. When I reached the road, I checked one last time that there was nothing and then I stopped the car and wondered if, after all, I should have knocked at his bedroom door before I left to tell him I was going. Because what if he woke and rushed to find me gone? He'd panic at not having had the chance to bless me with his warnings. But the note, I argued with myself.

Didn't want to wake you. All is well. See you tonight. Rx.

But was it enough? Should I run back in? What if he'd had a heart attack in the night after all the stress about *Aoibhneas* and me running the roads and had died?

I was sticking the car in neutral and opening the driver's door, turning to run back in, when I heard him: 'The oil,' he was shouting from the front door, his finger pointing towards the harbour off north, his dressing-gown only having made it around the right shoulder. 'Remember to check the oil.'

'I will,' I called, and gave a wave, shaking my head in wonder at this man. 'Now go back in. Rest.'

It was 7 a.m. as Iggy and I pulled up at the harbour. I glanced at Patsy's windows but there was no sign of life, her curtains still drawn.

'She's usually up by now.' I nodded at her house.

'Aye, it's not like her, Still, good thing for me, though. I don't feel like doing the butterfly, and I don't like disappointing her. You're not the only one who had a rough night. I slept on my shoulder wrong and now I've a knot in there the size of one of Diarmuid's scones. I think it'll be a simple doggy paddle for me today.' Iggy rotated his shoulder, squeezing at it.

On our journey down, I'd told him about Liam's ultimatum and my strange night-time apparition. Iggy didn't mind such otherworldly happenings. He said the island was full of them.

'Yes, your shoulder is totally comparable to me running around the island like a woman possessed.'

'You haven't got a tennis ball, have you?'

'I usually have one in the back there with my golf clubs and hockey gear.'

Iggy was not impressed with my sarcasm. 'Well, you might have had one for Ergo. Dogs love the whole fetch-the-tennis-ball thing.'

'What do you want it for anyway?'

'I could give my shoulder a good rolling-over with it against the shop wall.'

I looked at Patsy's windows again. 'It's curious, though, isn't it, that she isn't up the morning after the night I dreamed I saw her? Perhaps it wasn't my imagination after all. Maybe she really was coming to help us with *Aoibhneas*. Maybe she has a message, something I can do to save her.'

We stared at her house, but when not a curtain twitched, Iggy pressed on. 'So, what are you going to do? Wake her up or come and swim?'

'Swim, I suppose.' Although I knew my heart wasn't in it. 'By the time we're finished, she might be up.'

My swim that morning seemed as fraught as Iggy's: he only managed a short dip and an attempt at a one-armed crawl. We were two minutes in before we gave up, Iggy nevertheless swearing the cold water had sorted him. It had also, however, taken his sandals, which as far as I knew were his only pair. Iggy wore sandals right up until November, he proudly told whoever would listen. They had been perched on the rock I had sat on all summer watching him. But for some reason that morning a rogue wave had decided to mount the very place and make away with Iggy's only summer footwear. We watched them bob out towards the harbour opening.

'I could start up the ferry,' I offered, 'and you can hang overboard and try to catch them with the pole. Mind you, I could be done for it, if you fell in.'

'I'd hardly sue you.'

'It's not you I'm worried about. It's the boat and my licence. The way things are going now, one foot wrong and Liam would be on me.'

'Leave them.'

'I could go get the canoe from Carhoona?'

'By the time you're back they'd be well gone. No, they're the sea's now. I give them to her in the hope she gives me something back.'

'Like a stray fishing net? She seems to have loads of those.'

'Ugh.' Iggy tutted. 'I'm depressed now. I need a coffee.'

With no sign still of Patsy coming to life we headed for Iggy's roof and there, wrapped in a blanket, I closed my eyes against the sun. The still air brought the sound of birdsong and, to my surprise, a hammer bang. Someone somewhere was up early, working hard.

Iggy had now changed into navy cargo pants, which if I wasn't mistaken were once Críostóir's, and a white sweatshirt with fraying neck and a pair of white runners that he said were his mother Dora's, left after her summer visit when parent and child had played Nirvana and Nancy Griffith tunes in Páidíns. He was almost coordinated – not intentionally, I think, but definitely a first.

'What do you think?' he asked, looking at his new foot-wear as they dangled over the edge of his rooftop. He had cut away the heels, given his feet were too big for them, and tied an elastic strip through each eyelet that stretched around the back of his ankles. He seemed to be sporting a type of flip-flop or clog. 'I'm thinking of calling them flogs. They could catch on, you know.' And once again I was reminded of how in-sync we two often found ourselves. He turned his feet this way then that so he could appreciate his handiwork.

'Yeah, right, you should definitely patent them.'

'I think I just might.' He gave a contented sigh, then took the first sip of his coffee.

'You know, Rosie,' he said, after a moment, 'I've been giving the whole boat situation a lot of thought. Even before Liam's intervention yesterday.'

I'd told Iggy all about Liam's proposal on every occasion that we'd found ourselves alone since that first big dramatic visit. He'd listened patiently while I'd spouted and spewed, walking the length and breadth of his kitchen, each time wasting myself so that I had to sit on one of his mismatched seats, drained of the energy to curse any more.

'You should let Liam take it.'

'What?' I laughed, thinking he was joking. But Iggy wasn't laughing or smiling as I'd expected. 'Are you *actually* serious, Iggy?'

'Well . . .' he said, an uplift to his voice indicating his suggestion wasn't the worst.

'Jesus, Iggy.' I was amazed – no, more disgusted – that he might think I'd seriously let that fecker take *Aoibhneas* from under us.

'Would it be such a terrible thing to let your father retire? And let you . . . I dunno, not have to worry about it?'

It was one of those moments when you wondered how you could get someone so wrong. No, how they could get *you* so wrong, have not understood you, not seen what it was that held the precious pieces of you together.

'But it's all I have. If that ferry is taken away from me, I have nothing.'

The sting of threatened tears forced my eyes to close, and in that split second's darkness I heard the cry of a passing guillemot, the squawk louder in my ears than I ever recalled before. And I felt it, the rumble of madness that would surely ensue should *Aoibhneas* be taken from me.

'I've never told you about Hannah, have I?'

Iggy saying his wife's name was so unexpected that I was unable to connect it to him straight away. But it came, eventually.

'I ruined everything. I kept insisting, idiot that I am. Honestly, if I hadn't pushed her to take on the hotel we might still be OK. I might still be living up there, not shoe-less and penniless, like I am down here.'

It was the first time I'd seen Iggy so vulnerable as he sat considering his new footwear. I'd never realised the depth of the disappointment he felt in himself about his former life. He'd hidden it well for all of those months we'd shared as friends, letting his positivity and humour mask the hurt. And a hotel? I'd known of no hotel, but I said nothing and let him continue unhindered.

'It was her family's. And over all the years we were together they simply ran it into the ground. Hopeless, they were. And such a beautiful place. You should have seen it. A Gothic beauty.' His face lit up suddenly at the memories. 'In the photos you could see how magnificent she had been. And I wanted it, wanted to take it and make her great again. And they offered it to us. Hannah said no, though, said the place was full of too much sadness for her to want to go back. But I pushed and pushed and pushed. Ten years I was at it. Even before the kids were born. Never letting up. I did everything to convince her, used what little money we had to get architects to look at it, even did up a business plan. Oh, yeah, I was quite the go-getter back then. I know you wouldn't suspect it now, but we change, don't we? I showed it to her parents, the plan, even when she'd asked me not to. They were keen. They'd move into the gate lodge, they said. Their way out of the sink-hole, not that they added that. That was Hannah's summa-tion. They'd never been the kindest of parents. Hannah had been the only one of the three children to stay in Donegal – trapped by me, she used to laugh. We'd thought it a joke. But really it wasn't. In the end, she gave in, worn down by me. She allowed my plans to convince her that perhaps it would be different and she could be happy there this time, with me and the kids, this one molecule of change that would surely blow away those horrible memories, and somehow make the place happy and warm. We sold our little cottage that we'd had out on the peninsula. Jesus, I was so deluded. We hadn't a pot to piss in, not before and certainly not after. I couldn't make it work, we sank loan after loan into the thing. She hated it and had to raise the kids on her own because I was too busy running around trying to plug holes that only grew bigger. We barely spoke any more, and when we did, it was with the burden of the debt bearing down on us. Until one day I found her in the old scullery, sitting on the cold stone floor, watching the washing-machine as it spun. There wasn't even a wash in. She had simply turned it on. Still had on her flimsy nightdress. I mean, it was nearly six o'clock in the evening. When I touched her she was freezing. I put my jacket around her and tried to pull her up, but she wouldn't budge. I sat down beside her and held her hand and begged her to look at me. And when she eventually did, she told me to go. To pack everything I had and leave and not come back.

'She sold the place after. Her parents ended up in the local nursing home with enough to pay for their fees. They'd never actually signed the place over to her, you see, wise old fuckers, so what was left after the sale had to pay for their costs. Hannah's in a small council house now. Every penny I've ever sent, which I still do, by the way, she used only for the kids, and now, of course, it's the grandkids. Refused to buy herself a coffee with it. When I still lived up there and I called by, she couldn't even look at me. She'd leave the door open and tell the children I'd arrived. They were teenagers by then. When I'd ring, she wouldn't say a thing, just handed the phone to them. They'd talk to me, but not like before, you know. They couldn't get over it either, what I'd put them, or more, what I'd put *her* through. She was so very broken. That's why I won't be seeing my granddaughter any time soon. I don't think I'd be turned away, but I can't bear to see it, their disappointment in me.'

Out on the horizon, a tanker, lazy and long, came into view.

'So, things, they aren't worth it. They tend to ruin us. I don't want to see that happen to you or Danny. You are good people. And I know you love *Aoibhneas* but she's not worth the battle, the loans. Your dad's getting older, Rosie. Let his last few years be without worry.'

'God,' I said eventually, 'we really are alike, aren't we? Both of us being told to leave by the people they love. We are the unwanted.'

'Rosie, I wasn't telling you all this to make you more unhappy. It's simple, you and Danny don't need the debt.'

'And tell me, Iggy, what is it that we'll do then when we've handed her over to Liam do you think? Sit in the house, day in day out, watching the four walls that we saved, looking out of our window at *Aoibhneas* passing three times a day being driven by Liam and feel like we've done the right thing? We'd only be trading one for another, a boat for a house. They're all "things" as you put it, only *Aoibhneas* is who I am, Iggy. The *only* thing of me that I have left. Do you understand?'

I couldn't read him. Couldn't figure out if he got what I was saying.

'But you have me, Rosie, and Diarmuid and Patsy.'

I shook my head. 'You're really not getting this, are you?'

'Rosie, I—'

'Look, Iggy, I'm sorry your life is fucked, OK. I'm sorry your wife is a shell of herself for something you think you did. But enough with the sermons. Our lives are not the same. You can't possibly know what I feel. You can't possibly know what you're asking me to give up. No amount of trying to walk in my shoes here is going to cut it. I'm not giving up the boat. Never. So stop with this. Fucking leave it.'

The force of my words shocked even me.

But on he went nevertheless.

'You know he's kept it for you, Rosie? Your dad, all this time, he's kept it for you.'

'Dad loves that boat. If he didn't have it, it'd kill him too.'

'No, Rosie, if he didn't have *you*, it would kill him. The boat is just a boat.'

I made a noise, a kind of puffing out. 'It's not *just* a boat, Iggy. It's who we are, the Driscolls. And it's the one bloody thing that brings me any joy.' My breath was quick and sharp with indignation. 'I don't get this, I really don't. *We* don't do this, Iggy. We don't pass judgement on each other's lives. It's been a part of me for ever. Even when I wasn't living here she was still in my head. She's the only place I feel at peace now in this awful, shitty life. *That boat* is the only place I don't feel guilty. The only place I feel Saoirse beside me. She's right there, you know. And I talk to her and laugh with her. And I can't, I won't give that up.'

I stopped and wrapped my arms around me tightly. I shook my head in exasperation at this man suggesting for one second that I get rid of the one precious thing I had left.

'And what would you know anyway, Iggy,' I demanded of him, striking back, wanting to hurt him as he was hurting me, 'about what that boat has meant to us all these years, when you've only been here a wet week?'

'Ah,' he scoffed. 'And there it is. Something I didn't think we did either, thought less of each other because of our place of birth. I thought we left that kind of thing to all the other xenophobes.'

That stopped us. Forcing us even further apart.

'Perhaps it's best if we don't talk about this, Iggy. Forget I ever mentioned it to you.'

'Rosie, I just care about you, that's all.'

'Well, stop then. This wasn't the agreement.'

'Agreement, is it? I don't quite remember there being an *agreement*.'

'You know what I mean. We don't do that kind of stuff. We don't weigh in with our opinions.'

'Except we're friends. I'm not sure if you're aware that this is the kind of thing friends do for each other.'

'No, Iggy.' I felt the kind of exasperation normally reserved for a child who had been told a hundred times that their coat didn't belong on the floor. 'You don't get to care for me. You don't get to feel anything for me. We are simply . . .' And it was there I faltered.

'Simply what?'

I searched the sky for the right definition to encapsulate what we were. 'People who let each other be, without needing anything back.'

'Well, that seems like a fantastic recipe for a friendship you have there, Rosie.' He flung a stone from the roof in disgust.

The silence grew between us, and I was considering leaving – what was there left to say? – but it seemed he wasn't finished yet.

'Rosie, what do you think your vision was this morning? It's a warning that something needs to give.'

'Well, it won't be *Aoibhneas*, I can tell you that. And, anyway, you've no idea what you're talking about with Dad and all.'

'Don't I?'

He turned towards me again, but I would not engage him. Instead I let the breeze that had finally arrived to buffet the edges of the island, its gentle, feather-like touch stroking the hairs on my arm, tell me it was enough.

'I'm not talking about this any more, Iggy.'

I gathered myself up, sweeping the dust and grit from my rear with my palm. I climbed down the ladder as he sat still, not moving an inch. But when I thought there would be nothing more said between us, he offered a warning as I opened my jeep door.

'I'm not wrong, Rosie. Something has to give.'

His curls, fully dry now, shifted in the breeze. It was rare to see Iggy so troubled. And I wondered at this new place we had found ourselves, and what the future would hold for all we had been. I sat into the driver's seat and began to reverse. When I stopped to put the jeep into first, I glanced up one more time, but it was only the white of his newly acquired runners that I could see, one crossing defiantly over the other.

Within minutes I was rounding the coastal road, speeding perhaps more than was necessary to get back to the harbour. My foot hit the brake as I pulled up in front of Patsy's, jolting me forward.

Her curtains were now opened.

It was 8.20 a.m. and by rights I should have been over on the ferry, but I couldn't go yet. The pull towards Patsy was as deep as a well. I closed the jeep door with a bang so that she might see me before I knocked on her door. I stood for a moment, ridding myself of all that had happened with Iggy. Allowing some space for what I had to ask this seer of things.

To my left Fergal's car approached and I waved him down, curious on several counts: he never usually got to the ferry that early, and someone was with him. When he stopped, he rolled down his window, as deadpan as ever. With no greeting, he simply cocked his elbow on the door and waited to hear what I wanted of him.

In contrast, there came an enthusiastic 'Hi, Rosie' from his passenger.

I smirked at Fergal, who still refused to look at me, before replying.

'And good morning to you too, Éilísh.'

'Fergal offered to give me a lift this morning.' She beamed.

'That was awful good of you, Fergal. Must've been a big sacrifice leaving the Friesians so early.'

'Ah, you know yourself.' Embarrassed, he adjusted the pine-tree air-freshener, the same one that had hung from his rear-view mirror for years now.

'Indeed I do, Fergal, indeed I do.' How could I forget those wonderful feelings of something beginning, that willingness to do anything for the other person even if it meant intruding on your early morning routine? 'Anyway, I just wanted to say I'll be over in five minutes. Can you do the oil and water?'

'Consider it done,' Éilísh replied eagerly.

Fergal smiled – a thing he rarely did – then turned back to me to tip his head in salute. He dropped the handbrake and was gone.

I started up Patsy's path but before I reached the red-painted door it opened.

'The very woman. I was looking out for you.' Patsy smiled.

'Really, you were? I was here earlier. Did you not see the car?'

'Well, now.' She beckoned me in. 'I didn't have the best of nights, so I slept through. Am only up fifteen minutes. I possibly look a fright.'

'You look perfect, Patsy, as always.'

Following her, I passed her floral wellies and red-trimmed walking boots sitting on the hall rug. They couldn't have been bigger than a size two.

When we arrived in her sitting room, she beckoned me to a chair opposite hers – a high-backed purple-satin-covered armchair that looked so comfortable I felt I could sleep a whole night there. Between us was a low coffee table in front of the patio door that looked out at her hedgerows, which gave shelter to any bird coming in off the swell, not so high, though, that she couldn't see the harbour and the pier and all that might happen out there.

'Tea? Or are you a coffee woman? I forget.' Patsy was already heading to her kitchen but stopped and smiled. 'Do you remember your poor mother? I'd have to ply her with coffee when she came looking for those books of hers. I never knew where they were. I only ever borrowed them because I felt I should. Your mother and her education of this place, if I passed by her cabin and didn't go in, I'd feel guilty. I didn't want the books at all. I'm not a reader. I'm more into the Sudoku. But I loved chatting with her. Such an interesting woman. Always had some different take on this world that I couldn't get enough of.'

I laughed at her appreciation of Mammy and for the first time that morning felt settled, at my ease.

'Patsy, sit yourself back down. I've had a coffee already with Iggy.'

'Ah, Iggy. I missed him this morning. I like to see him swimming out there.' She indicated the water before taking her seat again. 'It reminds me of Prionsias. He used to swim there most mornings when we were children. I'd watch him from the wall. I was never one for it, though. Daddy didn't like that he swam. He always said if he wanted to be a fisherman, then it was best not to know how. That way he wouldn't be able to fight the might of the sea should she decide to take him.' Patsy was lost to me for a second, thinking of her older brother whom that very fate had befallen. A storm caught his trawler as they were coming back home. Both Prionsias and John-Joe, his fishing mate, drowned when both were thrown overboard.

'He didn't struggle, you know, well, only a little, but when he realised what he was up against, he stopped and let the power take him. That's what I see anyway in this old head of mine. His quiet acceptance. But sure would you listen to me. That's not what you came here for, me wittering on, was it?'

'You don't witter, Patsy. No one could ever say that about you.'

'Plenty do. Me and my "ways" aren't exactly popular with everyone.'

'Well, that's not the case with me. Actually, Patsy, I wanted to ask if you'd sensed anything recently. You said you had a bad night?' I stopped short of questioning whether she'd found herself sleepwalking.

'I did and in fact it concerns you.'

I smiled, so very relieved that I had not been wrong. Perhaps there was hope for *Aoibhneas* yet.

'I woke to the phone ringing. It must've been about one o'clock in the morning and I reached out to pick it up. I have one by the bed, you know, very handy altogether. But there was nothing except a dial tone. So, I thought, that's you at it again, Patsy, letting your dreams slip into your reality. And I go back to sleep. But off it goes a second time. Same thing. Ring, ring, dial tone. Warm milk, I think. That's what I need to shake me out of this. Down I go, sort myself out, and I come in here with the intention of sitting for a bit to look out at the sea, to maybe have a chat with Prionsias, and I pull up the blind only to see that friend of yours sitting on the wall, but not facing the tide, no, he was looking right in at my garden. Like he was happy to be there enjoying the view, maybe waiting to see a willow warbler fly in.'

I'd fully expected her to say she'd seen me, standing looking at her house, or Dad's car turning to bring me home. But, no, while I had imagined her at my door she had imagined someone else on the sea wall.

'What friend, Patsy?' I asked, keen to know who this new arrival was.

'That tall one. I've seen him with you on the telly. Grey at the temples. Dublin man. Something to do with Saoirse.'

'Saoirse?' I said, thrown. Then the penny dropped. 'Mick, you mean, the inspector who works on the case?'

Patsy clicked her fingers and pointed at me. 'The very one.' She sat forward a little in her chair, close to the edge. 'I couldn't think of his name, but I knew it was about her. He's not on the island at the minute, is he?'

'No,' I replied, bemused at this mention of Mick.

'I thought not. But there he was, clear as day.'

'Did he say anything?' I asked, still not understanding what all of this meant. 'Was he trying to tell you something, do you think?'

'Well, he was a bit of a distance away, but I got the binoculars out and I can tell you his lips didn't move once. He just sat there. I wish he *had* said something. I stood looking at him for a while. When that didn't work, I closed my eyes and concentrated, I even let my milk go cold in case he wanted to reach me, you know, in a telepathic way. But there was nothing. He stayed for a little bit. Looking right at me. And then he got up and smiled before waving and turning to walk off down the pier. Then he disappeared, like he was stepping into a fog, which there wasn't, not last night. I checked with Diarmuid this morning – he's the only one who can't sleep in the summer – and he told me it was as clear as the pane of glass in his shop door. You know he cleans it with—'

'Patsy.' I cut across her, pulling her away from Diarmuid and the cleanliness of his windows. 'I still don't understand what it could *mean*.'

'Oh, now, I'm not sure either. I was hoping you'd know what it might be. Has there been some advance in the case lately?'

'No, nothing.'

'Oh, I see.'

I considered the coffee table, the window, my hands, as if they held the answer.

'But, Patsy,' I said, something having actually occurred to me. 'Do you remember back in the beginning when she first disappeared you said you couldn't see her yet, but you knew she was coming?'

'Yes, I do recall that now that you say it.'

'Well, maybe this is it? Maybe you seeing Mick is the sign?'

'Of what, love?'

'That she's finally returning.'

'Oh, I see,' she said, more dubiously than I'd hoped.

'But it makes sense, doesn't it?'

I sat forward, surprised by all that had been said, and by all that I was now thinking, understanding that the pieces were finally falling into place.

'Patsy, I really think this is it. I think she's on her way home.'

'Perhaps, Rosie, but I don't know if you should go jumping to such conclusions yet. I was only really supposing it could mean that Mick might be about to phone you or something.'

'And to think I had this all wrong, that you'd come to the house last night to tell me how to save *Aoibhneas* but it was about Saoirse.'

'Your house? I wasn't at your house.'

'After all this time, she's alive. She's actually alive.'

She looked startled, tripped up by my assertion. Her mouth opened to speak, then closed again, defeated. She settled on a smile, one meant kindly, but where all I saw was pity.

'Now, Rosie, please, love. This isn't good, you getting so worked up.'

But she may as well have saved herself the effort. I was no more hearing her than the three short beats that sounded from the ferry right then, attempting to call my attention.

'Is she OK, Patsy, do you think? I mean is she happy or . . .' I searched for the right words, my smile more anxious than joyful '. . . is she hurt? Has someone hurt her?'

'Maybe, Rosie, maybe don't put so much store by this.'

But I would not listen to her caution. Eight years I'd waited, eight long, horrendous years.

I stood up to walk a stride or two, only to return to sit again. 'What should I do now? Should I wait here, do you think? Maybe I should call Mick.'

'Just take a moment, Rosie, please. I'm sorry now that I said a—'

'Or Hugh. I should really call Hugh.'

I wanted to. I so wanted to call Hugh and Cullie to tell them she was nearly home. To tell them I had been right all along, that she wasn't lost to us at all.

'No,' I said in answer, before Patsy could even begin. 'No, he wouldn't believe me. Neither of them would. They didn't agree with me keeping faith that she was alive.'

Again, the ferry hooted, deflating me.

'I don't know what to do, Patsy,' I appealed.

She reached across to take my hands, holding me tighter than I thought she was capable of. 'Listen to me, Rosie Driscoll. Nothing in what I've seen can tell me very much. You need to stop getting so worked up now, all right? You need to take a breath. A big, deep breath.' As she breathed in, encouraging me to do the same, I closed my eyes and followed as instructed, trying to calm myself.

'And again,' she said, and we repeated it four more times.

'Good. OK, now, Rosie, I want you to listen to me very carefully.' I did so dutifully. 'Don't dwell on this. Mick arrived in my head for a reason that I cannot explain. Maybe you should go on back home and forget the ferry for today. I could ring your father. I'm sure Liam would be happy to step in this once.'

How could she have known that mentioning that man's name would only stir my disquiet further.

'No,' I barked, frightening her a little, pulling myself from the restraint of those powerful hands and jumping up to point at this startled woman. 'That man isn't having *Aoibhneas*. No, I need her. I'm going to find Saoirse.'

I was at the front door then, wanting to get to *Aoibhneas* and to Saoirse before anyone else could. She was out there waiting for me, out there beyond on the mainland, and *Aoibhneas* and I were on the way.

'Oh, Rosie, what in God's name.' Patsy was behind me as I fumbled with the latch then ran down her pathway, tripping on a loose paving slab. 'Take your time,' she called.

I attempted a wave, trying to reassure her that I was fine, but I knew full well as soon as I got into my jeep she'd be ringing my father – none of that mattered now, though. I still had time to get to *Aoibhneas*, to be gone out into the sea's vastness before anyone could stop me.

I didn't look back at Patsy once, the woman who had given me so much. I didn't want to see it again, the doubt and worry that for years had darkened Hugh's eyes. I started my jeep and it screeched away to arrive seconds later at the pier steps.

On the ferry, I brushed past Fergal and Éilísh, not listening to them update me on the oil and the passenger numbers.

'The ropes. Untie them now,' I called, taking the wheelhouse steps two by two, to start *Aoibhneas*, and to turn her in her half-pirouette so that we were gone, away from the land and the possibility of anyone stopping me. At the mouth of the sea, I breathed out, slowing the force of my heartbeat for the first time since I'd left Patsy's door.

'I'm coming, Saoirse,' I said to her. 'Hold on, my beautiful girl. I'm nearly there.'

She slid the smiley face up and down the chain of her necklace as she watched street after street carry them further away from Dún Laoghaire.

My progress was steady. Determined and focused. My eyes straight ahead watching out for our approach to Rossban harbour. I counted down each nautical mile, each buoy and each natural occurring landmark.

Since I'd boarded, Fergal had pretty much stayed out of my way, but Éilísh had braved the urgent fury of me and had come up to give the passenger numbers almost as soon as we'd left the harbour. As I concentrated on our course ahead, I could sense her watching me, searching no doubt for some indication of what was wrong.

'Rosie,' she said eventually, 'is everything OK?'

'Everything could not be more perfect.'

'You're sure? You just don't seem yourself.'

'No, and thank God for that. I haven't liked that self in a very long time.'

'Rosie, are you positive you're all right to skipper today? Maybe you need me here with you. I can help. I nearly have the exams now and, well, given you seem . . .'

'Seem what? Happy?'

'I didn't mean—'

'Listen, Éilísh, I'm fine.' A rogue wave sprayed up onto the window as I felt the exhaustion of convincing her to leave me be, because that was all I wanted now.

'Don't you want to get back down to Fergal?' I asked. She looked away, embarrassed at my crassness. 'Oh, come on, there's nothing to be ashamed of. The first blossoms of love?'

To her credit she stood her ground and did not rise to my teasing.

'Go on,' I said, when I realised she wouldn't leave unless I ordered it. 'Go on back down. Make sure everything is OK.'

She left reluctantly, taking a concerned look at the panel and the sea beyond us, as if she were a mother leaving her baby alone for the first time with a sitter. Twenty minutes later, however, over halfway out, yet another knock came to the open wheelhouse door.

'Honestly, Éilísh, I'm absolutely fine,' I called snippily.

'Good to hear,' that soft Donegal voice replied.

I froze, disarmed and dismayed that Patsy had somehow worked more of her magic to get Iggy – of all people, given our row earlier – down onto *Aoibhneas* in the five minutes it had taken me to leave the pier and turn that boat for Rossban.

Those flog things of his scuffed their way towards me.

'I can see why you love it,' he said, looking out at the sea. 'I might give this whole wee skippering thing a go myself. Can't be that hard, really, can it?'

I didn't take the bait of his banter.

'So, she called you?' I said.

'She who?'

'Patsy. She sent you, right?'

'No, no one sent me.'

I glanced at him, to judge the veracity of what he'd said, that he really was here of his own accord. He smiled his wonderful calm smile that had always made me so comfortable – at least until this morning.

'Well, if that's the case, Iggy, can we hurry whatever this is up? I've more things to be concerned with than having another lecture on how to live my life.'

'Yeah, you know, about that, we didn't leave it very well, did we? We don't do that kind of thing you and me? It was . . . unsettling.'

'No, we don't, but then you don't normally form such definite opinions on my life, either.'

I tapped the pressure gauge, refusing to allow this to go as easily as he might have liked.

The weight of his stare bore down on me as if he was searching for something I just wasn't letting him see.

'I thought,' he said, giving up and turning to the waves again, 'that maybe I might be able to help.'

'To help? To help with what?' I asked defensively. His definition of 'help' was concerning. Help by commandeering the vessel and selling it to Liam? Or help by having me committed at the other end for another stint in Rossban hospital?

'Well, I was thinking when you get back this evening, we two could have a sit-down and try to come up with some way to sort this *Aoibhneas*-Liam thing. I do want to help, Rosie. I really, really do. I know I came across a bit harsh this morning, not reading the mood very well. I blame the shoulder, by the way. It's still not right, you know.' He gave it a good squeeze. 'I mean, I don't have the worst business brain in the world. I've only the one failed venture under my belt. Bill Gates failed, right? And now he's minted, so who knows what I could come up with?'

'Oh,' I said, softened for the umpteenth time in those last few months by his honesty and care. 'That's . . . em, well, that's actually really good of you, Iggy. But, em, I'm afraid I won't be back tonight.'

'What do you mean? How else is *Aoibhneas* going to get home?'

'I don't know,' I replied, as befuddled as he was as to how *Aoibhneas* and her passengers were going to make it across to Roaring Bay that day. 'It's Saoirse,' I qualified. 'I'm going to find her.'

'Saoirse?'

'She's on her way home.'

'Jesus, Rosie. Seriously?'

'I know.' I smiled, encouraged by him. 'Patsy said she sensed it last night. Around the time I was at her door. Can you believe that? The universe coming together to tell me she's on her way.'

'Wait, hold on, this is Patsy? This is what she told you this morning after you left me?'

I nodded, while noting his sudden scepticism.

'What did she say exactly?'

'I know what you're doing, Iggy, and you may as well give up now. I'm not going to listen to you. You can't talk me out of this. Patsy already tried. And I've had enough of that the last eight years.'

He held up his hands. 'No, no, that's not it. I'm just trying to understand.'

I repeated all that Patsy had said as succinctly as possible.

'Jesus,' he said again, when I had finished.

'I know. And it's all true, because I can feel her, Iggy. I can really feel her. I mean,' and this was where I started to cry, 'I know this is the place where I've always felt her the most, the wheelhouse. But this is different. I know she's on the mainland now and I just have to get to her.'

324

'OK.' He nodded.

'And I'm not coming back again, Iggy, you know. I'm going to Dublin to be with her – that's where she'll go, you see. And I have to get there as fast as I can. She'll be waiting. She'll expect me to be there. I mean, what if she gets there before me and she sees I don't live there any more? She'll think I gave up on her.'

'She won't, Rosie. She won't.'

'Oh, and Dad.' At this I stopped for a second, realising the immensity of my abandonment of my father right when Liam was breathing down his neck. 'Will you watch out for him?' I asked beseechingly. 'I mean, I'll call him as soon as I can. He'll understand and he'll be so happy she's back. But it's just with Liam and all.'

'Sure, Rosie, sure, no problem. I'll keep an eye on him.'

'It's just . . . I have to go now, you know.' I was growing more upset with each defence I gave for leaving my father. 'I can't stay. I don't have any choice.'

'Of course, Rosie. It's OK now.'

I nodded, reassured by his promise. As we passed No Man's Haven, I felt calmer somewhat, my lightness of spirit returning, smiling again at the thought of Saoirse. I slowed the engine slightly as we moved through the mouth of the harbour and as we began our approach to the pier.

It occurred to me as I saw the waiting passengers that she might be among them and not in Dublin as I had thought. As we drew closer I scanned those eager travellers, watched the shuffle of feet and bags being picked up already as if their departure was that imminent, but of course she wasn't there.

And then, just as I was about to return to the task of bringing in *Aoibhneas*, I saw them: two familiar faces, two people who made my heart break in an instant, staring directly at the wheelhouse.

'Oh, God,' I said, my knees immediately buckling.

'What?' Iggy's eyes followed mine to my husband and son.

'There's news.'

This can't be the right way, she said,
leaning between passenger and driver.
But they ignored her.

My arms weakened and I worried that I would lose my grip on steering her to safety. I looked around to say so but there was only Iggy and he had no idea how to guide that boat. I whimpered and tried to tell myself to concentrate on the wall, that there were passengers below who needed me to be their skipper and bring them in safely. I called out each instruction in desperation, but nothing was sticking, the words were slipping away, and I had missed it, the moment when I needed to inch her in. Too fast, still too fast.

Iggy called to me, then out of the door to Éilísh, and she was there, pushing Iggy to one side, taking over at the rudder, nudging me away so that I was standing in the middle of the wheelhouse with my arms slumped by my sides, Iggy holding me steady as I watched Hugh's solemn face. When we had finally docked securely, Éilísh left again, rushing to assist Fergal with the ropes and the passengers. Hugh and Cullie stepped back against the pier wall to allow them room to pass with their many bags.

Once there was just the crew and Iggy remaining, Éilísh returned to look at me with such concern.

'What do you want to do?' she asked. 'Can we shut her up now?'

Iggy had spoken to me that whole time since my near collapse and although none of his words had gone in, I knew they had the shape and sound of kindness.

I tested my voice that I was not sure would work: 'Close her up,' I croaked, then coughed.

When I finally left the wheelhouse, it was the first time they could fully see me. Serious and alert now, Cullie opened his mouth slightly, as if he wanted to say something, but closed it again almost as quickly, his mind changed. I waved cautiously to them, and they waved back in the same vein. Almost in unison. Two hands raised in perfect harmony, like the movement of synchronised swimmers. I took the pier steps, slowly, watching my foot hit each concrete slab until I came to stand in front of them, not knowing or caring where Iggy was now. They must have left Dublin in the early hours of the morning to be there at 9.45 a.m. They did not speak immediately, but both stepped towards me. Cullie took my hand.

'Rosie,' Hugh said quietly, his lips up against my ear so he could whisper. 'They've found her.'

The air around me, in that great expansive bay, felt as if it was escaping, being sucked away, out past No Man's Haven and further still, until I imagined it sweeping through the gap that lay between Shelley Island and Roaring Bay's coastline, because no matter how much my chest struggled to pull in that oxygen, it simply was not there.

I heard my son cry. And it was the first time in all those years. His face had been worn with worry many times, yes, but never had he let tears fall. I'd always thought that was a bad thing, but none of that mattered now, those wasted concerns, as he held onto me, his arms around my waist, his head bent to my shoulder. I raised a hand to comfort him, to rub his back. But my head was tilting longer and harder against his, and I was swaying as my weight pushed against him, and I was falling, falling onto him, letting my limbs be free of tension and effort, allowing them to crumble, to collapse. I was weightless, groundless. I was gone. My eyes closing on the world.

And she was there, at last in that other space, smiling.

'Mum,' she was saying, 'Mum, I tried. You know I tried.' And she looked so worried. It was me: I was worrying her. And so I smiled, and laughed, assuaging the anxiousness I was causing.

'I know, love, I know. Don't be worrying. Don't.' I touched her face, that seventeen-year-old face, not a wrinkle, just perfectly smooth.

'We all tried,' I was saying. 'We all did our best, didn't we? And that's all we ever asked of you, isn't that right? Remember the exams, when you got worried about them and we'd say: "Now, Saoirse, all you need to do is your best." You can't do any more than that. And you've always done your best, sweetheart. You are magnificent. "Outstanding in your field" – isn't that what Granddad says?' And we laughed together and touched foreheads, my hand cradling the back of her neck, tears streaming down our cheeks, lips pulled in trying to fight the sadness, trying not to let go of this precious moment we had before I knew she would leave me. 'Magnificent.' I repeated, watching those blue eyes of hers, letting them imprint in my brain, stamping their memory there so I would never forget, never ever lose sight of their brightness and beauty through all there was to come.

And can I have my
phone back now, please?

But the man simply laughed.

By the afternoon I was standing in our sitting room in Dublin. Don't ask me about the journey from Rossban to there. I remember none of it. The summer light streamed in on that south-facing room. And I was thinking that it wasn't as bright as it was on the island. I watched Mick's car pull up and heard his footsteps through the house after Hugh opened the front door. There were cameras outside all day, already ensconced when we'd arrived not half an hour before, all waiting to catch a glimpse of us. We were now hiding in that room: the angle of the driveway and the hedging meant they could not see us unless they trespassed, which was so very possible.

'Rosie,' Hugh said, and I smiled briefly to indicate that I was there, coping and would cope.

We sat. Mick rummaged for something in his inner pocket. I saw the fabric of his jacket move as his fingers uncovered what they were looking for. When he pulled it out, I could see it was small, in a zip-locked plastic bag. He started to tell me all that Hugh had already imparted on the journey up.

'Yesterday a body was discovered in the Dublin Mountains. Something had disturbed the earth, uncovering what appeared to be an arm. We don't know how long it was there exposed like that. A hill-walker who'd strayed from the track came across it at around seven p.m.' He stopped then, coughed once, swallowed hard and began again. 'Thankfully, the news only broke this morning after Hugh managed to get to you. We will, of course, have to wait for confirmation of the DNA match, but I contacted Hugh in the early hours when we identified this as being hers.'

He handed Hugh the bag and my husband's face crumpled on holding it for that tiny second. Cullie grabbed it before it fell to the floor, looked at it and nodded. He got up then to cross the room, to show me what I knew it was – her smiley face necklace. He hunkered down beside me, his hand on my back.

'We have to run tests to establish more. Obviously, what we're looking for now is evidence of not only how long she has been there but also how she came to be buried in that spot, or any clue as to who might have done it. But we believe she didn't get there by herself.' Mick lowered his head as if in apology. I watched as he pressed a thumb and index finger either side of his nose. He grunted then, pushing back his shoulders as he tried to find the courage, the will, to continue. 'The pathologist will be examining her for injuries, cause of death, which, I have to warn you, will take some time. But it is fairly clear at this point that we're dealing with a murder.'

Silence. There was silence in the room for a wisp, a click, a swallowing of time as we gathered in that word. The one word that Maggie was able to use so often over the years about her Claire. The word I had refused to let into my consciousness that was now here, defining my daughter also. I wished nothing more than to grab it and strangle its power over us, demanding it leave us be. But it was ours now, ours to have for ever, ours to offer a home, instead of our daughter.

I held the pendant in one hand as Cullie kept hold of the other. He was grasping it tighter now and I began to feel it shake. He watched it, too, as if it was not his, wondering why it was acting in this way. He placed his right hand on top of it, but that one, too, was trembling. I looked to see the swell of tears against the reddening hue of his face. I let the necklace drop into my lap, and I touched his clammy cheek. 'Oh, my boy,' I said. 'My poor beautiful boy.'

I wrapped my arms around this man who had been so brave, so utterly and totally brave for me and for us. This considerate soul who had gently navigated those many difficult lines that his father and I had drawn around ourselves. Navigating our loss and our heartache and our inability to be his parents, let alone be together any more, with a kindness that was now tearing me apart. All I wanted was his forgiveness. I rocked him back and forth as he clung to me. This grown man holding on like I was the rock that would save him from the oncoming surge.

'I'm so sorry, Cullie. Oh, my God, I am so, so sorry.'

Then it began, my crying, my wailing, moaning – a tormented soul, raging at herself for letting whoever it was lay a hand to her precious daughter and steal her away, hurting and damaging her, causing such unimaginable pain to someone who was full of goodness and hope and had had the brightest of futures. I wanted each blow inflicted, each depraved act erased from her defenceless body and meted out on me.

Do it to me. Give her back and do it to me.

I thought I was saying those words. I thought I was shouting them. So loudly that perhaps the journalists swarming at our boundary could hear and were taking down each syllable so we would see them printed in the papers the next day.

I did not care.

Print it all.

Hugh's arms surrounded me. He was not telling me to stop or trying to lull me into composure or something less horrific, as I had expected. He was leaning in, wrapping his love and sorrow around us. His voice joined mine in grief. His cries rising over mine. And I was reaching for him too. One arm for Cullie and one for Hugh. I was holding fists of them, their shirts, their skin, digging into them. Holding on tightly to our triumvirate of broken souls.

At the traffic lights, she tried to open the car door.

But it was locked.

A month ago, my brother Daniel came home to be with Dad. Early retirement, he'd said. He'd rung me in Dublin, where I was waiting for Saoirse to be given back, to ask nervously what I wanted to do about *Aoibhneas*. Liam had spoken to him, apparently, and he had spoken to Dad, who had told him to do nothing until he'd talked to me. *Aoibhneas* was, after all, mine, he'd said.

'Let her go,' I'd told him. 'Liam won't give up till she's his, Daniel. It's all he's ever wanted, and I don't have the will to fight him any more. Let her go.'

To fight over a boat with all that we were facing seemed by then ridiculous. Even if I could have been at her helm right there and then, she would not have given any release from all that I was going through, I knew that. Why stop the inevitable, when it held no importance for me now?

As we drew closer to getting Saoirse back to bury her, the knowledge that *Aoibhneas* was no longer the Driscolls' didn't kill me, as I had once thought it would. No, it was something else that had done that damage: those tests they had run on what was left of poor Saoirse, the final violations that made my body curl in on itself, as I begged that they would simply let her rest.

'But they have to, Rosie,' Hugh had said, 'they have to.'

And when at last they had told us they were done, I insisted on seeing her despite their vehement protestations.

They relented only when I told them I would prise open the coffin at the funeral if I had to. We all went, Hugh, Cullie and I, to be with what they deemed palatable. Bare bones, with no muscle, no skin, no hair, laid out on a bench. I breathed through my quaking body, deep breaths let out through tightly pursed lips. I needed her to feel me there, to know I had not abandoned her, that I would not abandon her even in that state. She was mine. My bones were her bones. She had come from me.

We three held each other's hands as we stood by her side until I stepped forward to kiss, then rub my hand along her right humerus and femur. Intact, undamaged bones. They did not allow us to see, let alone touch, the broken clavicle where she'd had the breath and life squeezed out of her, or the hip bone, also damaged, or the many other parts of her, so broken. They said it was most likely that she had died within a day or two of being abducted. The guards were now returning to the alibis they had taken so long ago of those predators that had once been ruled out and that Mick was now ruling very much back in. They appealed again to the public to think back to that time and that area, anything suspicious that anyone might have seen. One thing was for sure, Mick said. Someone, if only one, knew exactly what had happened, and he would not rest until they were found.

When I returned to my father's house three days ago, two months from when they had first found Saoirse, I sat at the end of the back garden, wrapped up in my winter coat, looking onto the water. The legs of the kitchen chair I'd carried out had sunk into the sodden land, but I didn't care. I wanted to look at Greystone Island and the tree that stood on it, feeling like somehow we were kindred souls. Ergo lay quietly by my side, and I dropped my hand to his head every now and again to give him a well-deserved petting.

Behind me, I heard the swish of footfall through the wet long-bladed grass. I had assumed it must have been Hugh or Cullie or Nina. We had all come to bury Saoirse. But it was Daniel arrived up from Michael-Fran's house, where he and Ellen, his wife, were now staying.

'The home place won't hold us all,' he'd argued, when I'd rung to tell him we were bringing her home. 'Michael-Fran is only dying for the company.'

'Not sure how his livestock will feel about their eviction.' I'd laughed softly in reply. I'd managed laughter, the sad, exhausted kind, a couple of times that last little while.

I stood to hug him. Of course I'd seen him since he'd come home from the States. They'd stayed with us a night in Dublin, but this time it felt like I really knew he was there. He seemed so much older now, even more so than in

Dublin. And heavier, his trouser belt having to dip under his belly. But he was still as tall, towering over me as he wrapped his arms around my tiny frame. I felt crushed by his sorrow as he held me against his chest.

'You know, I'm sorry, Sis, for what I said at Mammy's funeral.'

'I know, Daniel, I know,' I said. 'But we have her now.' Saoirse was waiting for us in Cullen's in Clonkill and would travel over later for her burial. 'No more now, Daniel.' I pulled away and smiled. 'It's OK.'

He looked around then to locate an old half-barrel that perhaps had once collected rain water, God knew why, way back in God knew when. He brought it over and turned it upside down. We sat, me on my chair and him on his low perch that I worried wouldn't hold.

'You'll get a cold sitting on that damp yoke. Mammy'd have a fit if she were here.'

'I'll be fine.'

We both concentrated on the sea ahead of us for a second or two.

'I love it here, you know,' he said, after a bit.

'As I recall you couldn't wait to get out of the place, you and Nathan, when you were young.'

He laughed. 'That was back then. It's different now. Now that I'm older.' He nodded, agreeing with himself. 'Nathan's coming, by the way. Should be here tomorrow.'

'Dad told me.'

We both clocked her then, over towards the north, *Aoibhneas* beginning to edge away from Roaring Bay's coastline, heading out into the expanse of sea.

'I can't believe Éilísh got her ticket,' I said. 'I'd forgotten she was so close before I left.'

Éilísh had brought us in that morning. I'd smiled up at her as we'd boarded. I hadn't seen her since they'd found Saoirse, and I'd left without even turning to say goodbye. She'd come down the steps to hug me tightly. 'Congratulations,' I'd whispered in her ear.

'Rosie, I don't know what to say.'

'I know.' I seemed to have been saying that a lot lately. 'Go on,' I said, releasing her, my eyes darting upwards to the bridge. 'Bring us home.'

'Yeah, heck of a girl,' Daniel enthused. 'Mad about that boat. Reminds me of someone.'

He smiled at me, then looked away north again.

'Actually, Rosie, about that, there's something you should know.'

I moved. A slight shuffle to my feet, an arching of my back. I didn't want to hear it, the explanation of *Aoibhneas*'s destiny. The reality of her not being ours any more had begun to hurt a little now that I was back, not so devastating as it might once have been, but a tiny thread in my heart that I reckoned might grow if I pulled on it too much.

'It's best I don't know, Daniel.'

'No, no, wait. Now, I'm sorry to do this with the funeral and all, but I thought it best you know before someone mentions it to you over the next couple of days. You'll have enough to contend with without having to figure out what the heck they're talking about. You need to hear this, but not from me.' He seemed nervous.

At first I thought he was referring to Dad, who was inside chatting with Hugh and Cullie. But then he said: 'There's some people here you might want to see.'

He looked back to the house then beckoned. And there he was, Iggy, wearing a smile, and behind him, Liam and Teresa.

Iggy said something to the pair, who then hung back. On he came towards us to shake Daniel's hand.

'I'll leave you to it, Sis, with this man. I'll get some refreshments with these fine folk over here.' He slapped Iggy on the back, then headed towards the others, calling out a hearty, 'Let's get that kettle on.'

I smiled at Iggy, genuinely glad to see him.

'So, I go away for two seconds and this happens.' My head indicated the others' retreat. 'Peace is declared. Was this all your fine work?'

He took me in his arms, and I laid my head against him.

'Christ, Rosie,' he said, 'I'm so sorry.'

No words followed. They remained stuck deep inside as he gently rocked me. I stayed there, lulled against him, holding on.

'We never got the chance to put things fully right the last time, did we?' he eventually said.

I gently pressed his arm as I pulled away to tell him it was OK, that this water was so far under the bridge that it had already reached the sea. Iggy sat on Daniel's barrel.

'I meant what I said. I heard you, Rosie. I heard what you were trying to say that day.'

'Honestly, Iggy,' I began, 'it doesn't matter—'

'No, listen, I have to say this quickly before Liam gets back out. I promised I'd let him explain it all. It was part of the deal.'

'The deal?'

'See, after you left, I couldn't rest. And I decided it was time to poke my nose into something that didn't concern me. I thought about it every day as I swam that harbour, trying all different solutions. And, unlike my bright idea with the hotel, I think this time I actually came up with something good. So I talked to Teresa.'

'Teresa?'

'You were right about her, by the way, a real head for business. After the swimming lessons with the lads over at the pool, we'd sometimes have a coffee, absolute muck, but you know, you have to be social. And I told her it had occurred to me that really *Aoibhneas* was everyone's, being, after all, our collective lifeline. And I suggested what if we all owned her, or at least anyone who was interested? Why couldn't we just form a company?'

I gave a quizzical look that encouraged him on.

'See, anyone on the island could buy a share or shares. That way your father gets bought out, bank gets paid, everyone's happy.'

'Right,' I said slowly, letting this information fully seep in.

'Would you believe we shareholders now number nearly thirty-two? Who knew we had so much cash hidden under mattresses around here? I've even scraped together a few bob myself. There'll be a bit left over for investment, too.'

'Wait,' I said, 'hold on, you're telling me this is done already?'

'Well, we're getting there, one or two final things to sort. A month, two no more, I'd say.'

'And Liam agreed to this and didn't throw a strop?'

'Thought that bit might come as a surprise.'

'But how?'

'Teresa. She got it right away. Even hugged me the day I explained it all. Looked almost relieved. Went home that night to talk to Liam. It took a couple of weeks but she pointed out his empire-building was not a good way to raise the boys in such a small community, that they'd done a pretty good job of making them level-headed young men and she wanted to keep them that way. And that if he didn't comply she'd have to seriously rethink whether Roaring Bay was in fact the best place to raise them. Hadn't her own family got a plot back in Tipp that would make for a great four-bedroomed house? Not that I'm supposed to know that – she swore me to secrecy.'

Behind us, footsteps approached, and I looked back to see Teresa with a tea tray holding four mugs and Liam with two more kitchen chairs that would soon have muck-covered feet.

Iggy leaned in to whisper to me before they reached us. 'You know none of this, by the way, none of it. Liam insisted he be the one to tell you. The only reason he let me come on ahead was that I said I had to sort out a personal matter and they agreed to hold back for a minute or two. Say nothing.'

'Tea time,' Teresa called brightly, passing the tray to Iggy so she could give me one of those hugs that I was so used to by then, the ones that lasted longer than a normal one, and allowed the hugger time to cry if they needed to, then compose themselves. She wiped at her eyes before standing back to allow Liam to offer me his hand.

'What do people normally say on such occasions?'

'All sorts. Take your pick.'

He hesitated a moment. 'I'm sorry for the cruelty of it all. Losing someone in that way isn't right.'

I dropped my eyes, unable to keep his gaze.

Teresa handed out the mugs. Iggy smiled as he took his before surreptitiously placing it out of sight behind the bar-rel. Later, he would tip it unseen into the grass.

When we had settled, I noticed Teresa glance at Liam, tilting her head quickly in my direction, encouraging him to begin.

'Yes, well, I hope you don't mind us coming here like this, Rosie. I know you have other things to be concerning yourself with now.'

I waved the hand that had just held his, dismissing any ill feeling on the matter.

Liam coughed before beginning. 'Teresa and I got talking there a while back, just before I was about to close the deal that you and I had discussed a few times, as you might remember, with your father and—'

'Indeed, I remember it perfectly.'

'Right. Yes.' He shifted a little in his chair. 'Well, it struck us, on reflection, that what this island really needed was community involvement. That it wasn't right that the boat, this place's beating heart, if you want to put it that way, should remain in the name of only one family. It was backward thinking when the boat, after all, is everyone's.'

'Wow.' I said, my hand, out of his sight, tapping at Iggy's leg. 'That's incredibly progressive of you, Liam.'

'Exactly. We decided a company of interested islanders was more the thing, to bring everyone in who wanted to be a part of it. And you won't believe your ears when I tell you that we shareholders now number thirty-one. Who knew we had so much—'

'Two actually,' Iggy interjected, stopping Liam's heroic tale mid-flow. 'It's thirty-two.'

Liam did not miss a beat, despite his double-take. 'And there you go, getting more popular by the day.'

'Yes, impressive,' I added.

'Absolutely. And we are all of the one mind that it is time to *finally* give the ferry the investment she deserves.'

'Can I just stop you there, Liam?' I said, holding up a hand at what I felt was a dig. 'My father is a good ferryman.

I'll not have his name tarnished with your suggestion that
he somehow failed in his duty to that boat or this island.
He's served us faithfully, as you well know, so let's not pre-
tend anything different.'

In the stillness that followed my words, I watched him,
daring him to contradict me. At the corner of my eye I saw
Teresa's hand reach for his knee.

'That's not what Liam meant,' she said. 'Isn't that right,
love?'

'The furthest thing from my mind.'

I let it go. Allowing peace to resume.

'As I was about to say,' he continued again, 'the shareholders elect a board. This board makes the strategic decisions
while the day-to-day management will be left to a manager.
As yet to be appointed.'

'Teresa's idea,' Iggy interrupted enthusiastically, his broad
smile receding as Liam bristled at another interference.

Teresa smiled shyly, but then turned to Liam as if asking permission to step in. He assented, a little reluctantly it
seemed to me – he never did like to share the limelight.

'Well, it's like in school, you see. The major decisions are
voted on by an elected board, but the day-to-day running
is done by me as the principal and, on the whole, it works
well. I'm always answerable to them but I'm still given a
reasonable level of freedom. Anyone can apply for the
post.' She beamed.

'I guess you're a shoo-in for that, then.' I turned to Liam.

'Well, we'll see. I haven't decided if I'm applying yet.'

I stopped myself scoffing just in time before Liam looked
at Teresa earnestly, a look that repeated all Iggy had tried to
tell me three months earlier, that power and land and wealth
and property did not matter when family was on the line.

'So,' I said, testing these new waters, totally intrigued, 'what if I wanted to go for this "manager" post, would that be OK?'

'Of course. The board would welcome it.' Iggy beamed at me.

'We would expect no less.' Liam held my eyes on that one. It was not so much a letting go, but an admission on his part, I suspected, that it no longer mattered who owned the boat or who managed her. The important thing was that she remained part of both our lives as she always had been, shared by us both, *loved*, I begrudgingly accepted, by us both, that this war was finally over – or, at least, would be if we both tried not to bark and snap at everything the other did. After forty long years of intermittent fighting, he was offering a ceasefire.

'Right,' I said, genuinely impressed. I looked again to *Aoibhneas*, slipping along our seas, our true heartbeat, our saviour.

'And what did my father say to all of this?'

'Well, you can ask him yourself.'

Liam looked around to the back door where Daniel had been waiting unbeknown to me. On receiving the nod, Daniel stepped back inside to get my father with whom he linked arms for the journey across the mucky ground. On seeing me, Dad, now wrapped up in scarf and hat, a thing I'd never seen him wear before, raised his eyes to Heaven at his eldest son's mothering.

'Wow,' I said, addressing the three beside me, 'you guys really had this all worked out. It's like a well-rehearsed play.'

Iggy laughed, and I turned slightly to him, grinning.

As Dad arrived, Liam offered him his chair. 'Here, Captain,' he said, holding it steady as my father got comfortable.

I smiled to myself, the first time the title had ever passed that man's lips. 'So, Dad,' I asked, 'what do you think of all of this?'

'Well, now, Rosie,' he began, 'it nearly broke my heart to think that you would lose *Aoibhneas*, but I could see no other way, and when these fine people came to tell me their idea, I could've cried. And I nearly did, didn't I?' He looked around at all three, and I saw Teresa give a little smile. 'This way,' he continued, turning back to me, 'you get to still have her. You've lost too much, my darling girl,' his voice weakened and his eyes welled as he concentrated on our joined hands, 'and that . . . well, that to me was all that mattered.'

I reached across to hug him tightly, imparting my love and gratitude for every time he had put me first: aged twenty-two when I had left these shores, aged forty-nine when he had welcomed me back, gifting me that precious time with Saoirse by my side. And as I cried, I felt my big brother's hand on my back, his other, I could see, on my father's shoulder.

How long we stayed that way, I do not know.

'So,' I said finally, letting my father go, sniffling, bringing us back to the issue at hand. 'Do we Driscolls have shares in this thing or what?'

'Oh, yes, DJ has sorted all of that,' Iggy answered.

'That apparently is me.' Daniel smiled, winking at me.

'Hmm. OK.' I considered that and everything they had told me as everyone waited for me at last to give my opinion on all they had explained.

'Well, I'll be upfront with you,' I admitted, looking from Iggy to Teresa and then to Liam, 'it's a pretty good plan.' And, no, there was no audible sigh of relief, just a small smile from each of them. 'But I'm not going to be applying for that manager job. Don't get me wrong, I still wouldn't mind the chance of skippering her, if it's being offered. No, I believe you'll do a fine job, Liam, if that's what you decide to do.'

He smiled, a genuine heartfelt smile, and it was only then it occurred to me that maybe, had this woman, whom he had been so jealous of for nearly fifty years, who unlike him had had parents who loved her and a boat to call her own, had she been the bigger person and acknowledged that he was worthy of the name skipper once in a while, we might never have found ourselves so locked in battle all of these years.

'Or Iggy, maybe?' I said, looking around at him. 'He's not bad when it comes to business, it turns out.'

'Ach, now.' Iggy laughed shyly.

'And in years to come maybe Lar and Paul,' I added. 'I'm sure they'll do a fine job too of being manager, taking care of her into the future.'

'And Éilísh.' Liam suggested, not turning to me but keeping his eyes on *Aoibhneas* as we both considered his words.

'And Éilísh,' I agreed. 'My goodness but this board will be spoiled for choice.'

The four of us then watched *Aoibhneas* continue her journey until she disappeared, rounding No Man's Haven, each smiling, contented in our shared fate.

EPILOGUE

And now we stand at my mother's grave. Everyone is here around us where we are laying Saoirse down: my father, my brothers, my uncle, Nina, holding Cullie's hand, Hugh's family, Mick and his colleagues, Maggie, and the Families of the Disappeared, Saoirse's friends, Aimee, Ross, Theo, all looking older, true adults now, as they circle us, protecting us from the wind that has whipped up this December day. The islanders are here too: Patsy, Iggy, Diarmuid, Phelan, Éilísh, Fergal, Teresa, Liam, Lar and Paul, and beyond them the rest of the islanders. The ferry is not running today in honour of Saoirse.

I glance down at *Aoibhneas*, as she sits silently in the bay. As if she is listening, paying attention to what is happening above her: the rhythmic prayers of Father Michael, the murmured responses of the congregation. I imagine I see that wheelhouse bowed in reverence for the girl who once adored her.

They are lowering Saoirse and I am watching them take her from me. I'm letting her go again when I had her for such a little space of time in this life, letting her go into the arms of my mother. It was Hugh who suggested it. I had thought of it, but I wasn't sure I had the right to ask he be parted from her any more than these last eight years. I thought he'd fight for her to be in Dublin and I would have agreed. But he has said it feels right that she is here with Evie, so she can tell his daughter all the stories she loved, and they can look out at the sea together and see *Aoibhneas* whenever they want. And the library, don't forget the library, I added with a tear-choked laugh. And the library, he said, with a kind smile, they can see the library. And, besides, he said, I'd like to visit more. And I had lifted my head to that and smiled back at him. He took my hand and raised it to his mouth to kiss it before giving it back.

Neither of us quite knows what that means and who we two will become but it is something, it is our version of this relationship we have been given and seem unable to let go of. I don't think he'll ever leave Dublin fully to live permanently on Roaring Bay, and I can't see me abandoning this island again now that she is back with me. But somewhere in between we will find a place, I think, a place of our own making.

I am holding his hand as her coffin disappears from view and final prayers are said around us, as the temporary wooden cover with its flowers gifted from so many is laid over the gaping hole that has taken her and it feels like I never want to lose his grip. But we are forced apart as he and I are overcome by the hugs of mourners. And I have to fight to reach him for one second longer, to kiss his lips and say sorry, sorry for all we have been through, sorry for how I slipped away from him for so many years, sorry for the times I never held his hand and consoled him as I should have, sorry for the loss that we must always and for ever endure.

Acknowledgements

Island life

The island depicted in this book is a work of my imagination. All characters and events are fictional. In helping me create this world I am indebted to the following: Muintir Chléire – who allowed me to live among them when this writing career of mine began in 2013 and who have welcomed me back summer after summer thereafter – but in particular for their kind hospitality, care and time: Bríd, Séamus, Aodh, Shane and Fay, and Maura and Seán Cadogan.

Published works that have helped inform island life are:

Island Stories: Tales and Legends from the West (O'Brien Press, 1977).

The Island of the White Cow, Deborah Tall (Atheneum, 1986).

Seven Year Island, Jerome Kiely (Geoffrey Chapman Ltd, 1969).

Ó *Charraig Aonair go Droichead Dóinneach, Poems by John K.Cotter*, edited by Éamon Lankford (Celium Publishing, Lankford Books, 2016).

The Natural History of Cape Clear 1959-2019, Steve Wing (Steve Wing, 2020).

Wing it with Steve, A Bird Guide for Cape Clear, Steve Wing (Steve Wing, 2021).

Ferrying

I am deeply grateful to Niamh Ní Dhrisceoil, one of the skippers of Cape Clear Ferries, who gave her time two summers in a row to help me understand what it is to skipper. Her wisdom and professionalism is inspiring.

To Séamus Ó Drisceoil and Karen Cottrell of Cape Clear Ferries. I am indebted to both for their corrections and encouragement.

To the crew of Cape Clear Ferries who work so hard especially in the summer months when we visitors insist on coming. Watching them work as I sat in the harbour with a cup of tea in hand has helped me shape this book.

The missing of Ireland

I am grateful to the families of all of the missing in Ireland who have given their time in the many newspaper and magazine articles that I have read and for the countless television archive programmes that I have watched. I do not claim that in this book I have touched on even a crumb of what they feel, of what they suffer every day. Their bravery has been foisted upon them by the cruelty of a fate none of us would wish for.

I am also grateful to the journalist Fintan Lambe for speaking with me about disappearances in Wexford.

Three books have helped in building this fictional world:

Missing: *The Unsolved Cases of Ireland's Vanished Women and Children*, Barry Cummins (Gill Books, 2003).

Searching: *The Story of Ireland's Missing People*, Valerie Cox (Blackwater Press, 2003).

Beyond The Tape, Dr Marie Cassidy (Hachette Books Ireland, 2021).

For all other things

For their support, encouragement, and expertise, these people deserve my thanks:

Helen Flood, Louise Court, Elaine Egan, Jim Binchy, Breda Purdue, Maria Garbutt-Lucero, Ruth Stern, Siobhán Tierney, Kim Nyanhomdera, Catherine Worsley, Drew Hunt, Kate Brunt, Alasdair Oliver, Juliette Winter, Hazel Orme, Kate Burton, Matilda Ayris, César Castañeda Gámez and Meredith Ford.

Lily Cooper and Carole Welch – not a day goes by where I do not feel I am the luckiest of writers having these two talented, considerate, professional women as my editors.

Sue Armstrong, who is so dedicated, supportive and wise. A brilliant agent who I am fortunate to have fighting my corner.

James and Adam, who give me the time, space and love to write.